TRISTAN

JENNIE LYNN ROBERTS

First paperback edition February 2021

Editor: O. Ventura at Hot Tree Editing
Cover design by Damonza.com

ISBN: 978-1-8383389-0-9 (paperback)
ISBN: 978-1-8383389-1-6 (e-book)

www.Jennielynnroberts.com

 Created with Vellum

For Mark, Alethea and Michael

Acknowledgments

A massive, heartfelt thank you to Gill Harvard and Hannah Huffelmann for reading early drafts, cheering me on, and being willing to spend many hours discussing all things *Tristan* related. It means the world to me!

A special thank you goes to Olivia Ventura at Hot Tree Editing whose insightful challenges and editing wizardry improved this book immensely. Thanks also to Donna Pemberton for keeping such a close eye on my book-baby, as well as Keeley Catarineau, Casey Ford, Ginny Gaylor and Maria Greenwood for all their support and help.

Thank you to the awesome design team at Damonza.com for this gorgeous cover.

And lastly, but most importantly, thank you to my ever-patient, always supportive family, and most especially to my husband, Mark, whose love and encouragement gave me the confidence to write this book.

Prologue

TRISTAN RODE NEXT TO LANVAL, glad of the breeze that stirred the warm summer air. Insects buzzed in the long, fragrant grasses on the side of the road while bees danced between the bright yellow hay rattle flowers. It was a perfect day.

Or, at least, it should have been.

He glanced sideways at Val. Damn, he missed his friend. Something had gone brutally wrong with their friendship, but for the life of him, he had no idea what it was.

He had hoped Val might use this chance to finally talk to him. Instead they had been riding in strained silence for hours.

Since they had both been promoted, Tristan to Captain of the Palace Guards and Val to Princess Alanna's personal guard, Val had changed completely. But not for the better.

It had been an unlikely friendship. Val, the golden boy,

the beloved oldest son of the Mabin magistrat, followed everywhere by his adoring baby sister. The complete opposite of Tristan—the unwanted, ignored when he wasn't being punished, and thank the gods, only child of a minor Tarasque baron and his beautiful, privileged wife.

Tristan couldn't remember the woman that had given him life. She had woken up one day when he was four years old, decided she was in love with a man that was not her husband, packed her bags, and left. Without even saying goodbye to her only child.

She had never come back.

He only ever heard from others about how beautiful and privileged she was. Although to be fair, the descriptions his father used were more likely to be "wanton harlot" and "spoilt bitch."

And yet, somehow, his friendship with Val had always worked. They had played together, grown up together— Tristan with his inner Tarasque beast, Val with his Mabin wings—as close as brothers despite their differences. Campaigned together. Laughed together. Even in the darkest, coldest, hungriest places in the kingdom.

But not anymore. Now, Val was hardly recognizable.

In the months since he had taken over responsibility for the new princess's personal safety, Val had become increasingly grim and withdrawn. Increasingly difficult to talk to. Even about the most innocuous subjects.

This new Val was irritable and secretive. His black eyebrows were permanently drawn together in a heavy frown. His heavy leather wings pulled back, tightly furled in attack position, as if he expected danger at all times.

Did Val ever laugh anymore? Tristan couldn't imagine it.

He had asked Val repeatedly whether something was

bothering him, but he had been shut down every time. The last time he'd said anything, Val had simply pushed away his ale, stood up, and walked away. Tristan hadn't seen him again since then.

Well, he couldn't stand up and walk away now, could he? He looked over at his friend and waited until Val met his eyes. "What's going on, Val?"

Val glanced at him briefly, then looked around carefully before replying with a short, "Nothing."

Tristan fought the urge to lean over and shake him. "I can tell that it's something."

Val's scowl deepened, and he ran a thumb down between his eyes as if his forehead ached. "It's nothing I can discuss."

Tristan grunted. He would rather stick his dagger in his thigh than talk about anything that hinted of feelings. His scales flickered along his arms as his discomfort grew, but he couldn't let it go. "If you don't tell me, how can I help you?"

Val's reply was so soft that he almost didn't hear it. "You can't."

Tristan leaned over Altair, the massive bay destrier that had been with him since their northern campaigns. "Please, Val, just—"

Val flinched, interrupting with a rough whisper, "No. Hell, Tris, don't you think I would tell you if I could?"

Tristan looked carefully at his friend. He seemed exhausted and miserable. The last time Tristan had seen him so unhappy was when his mama died.

In addition to this protracted, uncharacteristic unhappiness, Val was also obsessively vigilant. Even out in the pleasant summer sunshine, with a full company of Blues, his eyes were constantly searching. Constantly flicking back to the open carriage that trundled along, carrying

Princess Alanna and her father-in-law, King Geraint. Alanna and Geraint, but no Prince Ballanor.

Ballanor had been set to attend the meeting right up until that morning, but then Alanna had refused to get into the carriage if he joined them, and they'd been forced to go without him at the last minute.

That's what he'd heard, anyway—the princess had stamped her foot and told Ballanor not to come, and the crown prince had been only too glad to comply.

Personally, Tristan could see why Ballanor had no desire to spend the day with his wife. She was beautiful—if you liked skinny blondes. But frosty and aloof, disdainful, refusing to make friends or fit in at court. Prone to infantile tantrums. And a foreigner. All the other women hated her, and the men ignored her.

Not the kind of woman he would want in his own bed. He preferred warm, willing women and soft curves. Thank the gods he wasn't a prince, forced to marry a coldhearted shrew to cement a treaty.

Poor Val. What was it like having to spend all day with her? Tristan hated her on principle.

Although—since the whole trip was about cementing the new treaty—Prince Ballanor should have sucked it up and joined his wife. How difficult could it be? Meet up with Alanna's mother, queen of the Verturians, at a nice, neutral campground. Eat a few sandwiches. Drink some champagne. And walk away again, Verturia and Brythoria no longer at war.

Everyone knew that Ballanor had fought against ending the war. Fought even harder against the marriage. But in the end, King Geraint—supported by the Royal Brythorian Council—had put his foot down. The marriage cementing the new ties between Brythoria and Verturia had gone ahead, as had the treaty. And now it was up to Ballanor to endorse it.

Surely he could have ignored her tantrum and sucked up one day with Princess Peevish to ratify the treaty and save hundreds of lives? The people of the kingdom would have been grateful, if nothing else. Thank the gods that King Geraint had been prepared to continue without his son and sign the treaty.

He glanced up, his thoughts disturbed, as Val turned his horse back to the carriage, ending their stilted conversation to ride alongside and confer with Princess Peevish herself.

They had finally reached Ravenstone Meadow.

The cavalcade entered into a wide field of swaying grasses surrounded by softly rolling hills, with a small wood in the distance.

Everything had been searched and cleared before they arrived by Blues handpicked by Tristan and the king, and overseen by Prince Ballanor, but it didn't stop Tristan casting an experienced eye over the peaceful meadow, looking for anything amiss.

Everything looked calm. Sleepy and tranquil with the ticking of beetles in the hot sunshine. He sent out a squad to check the meadow once more anyway as they made their way to a colorful pavilion constructed out of fluttering silks.

Thick carpets lay over the ground, and a low table was set with a wide array of cold cooked meats, loaves of bread, pats of yellow butter, flagons of ale, and browned pies. As well as a mouthwatering selection of cakes and sweets. All set out by the small advance squad, only given the details of their destination the night before.

The Verturians had yet to arrive, and Tristan stood guard while the elderly King Geraint climbed gingerly down from the carriage.

He suppressed a shaft of annoyance at the princess who'd made her father-in-law suffer hours of discomfort on the road without his son rather than do her duty and allow her husband to accompany them.

And a tiny stab of irritation at the prince who had allowed it, however difficult his wife. He squashed it down; it wasn't his place to question the prince. His duty was to the king, and that included his only heir.

He turned away to run his eyes over the meadow and the woods in the distance while Val laid down a carpet at the edge of the carriage so that her royal iciness didn't have to get dirt on her hem.

The squad he'd sent out when they entered the meadow returned, confirming that all was well.

An hour passed, and then another, with no sign of the Verturian queen. Eventually the king and Princess Alanna sat together to eat some cold pie and drink a little ale. Neither of them spoke.

The soldiers around them grew restless, and Tristan growled out a few terse commands to stay focused.

He picked six men to take their horses and do another sweep of the meadow and the fringe of the forests beyond, but they were soon back with nothing to report.

He could see Reece and Tor standing vigilantly at the entrance of the tent and purposely relaxed his shoulders. He was glad that his own squad, the Hawks, was there. Men he'd known for years. Men who knew what they were doing.

Gods, he hated waiting.

When there was still no activity an hour later, Princess Alanna stood and asked the king if he would like to walk through the meadow with her. It was a little after noon, and she wanted to pick flowers in the sunshine.

Val, who had been standing behind her while she ate,

followed her, one pace behind, as she stepped daintily out of the tent. Gods. Tristan sighed. *Now* she didn't mind the dust.

The king, paced by Tristan, followed for a few minutes, but quickly lost his breath and decided to turn back.

They had no choice but to split up. Val followed Alanna, leading his massive stallion in case she grew tired and needed to ride back. Tristan accompanied the king.

The king called for a chair, and a pageboy set it for him to sit with his face to the sun. Tristan stood guard at his side as they all watched the princess and Val meandering farther and farther away into the hot, dry meadow, heat haze shimmering around them.

Suddenly, Val flung himself forward. Even from such a distance, Tristan could see his friend leap toward the princess, and then there was a flurry as he seemed to grab Alanna and shove her toward his destrier.

Tristan was already pulling out his sword when, seconds later, he heard Val let out a sharp whistle, the battle call of the Hawks. A piercing blast that guaranteed, after years of campaigning together, that every single Hawk would look his way.

Tristan twisted his head, trying to see what had alarmed Val.

And when he turned back it was to the most horrific sight of his life: a quivering black arrow embedded deep in the king's neck. Someone had shot him from behind the pavilion. An assassin with impeccable aim—a few inches to the side and Tristan would have taken the arrow instead.

A hoarse voice shouted orders, and he distantly realized it was his own. Desperate commands to protect the king. To defend their position. Even as he leaped toward the king, pulling him into his arms and out of sight, fumbling to press his fingers against the wound and stop the pumping blood that poured, hot and sticky, down his hands.

Horror mingled in his blood with the violent red haze of battle rage as his inner beast roared to the surface. His scales swept over his skin in a gleaming green-and-pewter armored wave.

The primal surge of bloodlust sang through him. The savage drive to run, screaming, into battle. But he kept himself under iron control. His first duty was to the king.

Arrows flew all around him, thudding into the pavilion, hitting the ground with sharp sprays of dust and stones. The king's page screamed as he was hit, falling to the ground beside them.

Sharp whistles and screams filled the air with chaos as hundreds more arrows flew toward them. Everywhere, men were shouting, cavalry mounting, pulling out swords. And everywhere men were dying. Cut down by the relentless flights of arrows from some unseen enemy, hidden in the nearby woods and swooping down from the soft hills. Men in brown leather, but no other markings. No tabards or pennants.

Beside him, the pageboy gave a last choking gasp as he drowned in his own blood. Tristan couldn't reach him. He had to stay with the king and accept that there was nothing he could do to save the boy.

He looked up from his huddled crouch over the king to see Val, in the distance, throw himself onto his destrier behind Alanna and gallop away. Leaving everyone else behind.

He turned, glad to find Reece and Tor crowding behind him, swords drawn and shields up. Between the three of them, huddling over against the blinding fall of arrows, they carried King Geraint back to the carriage.

Desperately shouting to retreat, he whistled again, calling the Hawks to him. Calling all the squads to follow—those few men that had survived.

Around them the fall of arrows slowed as the vicious attacking force melted away, back into the long grasses and the distant woods. Was it a decoy? He didn't know. Still frantically protecting the king with his own body, Tristan called the order for all men to fall in and withdraw.

The frantic ride back to safety was a blur of thundering hooves, clenched muscles, and sweat dripping down his neck as they fled with the king.

As soon as they reached a defensible rocky outcrop, he sent half his men back under Mathos's command to the pavilion to hunt down the cowards that had ambushed them.

He arrayed the rest in defense around them and then turned to Rafe where he knelt beside the king. His friend looked up, purple-blue eyes dark and sorrowful. It was too late. King Geraint was already gone, his life bled out on the stony ground.

They stood together, shocked and silent, waiting for Mathos and the men to return.

It was a grimly furious group of men that returned. The meadow and the woods were empty once more. Their attacker had known exactly where they would be and when they would be there. They had swooped in from a distance, their lethal assault perfectly timed, perfectly coordinated for maximum destruction. Then, in minutes, they had melted away again.

But they had left evidence. The soldiers carried some of the enemies' arrows back with them. All carved with small runes and fletched in black.

Verturian. Just like Princess Alanna.

Someone had betrayed them. Shared the details of a meeting so secret that only four people knew the venue before the day. Someone who didn't want the treaty to go ahead. Someone who hated the Brythorians. Who repeatedly rejected their culture and disdained their court.

A cold certainty filled him. They had been set up. Lured into a trap by the northern bitch and left to die.

Where was she now? And what had she done with Val?

He sent a messenger ahead, carrying the arrows back to the palace. Then, with the king's blood still drying on his tunic, he gave the order to retreat.

The ride back to Kaerlud passed in silent horror. Mourning their friends and carrying the body of the man they had sworn to protect, they reached the castle in the middle of the night, in a stampede of clattering hooves and clouds of dust, powered by grief and fury.

Tristan carried the king's remains himself and laid them gently on the covers of his state bed as the court healers and physics rushed around him.

He knew, and they knew, that there was nothing that they could do. But they tried anyway. No one wanted to be the first to admit the truth. The king was dead.

Slowly, as if he carried all the stone of the castle on his back, he backed out of the king's rooms and, still wearing his blood-soaked Blues, made his way to Prince Ballanor. His new liege.

He knocked heavily, and Prince Ballanor called a loud, "Come."

The room was filled with polished tables and crystal. King Geraint's favorite greatsword, with its intricate gold and black pommel, hung over the mantelpiece. Everything sparkled in the red flicker of firelight—the fire far too substantial for summer—as sweat beaded on Tristan's forehead.

The prince was sprawled over a chair, dressed only in a half-open burgundy robe revealing a muscular chest, the typical heavy build of an Apollyon in his prime. Ballanor's chestnut brown hair curled damply as if he had just bathed, and his black eyes glittered as he drank from a silver goblet.

In the corner of the room sat the impeccably dressed Lord Grendel, the High Chancellor. Another Apollyon and the prince's favorite. His hair darker, skin a little paler than Ballanor's, his frame only slightly less muscular, but with the same refined features of the upper nobility.

Handsome, the palace women thought them, flocking to watch them at their daily sword practice. But their black eyes were as cold as the ice crust on the banks of the Tamasa in winter.

The air was thick and musty, and Tristan would swear he could smell the faint sweetness of perfume in the heated air. He ignored it and Grendel as he lowered himself to his knees before his prince.

Not his prince; his king.

Gods.

The luxurious room, the jewels glittering at Grendel's wrists, the gleam of the silver goblet in Ballanor's hand, the musty heat, everything conflicted with the bitter horror that filled him.

It was a struggle to get the words out. To explain what had happened, his appalling shame. How the king had died on his watch. Not two feet away. And he kept his eyes lowered, watching the dance of firelight over the rugs and furs that warmed the floor.

The new king said nothing, only continued to sit, one

leg flung over the arm of the chair, as Tristan's report trailed to a close.

There was only one thing left to say. He closed his eyes for a moment and let his scales harden, taking strength from his inner beast. Then he gritted his teeth and informed the new king of his suspicions about Princess Alanna.

And finally, Ballanor responded. Shockingly loud in the oppressive quiet. He laughed.

King Ballanor's eyes glittered as he pushed himself out of his chair and walked over to stand before Tristan, uncaring that his robe hung loose.

Tristan stayed on his knees, eyes on the carpet, as Ballanor plucked one of the Verturian arrows from a low table beside the fire, its unique markings and black fletching offering silent condemnation.

"We realized the truth immediately," Ballanor admitted in a dangerous voice, his words falling heavily into the airless room. "After all, who else sent the missive to Queen Moireach with the details of the meeting place? Princess Alanna knew exactly where we were going and when we would be there. And who stood to gain as much as her? With the king dead, the Verturian princess hopes to leave us leaderless. Vulnerable to her clans sweeping south."

Ballanor put the arrow back onto the table with a loud click. "Deceit is in their blood, those northern bitches. We've known it for a hundred and fifty years—ever since they murdered Princess Mildritha barely a month after she produced an heir. It's exactly why we never should have agreed to end this war. Why I fought against this ludicrous marriage."

Tristan kept quiet—he knew this story. Six generations before, a young Brythorian princess had married a Verturian prince in a political attempt to tie the two kingdoms into one great nation. When she had died shortly after giving birth to a son, the Brythorian royal family had accused Verturia of murder. The feud had escalated year upon year since then, finally culminating in the brutal northern campaign. The war that Geraint had waged, unsuccessfully, for so many years.

Grendel's lip twitched. "You should never have been forced to marry. Brythorian blood runs in their northern veins, however diluted. You are the King of Brythoria… and by extension, Verturia."

The king crossed his arms and gave the Lord High Chancellor a slow look. "They'll be grateful for our rule. Our firm hand."

"Our guidance on running their mines," Grendel added almost too low to hear, but Ballanor ignored him as he continued, "They think they've weakened us, but they're about to learn that my father was the weak one. He couldn't finish this, but I can. Starting with that bitch, Alanna."

Tristan couldn't agree more; Alanna was the poison they had to purge. "We should send out a squad to arrest—"

King Ballanor cut him off, his eyes flicking toward Grendel with a darkly satisfied look. "You needn't trouble yourself; she's already in custody. The Black Guards were deployed as soon as your messenger finished his report. They have her."

Tristan wiped a tired hand down his dirt-streaked face. Good. That was good.

He would have liked to have arrested her himself. But the cavalry had her already. It would have to be enough.

She deserved to hang. Deserved whatever agonizing punishment Ballanor devised. And by the grim look on the new king's face, it would be agonizing.

Tristan rocked back onto his heels and got up slowly, a thousand years older than he had been that morning.

"Thank you, Your Majesty." He gritted his teeth and tried to find the right words to ask after his friend. "And, ah, Captain Lanval?"

"Her personal guard?"

Tristan nodded, his head aching in the cloying heat.

Ballanor tapped his fingers on his lips, his eyes narrowed. He looked over at Grendel, a silent communication passing between them. "Captain Lanval has become increasingly unreliable. He has put the wishes of the princess before his orders on more than one occasion. We realize now just how bad it had become—his loyalty has shifted to Verturia."

"No!" The word burst out before Tristan's exhausted mind could stop it, but he dipped his head immediately at the flare of rage in his king's eyes. "Please accept my humble apology, Your Majesty, I just couldn't imagine…."

He left the sentence unfinished. Was it that impossible to imagine?

Val had been with Alanna, hurrying her away a minute before the trap sprang closed. Almost as if he had seen some kind of signal. Or knew what was coming beforehand. And Alanna couldn't have arranged the massacre alone. She needed a veteran. Someone with strategic military experience.

Val had even whistled to the Hawks, ensuring that Tristan would look away from the king, just for a second.

Fuck.

He thought back on the months of increasing distance between him and Val. How much Val had changed ever since he had started protecting the princess. His refusal to tell Tristan anything.

Val's words came back to him. *It's nothing I can discuss....* What did that mean?

He remembered his friend's strangely obsessive vigilance, the way he seemed to be looking for danger at all times, even before they'd left the palace.

He didn't want it to be true. The very thought filled him with sickening horror, sending his beast into a frenzy of agitated discomfort, his scales flickering restlessly on his wrists.

Val might, in fact, have known of the betrayal about to decimate them.

Had he been recruited by the princess? Was that what he had refused to say? What on earth could she be paying him? Had Val allowed his friends, his king, to die? All in some twisted support for the most hated woman in the palace?

Tristan shook his head slowly. It was too hideous to contemplate. He didn't believe it. Wouldn't.

The room closed in on him. Too hot. Too perfumed. His head throbbed, and he fought to keep his face calm as the king watched him through hard black eyes.

Grendel slid from his place in the corner to stand next to Ballanor, his hands clasped behind his back as he gave Tristan a pitying look. "It's obvious that he helped her. She could never have done it alone... and no one else in the palace will go near her."

Could it really have been Val? The king seemed so certain, but Tristan didn't want to live in a world where that was true.

Grendel's eyes narrowed. "Your friend betrayed you. For a woman he's been fucking."

"Val was...." He couldn't say the words.

"He's been seen coming out of her room by a few of the

other guards," Grendel admitted. "After what happened today, they decided to come forward. There is no doubt."

Tristan felt as if he'd been punched in the gut. Gods. The words rang in his ears. *There was no doubt.*

Val was fucking her. It suddenly made so much sense.

But would Val do that? Betray him like that? Val was obsessive about honor, but who did he believe his loyalty belonged to—his oldest friend or the woman in his bed?

Of all people, Tristan knew just how easily a person could break faith with someone they were supposed to love. He'd had it beaten into him since he was four years old. And they had evidence. Other guards had seen it. His fellow Blues would never lie, not about something like this. Gods.

Tristan could hardly breathe, let alone think. "We should start a search, ah, arrest him. I—"

King Ballanor cut him off with a wave of his hand. "Captain Lanval was captured with the princess. Both are under guard on the Great North Road. They'll be back here before morning."

Tristan blinked, trying to process everything that had happened.

Grendel turned to King Ballanor. "We have much to do if we are to reestablish the military power your father has dismantled."

Ballanor gave a curt nod. "Assemble the council. We prepare for war."

It was inevitable. There had been no other possible response to the death of the king and the treachery of the princess.

Something deep inside Tristan grieved for the loss of life to come. And burned with hatred for the traitors that had made it happen.

Ballanor turned to face him. "Take what's left of your

squad and report to the cavalry barracks. Tell them I said to send you to the forty-ninth. You can hand in your captain's insignia while you're there. After all, you are responsible for the death of the king. You were friends with the man that betrayed us all. We can hardly trust you with our safety after that, now can we?"

Tristan kept his face completely blank as his entire world fell to ruin around him. Everything he had worked for. Everything he had believed in. Gone.

"You're dismissed," Ballanor commanded as he tied the belt of his robe and settled himself back into his chair.

Tristan bowed and let himself silently out the room.

There was nothing he could do to take back that terrible day. Or to ease his horrendous guilt for failing the king. No personal recourse against the princess or the man that had helped her and deceived them all.

His best friend. Gods. The betrayal burned all the way down to his soul.

If he never heard the name Lanval again, it would be too fucking soon.

He didn't have time to wait for Val and confront him. He had to pack up his life and ship out in disgrace— immediately—as per the king's orders. And, frankly, he didn't want to see him anyway. Didn't want to see his friend hauled back in chains. Didn't want to have to look Val in the eye and hear just how little their friendship had meant.

Betrayed for a woman. Fuck.

The only thing he could do now was to gather up the men that remained of the Hawks and get the hell out of the palace.

Chapter One

September

HER WINGS HURT.

Not just a low background thrum. Nor the deep throbbing ache she'd left behind hours ago. No, this was constant, stabbing agony as something wrenched deep inside her with every flex of her right wing.

The rest of her was faring only slightly better—throat and wrists bruised to deep purple, a clump of her long dark hair was missing. And, down her right side, a blistering burn surrounded by pits and pockmarks, flanked a deep laceration through her wing. The harsh results of catching herself against the blazing rafters in her frantic flight to freedom.

Nim flew in a haze of pain, hardly aware of her surroundings. Focusing everything she had on moving forward. Staying low against the trees.

Eventually she had to take a break. The frantic pace and

constant pain were making it hard to think, and she needed a moment to assess and plan. She had fled into the sky, taking nothing other than the clothes on her back and Val's ring clenched in her fist. No thought other than to get far away.

She had flown at least a mile before she felt safe enough to hover, just for a few seconds, and tuck the ring into the small pocket in her waistband.

But now she was past the initial rush of panic and tiring fast. She desperately needed a moment to regroup.

She allowed herself to drop down a few feet so that she was in amongst the top of the trees and flew jerkily toward a massive beech, thankfully still thick with leaves in reds and golds as autumn approached. A good place to hide. The kind of place she and Val had loved to play when they were children, pretending to be warriors with Tristan.

Hurt followed the thought, swift and brutal. She pushed it all away—there would be time for self-pity after she survived.

She hovered for a moment as she reached out to hold a branch and then swung herself upward. Only to slip, lose her handhold, and slide down the branch, tearing up her palms on the rough bark.

She frantically kicked up her leg and hooked her knee around the branch, jerking to a stop.

Nim hung upside down from the branch for a few seconds, breathing and getting her pulse back under control. Then she swung herself up to sit among the leaves.

She lifted her aching hands and stifled a gasp. They were slick with blood. And not just from her frantic slide. This was an hour's worth of blood. Twisting, she saw that the tear in her wing had been weeping silver, running in a steady trickle down her arms, the entire time she'd been flying. She had been so afraid, so desperate to get away, that she hadn't noticed.

A glance back showed a shining silver path for anyone to follow. Bile rose in her mouth at the thought, and she swallowed reflexively.

She could feel her long dark hair escaping from its loose braid and tucked a curl behind her ear with trembling, blood-sticky fingers.

She had to think. Had to stop the bleeding.

She had no bandages. And even if she had, she couldn't bind her torn wing without limiting her flight. Her precious salves were abandoned along with everything else. As much as she wanted to curl up in a ball and cry, that wasn't an option either.

She only had one, horrible option. She broke off a small dead branch and then flew down to the ground and sat on a large stone at the base of the tree. She used the flint she always wore to strike a spark into the dried twigs at its end. Then cupped it, blowing gently.

Once she had a good flame, she stubbed it against the tree trunk until she had a small glowing point, scarlet red and scorching hot. She opened her bleeding wing and then pulled the soft silver-gray leather forward and held it firmly with her free hand.

This was going to hurt like hell.

Nim wished she could close her eyes, but then she wouldn't be able to see what she was doing. Instead, she gritted her teeth and pressed the torch into the wound to cauterize it. The acrid stink of burning flesh was almost as bad as the agony of the burn, and she couldn't help her soft whimper or the tears that stung her eyes.

She blinked them away angrily and then stubbed out the torch in the damp ground of the forest and slowly let her wing go. It was trembling slightly; whether from her brutal treatment or the damage inside her muscle, she didn't know. But it had stopped bleeding. Thank the gods.

She hung her head and gave herself a moment. Allowed herself to stand still, steeped in the devastation of it all.

And then she straightened her spine and jumped tiredly back into the air.

She rose to the top branches of her tree and then spun slowly. She couldn't keep going in the same direction with a huge silver blood trail pointing like an arrow straight at her. All she could see were trees and dark, clouded sky. She didn't know where she was or where the forest led. Or where in Brythoria she could possibly go.

Eventually she closed her eyes for a few seconds while she spun. Then opened them at random, briefly checked that she was facing a new direction, and simply started flying again.

For the next hour, she was alone with the trees and the faint stench of burnt flesh. Beech gave way to horse chestnut, gold and fiery in the long bars of late afternoon sunlight as the sun dipped into the pale, clear band along the horizon. Beneath the ominous gray clouds that had lurked above her all afternoon.

By the time the sun began to sink, the trees had been replaced by gorse and heather. Then long rolling dunes down to an angry gray sea.

Far in the distance, she saw a glimmer of light shimmering against the darkness. It became her lodestar. Calling her forward. She was too physically battered, too mentally overwhelmed, to know where else to go.

Everything was lost. Everyone was lost. She was twenty-four and completely alone.

But she had the lights.

Their glow gradually solidified as she lurched ever forward. The one blurry orb slowly separated into strings of tiny colored lamps, leading toward a brighter cluster of lights. Some kind of structure, obviously massive, even from such a distance, lit as if for a carnival. Behind it, the twinkling spread of a seaside town.

She was slowing dramatically, flying erratically as her strength started to give out. Only her gaze fixed on the lights kept her moving forward.

Forward toward a huge pier flanked by colored lanterns, held proudly by their curling wrought iron posts. Ending in an opulent pavilion ablaze with lamps, their light reflecting off a hundred windows and mirrors.

The sound of giddy crowds spilled out into the damp, salty air. Beneath it all there was a deep pounding of drums and tambourines. The heavy, heady, pulse-like beat was woven through with a plaintive, mystical aria.

Nim flew raggedly along the side of the pier, staying in the shadows, following the music. Drifting dazedly with the haunting lilt of the soprano's voice. Until, at the pier's very end, deep within the struts below the pavilion, she finally found a perch.

No one would look for her there, miles from home, surrounded by iron, beneath an unfamiliar pier.

She pushed herself deep into the V of two joining girders, wedging herself tightly so that she wouldn't fall if she closed her eyes. Finally, she patted her pocket to check Val's ring, letting out a small huff of relief that it was still safe.

She had to close her eyes. She couldn't go forward for even one more minute. It was as if, in reaching her nameless destination, she had also reached the end of her endurance. She groaned, partly in relief to not be flying, partly with the pain of her torn and burnt wing settling against the cold girders.

She shivered as the icy metal against her wings leached away her body heat, leached away her sense of self, the iron and the cold working together to drain whatever small amount of will she had left.

It was as if she was floating out of her body, following the strange, winding siren song from above. Drawn inevitably down, through the darkness, to the sea below. What would it be like to drop down into the murky depths?

She had lost so much. Mama. Papa. Val. Tristan. Not that she had ever actually had Tristan—he had been a dream. The kind of dream that hurt to think about.

No other man had ever been Tristan, so she had turned them all away. He hadn't wanted her back, or even thought of her again once he'd left. But she hadn't been able to let him go. She had kept her love for him close, her secret source of comfort and of pain.

Now, it was only pain. He was as dead to her as everybody else.

No one would ever know if she let herself fall. No one would ever care. Everyone who had ever loved her was gone. Why not do it? Allow herself to fall off the girder, close her wings and drop, then simply slide into the cold, dark water and let the sea take her.

Chapter Two

THE CAMP WAS silent in the pale gray light of early morning. They were surrounded by rough hills and still in deep shadow, but Tristan had a good vantage point—high up on a rocky outcrop with a clear view of the entire camp and the path through the hills to the local village.

For as long as he could remember, he had always sought out the loftiest lookout points. The best places to keep watch.

He could see the tents rippling slightly in the cold breeze. A fall of autumn leaves swirled in the dirt, but nothing else stirred. The fires had been banked before the last of the squad made their way to their tents, maintaining discipline despite the debauchery of the night before.

Maintaining discipline despite everything else they'd done. Everything they'd lost.

He had taken the last watch, giving his men a chance to celebrate their success, the coin they'd been paid for bringing in a local gang of poachers. Gods knew they needed it.

Truthfully, he needed it too. But he just couldn't face it.

It had been a relief to have an excuse as to why he was staying sober. Well, relatively sober. And why no giggling woman from the nearby village would be staying in his tent. Expecting him to smile. To talk. To be vaguely friendly. He couldn't bear the thought.

He scrubbed a hand down his face, several weeks' beard scratching against his palm, and rolled his tired shoulders to loosen them. If they had still been in the palace, he would have been disciplined by now. He would have disciplined himself.

He allowed himself a mirthless snort. The beard was the least of it.

The men should be waking soon, but he wanted to give them a chance to enjoy themselves. A night of hot food and too much ale followed by one moment of peace, lying wrapped up in a warm pair of arms and a willing body. It was the kind of luxury they had been dreaming of ever since they took this post, out in the ass-end of nowhere.

This squad of eight men that was all that was left of their original two-hundred-strong company. So many men from other squads had been slaughtered, but by some miracle the Hawks had survived. Thank the gods—he couldn't have borne the loss of another of these men.

Well, nine of them had survived, the eight that were exiled and Lanval, imprisoned by the king. Not that Val would be alive much longer. but Tristan sure as fuck was not thinking about that.

A tiny dot flew into the air in the distance, and Tristan narrowed his eyes. It was far in the distance, over the top of the hill. He wouldn't have seen it at all if it hadn't caught a shaft of rising sunlight just as his eyes roamed over that spot.

It looked like a bird, perhaps disturbed by some larger animal.

He sat absolutely still. Listening. The wind swirled, bringing with it the rich scent of autumn trees and damp forest earth. Nothing else moved.

Some unnamable sense got him up and striding down into the camp without any logical reason to do so.

His wrists burned, and he knew, without looking, that below his sleeveless jerkin a fine sheen of deep, emerald green and pewter scales would be flickering up his arms, his body preparing for a battle that his brain couldn't yet identify.

"Up! Hawks. Up," he roared as he walked. They were expecting a lie-in, but they were going to be disappointed.

Mathos stumbled out of his tent first, dark blond hair mussed, still pulling up his leather breeches as he threw a lazy salute. "Morning, Captain."

Tristan grunted. He was no one's captain now. But they point blank refused to call him sergeant. What was he supposed to do? Put them in stocks?

"Sergeant," he reminded his second anyway. Then added, "Get them all up; something's coming."

It only took a few minutes to get the rest of the men out of bed and the group of grumbling, hastily dressed women dispatched back to the village. Everyone worked fast, quickly breaking camp and getting the tents rolled and onto the horses. Uniforms were straightened. Fires covered. Knives strapped, swords in scabbards, crossbows strapped to saddlebags.

Tristan pulled his hair into a tight queue and tucked it into his collar. It was too long, but there wasn't time to deal with that now.

Nearby birds screeched in disgust at being disturbed as he called to the squad to fall in.

They did so immediately, moving efficiently into formation. Each man next to his horse, standing loosely at attention. Some had scales in different shades gleaming on their arms, their bodies reacting to the potential threat. Those who had wings had them tucked behind them, battle ready.

They stood silently, listening to the sounds of the forest around them. No one moved. They remained still, focused, even as the sound of hoofbeats began to emerge from the other forest sounds.

He stood in front of his men, legs braced. His massive stallion was held firmly by Tor behind him, ready.

Within minutes, a pair of grays thundered into the clearing, and he stiffened. It was worse than he thought. Dark blue tunics over gleaming silver mail. The locked fighting boars on their chests. Supercilious, arrogant, and pretentious. And he should know; he'd been one of them.

He took a step forward, arms clasped loosely behind his back, and nodded to the two men wearing his former uniform. He recognized them both but didn't know them personally. He vaguely remembered that they had been amongst the new king's advisors last time he'd been in the palace.

Not real soldiers, just spoilt rich boys with a whole lot of power.

The heavier of the two men slid off his horse and landed lightly on his feet despite his bulk. Not as tall as Tristan, but heavy with bulging muscles. Black eyes combined with a swathe of black and red tattoos swirling up his naked arms marked him as Apollyon. Tough to beat. But not impossible.

He flicked his eyes to the second man, taller but slightly less broad. The same dark eyes and tattooed skin.

The first Apollyon stepped forward, captain's badge gleaming, and Tristan felt the shift behind him as the entire squad focused their attention on him.

The captain merely grinned, as if he would enjoy the challenge. He narrowed his eyes, lip curled in a supercilious sneer. "Sergeant Tristan of the," his lip twitched, "forty-ninth Cavalry division?"

Tristan wasn't taking the bait. He'd been in the military since he was seventeen, and he knew better. "Sir."

"We have a commission for you."

That didn't make sense at all. You banish the handful of survivors of a shamed and decimated company to fuck around with no real duty, no supplies, no wages and no orders. Then you send two of the new palace guards with a commission?

But there was no way he was saying any of that.

"Yes, sir," he agreed as he put his hand out for the sealed vellum that would contain their orders.

But the guard shook his head, his sneer growing. "A verbal commission."

Nothing good ever came of a verbal commission. But then, nothing good had come of anything recently. "Sir?"

"We believe you knew the queen's lover. Former Captain Lanval."

The men behind Tristan became, if possible, even more still.

They hated Alanna. She was the one responsible for what had happened to their comrades. To their king. To their lives. But they hated Lanval for his part in it even more. She was Verturian, they expected her lack of honor, *he* was a traitor.

His arms burned as his scales thickened around his wrists and flickered up to his biceps. He gave a curt nod. Everyone in the palace knew that they'd been friends.

"Good," the guard agreed with a smirk. "I'm pleased you haven't forgotten, out here, so far from home."

"What do you want from us…, sir?" Tristan asked, ignoring the taunt.

"Lanval refuses to confess the details of his treachery, although we all know what he did. Before he hangs, the king would like to hear him admit the truth." The guard's smirk grew. "Lord Grendel feels it would help Lanval to remember if those that helped him were to join him. He wants the whole nest destroyed."

His scales hardened as his beast prepared for battle— referring to a family of Mabin as a nest was extraordinarily offensive—but he kept his tone polite. "How can we help?"

"The traitor that supported Lanval has escaped arrest and fled. The Lord High Chancellor believes that you have the knowledge we need to resolve this most efficiently. Luckily, you're also the closest."

Tristan could only think of one place nearby that might be relevant, and he had planned never to go there again. Ever.

The Apollyon continued, "The Lord High Chancellor is offering you this one chance to redeem yourselves. Do this, find the traitor, and you will all be reinstated and returned to the Blue Guards."

Returned to the palace. Blues once more. Having redeemed themselves and brought down those working with Val to betray their king. Now there was a carrot. The one thing they all desperately wanted.

There was a slight rustle behind him, but no other

sound or movement. That anyone had twitched at all showed just how affected they were.

Was this some kind of test? Maybe the king and the Lord High Chancellor wanted proof that they were loyal to the kingdom and not their former friend?

Well. That wasn't a problem. This was a test they would pass with flying colors. The Lord High Chancellor could have just asked; the entire squad hated Lanval. And they loathed traitors. They wouldn't hesitate to take him down or the rest of his conspiracy. And then they would be the ones in the Blue tunics. Back where they should have always been.

"We would be glad to help." He looked the smug ass in front of him up and down. "And we look forward to seeing you again at the palace."

The guard took a sketch out of his saddlebag and passed it over. Tristan turned it round, keeping his face carefully blank as he recognized the subject.

Stupidly, at no point in the conversation had he imagined it would be her.

She was older. The last time he'd seen her, she'd been a teenager. Shy, just on the verge of womanhood, growing out of her baby softness. He and Val had been visiting their families before their first campaign, both newly accepted into the Royal Cavalry, eyes already firmly set on the Blue Guards.

He'd thought her a child. Sweet and harmless. Slightly annoying. Forever following them around. He and Val had alternated between teasing her and including her in their games.

No longer a child, she was entirely a woman now. And gods, she was beautiful. Long dark hair in a loose braid, wings curled softly at her sides. Eyes wide, with a delicate, innocent look on her face, as if the artist couldn't help capturing it.

And she was all that stood between him and getting his squad back home. A traitor who had resisted arrest and fled.

Val's sister, Nim.

Chapter Three

THE SHRIEKING of the seagulls woke her, mournful and discordant as they flocked around the pavilion. The sun had just risen, but the heavy clouds were dark and ominous, the world still misty and blurred with slow-rolling fog in the dim early morning light.

Nim stretched wearily, her body trembling with cold and pain. Her mouth was dry and tasted of salt. Conscious that she could easily fall, she glanced down at the gray waves lapping against the iron struts and away again. No matter what happened, she would not look down again—she was going to fight.

When she was steady, she forced herself to pull her injured wing across her body and prodded the wound. Her burns were angry, blistering, scarlet welts, swollen and hot. Left untreated, infection was only a matter of time.

Gods. All her shelves of ointments, tinctures, and remedies. All the work that she'd done. All the precious bottles that she had inherited from Mama. All gone forever. And no time to grieve; she had to keep moving.

She pushed up into the air to fly away… and nearly fell out of the sky as her wing muscles seized in agony. Her feet scrabbled back onto the beam, and she stood, panting in shock, trying to regroup. How ironic to fall into the sea now, having avoided its pull through the long nightmare-riddled night.

She moved her wings backward and forward, rolling her shoulders and stretching. Feeling the aching pull of tears and bruises. Acclimatizing herself to the torment of movement. Then, rather than trying to fly up, she jumped off the beam, angling downward toward the wet sand at the base of the pier.

It was a jarring and disorderly flight down to the lonely beach. A barely controlled fall more than flying. She stumbled as she landed, falling heavily to her knees before hauling herself up and carefully checking that no one was watching from the top of the pier.

It was gray and silent, like the beach.

Finally, away from the leaching iron, her brain cleared. Enough that she could start to think and plan. Enough that she recognized the miserable truth of what she had to do. She was going to lose her last tie to Val.

The leather jerkin she'd been wearing when the house was attacked was well worn and comfortable, but it was no good without a warm cloak to put over her bare arms. Her breeches and lace-up knee-high boots had kept her legs marginally warmer, but if the autumn night had been any colder, she would have been in real trouble. Far more urgent, though, was treatment for her wounds. And water. Her empty stomach clenched on itself—food, too.

Small white and gray birds scampered along the shore, back and forth through the foam of the rolling wavelets as

Nim trudged through the sand. Over the dunes and onto the well-paved road that led to the pier.

She darted over the road as quickly as she could, too worried about being seen to linger. The cobbles were flanked by a huge pleasure garden, and she followed a well-trodden path through formal flower beds filled with vibrant blooms and carefully maintained walks.

The gardens told her where she was. She vaguely remembered that the long-dead queen mother had commissioned the design years before. After she and her newborn baby girl had both died in the birthing bed, the gardens had been maintained in her honor. King Geraint had come down to take the sea air and enjoy the pleasure pavilion right up until his death at Ravenstone.

No doubt his son, the new king, would make use of them now. Part of her wished she could be there when Ballanor next arrived. To tell him exactly what she thought of him, his guards, and particularly his Lord High Chancellor.

But what would be the point? Her aching wings sagged. Yes, she was going to fight—but she wasn't an idiot. Val would want her to survive, not pick pointless fights with vicious, murdering bullies. That would only play right back into their hands. Bastards.

Gods. So many years she'd stayed at home. The dutiful daughter. The loving sister. The caring apothecary. Doing what was best for everyone else without much thought to what she wanted. What she needed. And look where that had gotten her—now she had nothing.

In future, she was going to stand up and take what she wanted.

She made her way through the gardens, staying in the

shadows as she flitted quietly from tree to tree. The paving of the gardens gave way to a dirt crossroads, dominated by a wooden cross pointing east to Brichtelmes or north to Kaerlud.

She paused for a moment beneath the sign, took a deep breath, and then turned to the nearby town. Away from the capital—the place where Val died.

She didn't want to go to Brichtelmes either, but she needed a cloak and supplies, and there was nowhere else for miles. Once she had what she needed, she could disappear into the countryside and nurse her wounds.

She would simply have to keep her head down and stay far away from any soldiers. And there would be soldiers. They had a large barracks outposted here as part of the sea defenses. Gods, the very barracks that Val would have stayed in when he first enlisted. Val, Tristan, and all their friends.

She wiped her dirty hands over her stinging eyes, refusing to give in to tears. Her brother was dead. Hanged for treason. Abandoned by those very friends. And nothing would bring him back.

It still didn't make sense to her; none of it did.

Begging for his life and weeping as he confessed. *He* had said so, laughing as he described it. But Nim couldn't imagine Val begging for anything. It made less sense to her than Val as a traitor, which was utterly ridiculous.

And abandoned by Tristan. Gods. Tristan, who had been closer to him than a brother. Tristan, whom they had played with as children. She had been prepared to play any role in their game, so long as they included her. All she had wanted was to be close to them. Her brother. And Tristan.

Tristan, whom she had loved secretly and hopelessly for so many years, even after he and Val were both soldiers and away on campaign far more than they were home.

The bastard. How could he have abandoned Val?

She couldn't imagine Val dead. Wouldn't. But her heart felt broken just the same. First Mama, so long ago. Then Papa just three weeks ago, a few hours after they heard of Val's arrest. Now Val. Her big, brave brother. Gone.

She patted the small pocket sewn into the waist of her breeches again. She still had Val's signet ring. *He* had thrown it at her feet, jeering as she scrabbled in the dirt to snatch it back. But she hadn't cared; she wasn't leaving it. And, by some miracle, she hadn't lost it through everything that had come after.

But she wasn't ready to think about that. Instead, she concentrated on battling her way along the tiny animal paths through the thorny gorse that flanked the road. Staying out of sight.

The town, when she finally got there, was bustling with midmorning commerce. Servants scurried, costermongers called their wares, and a colorful array of different people and different races thronged the streets. Some with wings, others proudly displaying their black and red tattoos, a few with glittering metallic scales.

She stayed away from all of them. Eyes down, hair over her face, she walked only in the shadows.

There seemed to be troops everywhere she looked. Deep voices calling commands and the stamp of booted feet. More than once, she crept around a corner only to flinch back at the sight of gleaming buckles and sword pommels. The black coats of the cavalry and the green uniforms of the military.

It was midday before she finally found what she was looking for, her feet hurting and her stomach rumbling, exhausted from constantly scanning for danger. A gloomy pawnbroker's shop stood on the street corner, its rough sign of three golden spheres swinging in the light breeze.

She waited until no one was watching and then darted through the narrow doorway. The dark-skinned proprietress watched her with narrowed eyes, the plum-colored scales flickering on her arms betraying both her Tarasque heritage and her distrust of Nim.

Nim forced herself to lower her shoulders and smile, keeping her hurt wing tucked well back, and stooping a little as she made her way to the dusty counter.

She took out Val's ring and put the heavy gold band on the counter with a small click. "I would like to trade this."

Damn. It hurt. More than she was prepared for, even knowing she had to do it. More than the moment she flung herself into the burning roof knowing she could die.

The broker flicked a glance at her wrists, and Nim shoved them behind her back, thankful she had laced her jerkin up high to her neck.

The old woman's eyes grew even more suspicious, but she lifted the ring in her gnarled fingers and held it up to her eye before putting it between her teeth and biting.

"It's gold," Nim stated firmly, offended, squashing down her wish that she could climb over the counter and snatch it back.

The woman assessed it once more, shrewd eyes noting the distinctive family crest of a wyvern, wings spread in flight, tail curled around a gleaming sapphire. "What do you want for it?"

"Your best cloak, water bottles, and five hundred groats."

The old woman laughed. "Fifty groats and a cloak, and take the satchel." She gestured to a worn leather bag displayed against a wall.

Nim swallowed down the acid burning her throat. "The satchel, cloak, and bottles, and two hundred groats."

"Eighty."

"One hundred and fifty, throw in a good blade, and you forget to sell the ring for at least a week."

"One hundred, no more. I can keep it until tomorrow."

Tears burned at the back of her eyes, and her throat was so tight that she could hardly breathe. But she knew what Val would have wanted. She could almost hear him, ruffling her hair and chuckling at her. *It's just a ring, Nimmy.*

She nodded, not trusting her voice, and turned away so that she didn't have to see the greedy satisfaction in the old woman's eyes.

She strapped her new dagger to her thigh, secured her new coin pouch in her pocket, and swung the satchel onto her back, wincing as it scraped at her wing, then covered everything with the slightly stained—but thankfully clean and warm—woolen cloak. Then, pulling the large hood up to cover her hair, and shadow her face, she stepped cautiously out of the pawnshop, back into the dusty, teeming road.

With money in her pouch and her hair covered, she decided to risk returning to a small apothecary she had passed a few streets back.

The sharp scent of pungent herbs mixing with warmer notes of lavender and geranium filled her with a deep longing for her stillroom. Half of her wished she could stand there, surrounded by the reassuring scents of home and safety. The other half wanted to get far away from the hurtful reminders of everything she'd lost. The need to escape won, and she hurried to purchase her honey and thyme poultice and leave.

Finally, exhausted, she made her way down the main street, looking for something to eat.

A hawker stood beside a large iron firepot, calling out his hot fried fish and cups of green peas. It smelled fantastic, of hot grease and fresh fish, and Nim's mouth watered as she paid for her first meal since her entire life had collapsed around her.

The hawker was handing over her bundle of paper wrapped fish, its heat scorching the tips of her fingers, when Nim heard movement behind her. The tread of booted feet and the telltale jingle of buckles and weapons.

Her heart raced hard in her chest, but she managed not to flinch. Managed to smile her thanks. To slowly take the greasy parcel. To stay calm as she turned away, doing everything she could to avoid attention.

Keeping her face deep inside her hood, she stepped carefully around the soldiers, flicking her eyes up only for a moment to check their uniforms. Black. Thank gods. Not the palace guards. Not *him*.

The younger of the two soldiers was speaking as she passed, and she almost stumbled right into his arms as she heard his words. "You mean they didn't actually hang him yet?"

Her hands started shaking so badly that she could hear the paper around her fish rustling, but she held it tightly and slowly eased into a deep alcove next to the hawker.

"No," the second soldier answered. "Apparently the king is enjoying spending a bit of time with him." They both laughed maliciously, and Nim's stomach dropped with a sudden rush of churning nausea.

"But surely he won't take much longer? Aren't we all being posted north? It's been weeks, and we still haven't declared war."

"Well, what I heard is that they're gonna do him on Thursday, no matter what happens. And then we ready for war. The king's spent all this time gathering the troops back after his father released all the conscripts. My mate said that he's been fortifying the palace…."

She didn't hear the rest, simply eased out of the shadows and started to walk. Somehow, she knew they were discussing Val.

Grendel had lied. Stinking bastard. Of course he had. He would have loved anything that caused her pain.

Her brother was still alive.

But only for three more days.

Chapter Four

"WHAT THE FUCK HAPPENED HERE?"

Tristan raised his eyebrow as Mathos added a belated, "Captain, sir."

"Sergeant," Tristan corrected half-heartedly, in total agreement with his friend. What the fuck had happened? In no way had he been prepared to find this kind of carnage.

The elegant manor home that he had played in as a child had been destroyed. Two walls had collapsed, and the roof was a blackened ruin of charred rafters. The kitchen garden was a trampled mess of uprooted plants still reeking of smoke.

He turned to Tor and Reece. "Go down to the local village, find someone who can tell us what happened."

Keeping his face carefully blank, Tristan stepped through the splintered door into the main hall. It had been violently looted. Nothing whole was left, just torn tapestries and fire-ruined furniture tumbled in amongst fallen roof tiles.

He stepped through into the kitchen where there had

once been a bustle of busy cooks and delicious smells. Now just broken glass crunching underfoot, and a single dented pot on the floor, lying in front of a massive, blackened, burned-out V that spread up most of the wall. The fire had started there.

A glance into the stillroom showed everything smashed, the strange smell of astringent herbs mixing rankly with the acrid stench of recent fire.

He had thought his heart completely immune to further pain. But the broken ruin of his childhood playground sent an unexpectedly vicious stab through him. He didn't need to see the rest of the rooms to know that the house was destroyed. Didn't want to see what had become of the bedrooms that he'd slept in as a boy. Or the sunny reception rooms where he and Val had mocked up epic battles.

He didn't want to, but he did it. Forced himself to make a slow and thorough tour of the devastation. The final decimation of his childhood memories.

Voices outside broke through his thoughts, and he shook off the sentimental idiocy as he strode back out the house, into the cold, fresh air.

"I've found the cook." Tor gently pushed a thickset, middle-aged woman forward as the rest of the squad stood listening nearby. He didn't recognize her. Not surprising, given how many years it was since he'd been back.

The woman was visibly trembling, and Tristan gave her a moment to collect herself before asking, "What's your name?"

"Tilda, sir." She bobbed an uneven curtsey, hands fluttering against her belly as she rose.

He kept his own hands folded behind his back, nonthreatening, his face calm. "We're not here to hurt you, Tilda. We just want to speak to you."

"Yes, sir. Sorry, sir."

"Where is everyone, Tilda?"

"Gone, sir." She looked at him for a second and then away.

"Because of the fire?"

"No, sir. I mean, me and the stable boy, yes," her voice wobbled, "but everyone else was gone already."

Tristan's scales slithered up his arms, under his vambraces and over his shoulders, but he kept his voice steady. "You can tell me, Tilda. Nothing will happen to you. The entire household was already gone?"

The woman seemed to relax slightly as she realized that he wasn't planning any immediate harm and answered more thoroughly. "After the master was bedridden, the young mistress had to let them go to yon Tarasque baron. He took over as magistrat for the district, so the steward and the marshal and all the pages went to him. Actually," Tilda looked at him more closely, "you have the look—"

"Thank you," he interrupted in a stern voice, and she flinched away again. He didn't need a reminder of the father he had spent his childhood hiding from. And didn't need to be judged by the old man's callous actions either. "Then what happened?"

Her wrinkled face collapsed into deeper lines of grief. "When we got the news—the news about young Lanval's arrest. Well, it was too much for the master. His heart... He couldn't...." She drifted into wet snivels.

"He died?" Tristan prompted.

"Three weeks ago. A few hours after they got the news."

That hurt more than he'd imagined. Val's father, Morgan, had taken him in, treated him like a part of the family. He'd been the closest thing Tristan had to a father. And now he was gone.

Yet another death that could be laid at Val's feet.

The woman shuffled back at the look on his face, and he forced himself to lower his shoulders. "And then what happened?"

A flash of genuine terror crossed her fleshy face, causing her chins to tremble. "And then the others came."

Tristan had to force himself to speak patiently and softly. Gods knew that it wouldn't help to shout at her. "What others?"

"The soldiers and the Lord High Chancellor."

"Lord High Chancellor?" He couldn't keep the note of disbelief from his voice. Grendel hated leaving the palace.

"Yes. And two Blues. Said the king sent them special. They wanted to take the master, but he was already in the ground. She showed them the grave, over yon, but it wasn't enough. They were looking for treason. Traitors. She told us to run and hide, but we couldn't just leave her. They made us stand outside while they ripped the house apart. Couldn't find anything though, could they? Broke milady's bottles. All her remedies. But it still wasn't enough."

Cold slithered up his spine. "What did they do then?" he asked softly.

"Said he'd prove that she had conspired with the traitor, didn't he?" She pressed her hands against her chest as she spoke, as if to hold herself together. "Took her by her hair and dragged her. The mistress. Back into the house. We could hear her screaming, but we couldn't follow, just me and Bertie, could we? Not with two soldiers standing over us, swords drawn. Bertie tried, but they walloped him so hard he fell. Took out a tooth. He's only fourteen. But gods. We heard her screaming." Her eyes closed as she whispered, "I'll never forget that sound...."

The men at Tristan's back stiffened into a rigid line. Not

one of them would ever harm a helpless woman in that way, no matter what she'd done. To imagine the palace guards.... His brain rejected the thought. Surely it wasn't possible. The cook was clearly overwrought.

The soldiers had come to arrest Nim, and she had resisted, that was all.

He shut down the shimmer of doubt that had crept through him. Val was a traitor. He knew that for a fact. Nim supporting her brother's treachery wasn't at all surprising. That was the whole point of taking her into custody—she would be tried by the assizes, the justice would hear the truth, and then she would be punished as she deserved. Just like Val.

He brought his concentration back to the cook's weepy description. "And then there was the fireball," she continued, "straight up through the roof. Flames running down the walls, sparks flying everywhere. The soldiers ran in, and the Lord High Chancellor ran out, but Mistress Nim was gone. Couldn't find her anywhere."

Gods, his chest ached. He rubbed it roughly, wondering if he'd eaten something spoiled.

"And where is Mistress Nim now?"

For the first time, Tilda looked him square in the eye, and suddenly he could see how much she hated him. And not just him; her eyes flickered over the soldiers at his back, filled with revulsion.

It was a shock. He was, had been, a Blue Guard. The best of the best. No one looked at them like that.

Tilda kept her eyes locked on his. "Gone. No one knows where."

Tristan glanced over at Jeremiel, needing his special talent. The red-haired man nodded once, "Truth."

Tristan grunted. Surely Tilda would have at least

noticed the direction Nim had gone in. "Did she go for the hills?"

The cook gave him a fierce look, fear and hatred mixing with her pleasure in delivering bad news. "She did not. Took the dogs out, didn't they? Never found her."

"Truth," Jeremiel agreed quietly.

Tristan pulled out a coin and passed it to the woman, letting her go. Then watched her, grim-faced, as she fled as fast as if she had been granted an unexpected reprieve from the Abyss.

Had he simply never noticed how much the ordinary people hated the black uniform? Or was this something new? Was it the same for the Blues? What the fuck was going on?

He glanced at the loose line of soldiers behind him. They looked like he felt. Grim. Concerned. But resolute.

He would think about it all later. For now, they needed to reassess. They had ridden hard all morning, expecting to quickly find one small woman hiding comfortably somewhere near her home. They could hand her to the authorities who would easily determine her guilt and be done with the whole thing by dinner and back in the palace —wearing their Blues—within a day.

But this was nothing like he'd expected. And now they had to hunt down Val's little sister. Morgan's daughter.

He swallowed against the worsening burn in his chest, and clasped his hands behind his back. If there was one thing he knew, it was that no one could just disappear.

He looked carefully at the house again. At the broken tiles. The collapsed beams. Damn, it was so obvious. The Blue Guards he'd met were both wingless. And bloody arrogant. It would never have occurred to either of them.

"Garet, Jos, fly up, please. Look on the roof."

The two Mabin soldiers unfurled their wide leathery wings and launched themselves into the sky. It was only a minute before a satisfied voice came floating down. "You're right, Captain, she went this way."

Jos landed next to the rest of the squad, Garet a few seconds later. "Looks like the fire tore through the ceiling and then the girl broke through the rest of the way. There's blood, thick on one of the rafters. I reckon she caught her wing as she fought her way out." His voice held a reluctant respect.

"And we're in luck," Garet added. "There's a trail. Hard to see from the ground, but from the air…." He shrugged. He didn't speak much, and they already had the gist.

No wonder the two Blues had been so pissed. She'd made them look like idiots in front of the Lord High Chancellor.

And they were idiots. Who the hell sent dogs to scent for someone that could fly?

Tristan clasped his hands behind his back, willing his scales to settle. This was good. The Blues' ineptness worked in their favor. They couldn't track her, but the Hawks could. She was alone and injured; it wouldn't take long.

Fuck, now he had a picture in his head of Nim, hurting and all alone.

He shook it away, but his voice was rough as turned his back on the burned-out ruin. "Mount up, Hawks. Garet, you're in the air. Find her."

Chapter Five

THE OINTMENTS HAD SOOTHED the burns down to a dull ache, but she couldn't do anything about her torn wing muscle. Rest, ice, compression... all things she couldn't do.

Flying was out. But she could still run.

She had to be in Kaerlud before Thursday. What she would do once she was there, she had no idea, but she knew she had to go. And so, she ran.

And when she couldn't run anymore, she walked.

Eventually a farmer passed her with a cart laden down with hessian sacks filled with recently harvested barley and offered her a ride. She accepted gratefully, allowing herself to rest among the rough bags, and finally eat her lunch. The fish was cold and oily, the peas grown bitter, and the smell turned her stomach. But she forced it down as she watched the coastal gorse and scrubby blackthorn give way to chalk down land with its rolling hills of springy grasses and the occasional wind-twisted hawthorn tree.

When the farmer reached his turn, she hopped off, thanked him gratefully, and continued to walk. She was used to being on her feet all day, but not like this. Her whole body hurt. And she was travelling far too slowly. Gods, she wished she could fly.

The mileposts at the crossroad showed fifty-four miles to the city. By her reckoning, so long as she only took short breaks, she could walk it in a little less than a day. Two days if she allowed time to sleep, which she would have to do.

It was doable, but only just.

If she'd been able to fly, she could have halved that time. She stretched out her wing, just to test it, and nearly went to her knees as the torn muscles clenched in agony.

She put her head down and carried on walking.

By the time the sun started to sink behind the hills, she had crossed the down lands and entered a stretch of woodland interlaced with little streams and ponds. It would offer her the best chance of finding somewhere to hide, which she needed before it became completely dark.

She left the road and walked a good length into the woods before she found a dense copse of trees that she could rest amongst.

The thick moss and ferns that surrounded her were soft but damp and cold. She wrapped herself tightly in her woolen cloak before sinking down, knees bent, back against a tree, and closed her eyes.

Frogs and nightjars called in the clammy air, and Nim sighed. Was Val sitting in a cell while she sat out in the woods? Was he being tortured? Did he know what Grendel had done?

She shivered, not wanting to think about it.

He was alive. She knew it in every cell of her body. She would find him and figure out some way to get him free. To prove that he was innocent of whatever stupidity he'd been accused of. And then they would both tell Tristan to fuck off.

She groaned softly, wishing she could stop thinking about the man that had abandoned her brother. He sure as hell wasn't thinking about *her*.

It was the sudden shocking destruction of her life—the loss of Papa, Val's arrest, the attack on their home—that had brought Tristan so powerfully to mind. It was the only explanation. After years of her love for him being a small, unspoken grief, suddenly it was all she could think about. Tristan's betrayal and Val's arrest, intrinsically linked and equally impossible to understand.

Tristan and the rest of the Hawks should have stayed with Val. Helped him to clear his name. But instead they'd abandoned him. Grendel had been only too delighted to tell her just how quickly they'd walked away.

She hated them. Them and all the Blues. For everything they'd done. Everything they'd allowed.

Oh, she knew how strangely Val had been acting in the weeks before his arrest. His grim silence on his final visit home, combined with dire warnings and strangely intense goodbyes was evidence that something had been terribly wrong. Something his friends should have had the loyalty to help him solve. Val was a good man; she just had to find a way to prove it.

Nim drifted into a disturbed sleep, cold and uncomfortable, wracked by nightmares. She twitched and whimpered, occasionally opening her eyes and staring into the darkness of the woods as hunting owls called and small creatures rustled through the undergrowth. Listening intently for any movement, any danger, before drifting off again. It was a relief when the birds began their morning chorus and she finally opened her eyes to a hazy green-gray light.

She washed her face and filled her water bottles in one of the small streams lacing through the woods. Then she picked her way through the roots and stones back to the road.

She stood under a tree for long moments, watching. No one was nearby. Long golden streaks of light and shadow lay prettily over the road, and birds sang undisturbed.

Her whole body felt chilled and stiff, so she decided to walk for the first hour or two, and then, when she was warmed, try her wings again.

She took a few steps out onto the road and then stopped. The birds had gone eerily silent.

The hair stood up on her arms as she was suddenly filled with an overwhelming sense of danger, and she stumbled back into the shadow of the trees.

She whirled, ready to run.

Too late.

A man leaped from a nearby tree, wings spread wide, letting out a high, piercing whistle as he flew. Just like the sound of a hunting bird of prey. Oh gods, like a hawk.

Nim ducked under a low branch, tripped on the twisted roots at her feet, and only just righted herself as she fled.

She could hear answering whistles from up and down the road and knew that she would soon be surrounded. They were hunting her from the air, and there was nowhere to run. She would have to fight.

She ripped off her cloak and flung the satchel to the ground, freeing her arms. Pulled the knife out of its holster and backed against a tree, facing into a small clearing.

Her breath came in sharp pants as she watched the man who'd found her stalk into the forest, taking agile steps over the roots and rocks, closer and closer. Crashes behind her told her what she already knew: there was no escape that way. Hoofbeats on the road added to her hopelessness.

She clenched the knife tighter in her hand and forced herself to look at her attacker. Black uniform, too-long blond hair, a smug grin on a face that she might have thought handsome if he hadn't been stalking toward her, intent on capturing her.

"I win!" he called out to his unseen team with a chuckle. "Told you she'd turn off at the forest."

The answering chuckles were closer than she'd expected.

Nim stayed silent.

The man held up his empty hands as if to show her that he had no weapons. But Nim wasn't falling for that. She knew all about this new crop of soldiers and how they treated women.

He took a step closer. And another.

Someone moved behind her tree, and the soldier's eyes flicked to the side. Disregarding her as a danger.

It was her opening. Nim dove, scraping herself along the rocky floor. He reached for her, but she had tucked her wings in tight, and before he could grab her, she was past. Past and running for her life.

She could hear him behind her, him and others. She whimpered, heart hammering as she flung herself around another tree. And straight into a wall of hard muscles and leather armor.

She screamed and slashed out desperately with her knife, unable to see past the blur of leather and black. She felt her blade catch against his belted vambrace, but then he grabbed her wrist and spun her, pulling her hard, her back to his front. One thick, scaled arm descended over her chest, still gripping her wrist, the other at her waist, trapping her as effectively as if she was a small child.

He lifted her off the ground and carried her back, stopping when he reached the clearing.

She couldn't see the man, only knew he wore the black armor and that she had to get away.

She threw her body back, bucking and kicking viciously behind her, but he simply spread his legs and gripped her tighter.

"Stop that," his deep voice growled at her ear, but she was lost in her terror, trapped.

She flailed against him desperately, flinging her head forward, teeth bared, looking for somewhere not covered in leather that she could bite.

He shook her, hard, and ordered again, "Stop. Now. Before you get hurt."

The cold order filled her with utter despair, and she quietened, hanging limply from his arms as a hot tear tracked down her cheek.

Several other men had surrounded them, watching with interest as he spoke again. "Can I put you down?"

She nodded, numb, and he lowered her back onto her feet, still gripping her wrist.

"Drop the knife."

She opened her hand and let the knife fall. He kicked it away to the other men before releasing her wrist.

She felt him stiffen behind her and glanced down. He'd seen the deep purple fingerprints bruising the pale skin of the wrist he'd just released. And, by the grim looks, so had everyone else.

She pulled her arm away and wrapped it around her belly. But he wasn't done. She'd opened her collar to wash her face in the stream and had left it hanging, enjoying the comfort of fewer buttons. Oh, how she regretted that now. He pulled her jerkin to one side, not roughly, but firmly, exposing her neck down to her collarbone. And she knew what they all would see, the mottled green and blues, thumbprint-shaped bruises.

She felt a flood of shame. And then anger. And a deep abiding hatred for these men that made her feel that way.

Her braid had come loose in the fight, and she let her head hang, covering her tears of pain and rage behind a fall of hair as she frantically laced her jerkin.

"Nim?"

For the first time, she recognized that voice. Older, deeper, but definitely *his*. Gods. Of all the people to find her. As if her own treacherous thoughts had summoned him. How could the gods hate her so much that he was the one to hunt her down?

She wanted to fall to the ground and disappear beneath the leaves.

But she wasn't a coward. She turned, lifted her chin, and looked him in the eye. Tristan. Wearing the black uniform and sword of the cavalry divisions.

His face matched his voice. It was harder, with frown lines where once he'd smiled. Green eyes deeper, colder, and more cynical. Unshaved. A jagged scar under his left eye. His dark hair was too long, curling slightly as it touched his collar. Emerald and pewter scales on his arms that she should have recognized.

Just as handsome; more, maybe, than he had been. Her teenage crush, grown-up and devastating. And the bastard who had abandoned her brother. Who had tracked her down like an animal.

She took a step forward and let her hand fly with a hard slap to that rough cheek.

Chapter Six

Tristan knew what she was going to do a second before she even lifted her hand. And, in the same second, he also knew that he would let her. He stood still and took it.

The deep disgust he'd felt at himself when he saw how his big, calloused hands had pressed into the existing bruises on her delicate wrists had almost overwhelmed him, and he had no intention of making the same mistake again.

But more than that, a small voice inside him whispered that he deserved her scorn. Hunting down an injured woman. What would Morgan have thought of that?

Morgan's own daughter. Fuck, the man was probably cursing him from the grave.

He shook his head slightly but made no move to cover the bright red handprint as he stared down at her. There were a hundred things he should ask, but he couldn't think of any of them.

She stared back, her face tearstained and defiant. It was him that looked away, unable to bear her withering gaze. Or the unsettling flicker of interest from his beast.

He took a step back, needing distance, and shouted orders. "Hawks, rations. Jos, Garet, lookout, please."

The two Mabin soldiers flew off while the rest of the men rapidly dug a firepit and began setting out bread and eggs.

Mathos brought Nim her cloak and satchel and handed them over with a wink and a dramatic flourish that was so overdone, Tristan could swear he saw her almost smile.

It certainly did not make him want to smile. His beast turned in his belly, irritated, and he grunted a stern, "That's enough!" to Mathos, and then sighed when Nim went back to her blank-faced withdrawal, arms clasped around her belly.

He led her to a pile of rocks, and she sank down, huddled over her satchel.

He sat down next to her, elbows balanced on his knees as he tilted his head to watch her. She was even more beautiful than he'd imagined. Dark hair tumbled around her graceful shoulders. Soft curves and creamy skin that he had the strangest compulsion to touch. Big eyes such a deep blue, with tiny flecks of silver, that they reminded him of a lapis lazuli he'd seen once, long ago.

At that moment, her eyes were glancing at the position of the sun and then darting around the woods, noting the movement of the soldiers. Intelligent as well as beautiful— but a terrible spy. She was broadcasting every thought so loudly, she might as well shout it.

He leaned back and folded his arms as he spoke. "You can forget it. Any one of us would catch you before you took two steps. And in the extremely unlikely event you made it to the road, Garet and Jos will see you from the air."

She turned her face to him, assessing. Blinked, and then looked away without bothering to reply.

He cleared his throat, not used to being ignored. "Tell me what happened at the manor house."

"You've been?" she asked, voice soft and husky in a way that made him inexplicably uncomfortable. "Does anything stand?"

"No." He shook his head, frustrated at his own gruff response.

"Then you know what happened," she said quietly and looked away again.

"I want you to tell me."

She turned her body toward him, watching him carefully as she asked, "Why do you care about the house?"

"I don't," he started, realizing as he watched her face shut down completely that it was the wrong thing to say.

"Nim," he tried to reason with her, "I'm trying to get some kind of understanding of what's happened."

"And this," she waved her hand, taking in the armed soldiers, "is you being understanding?"

"No," said an angry voice beside him.

Tor. The angriest of all of them over what had happened. The others had lost their commissions, but Tor had been disowned. He'd brought shame on his illustrious family, and they had cut him out completely in response.

Now he was staring at Nim with a belligerent scowl. "This is the Hawks taking a traitor's sister, a traitor herself, into custody to face justice. With a bit of luck, you'll hang together."

If he hadn't been sitting right next to her, Tristan wouldn't have been able to see the repressed flinch. As it was, Nim's face drained to a deathly pale.

He could feel his scales flickering. That primal part of him, his inner beast—that part that turned him into a berserker, indifferent to pain, deadly in bloodlust—was rearing its head in frustrated rage and an inexplicable need to protect this small, treacherous woman.

He frowned at Tor, trying to keep calm. "Shut up and get back to work. You can patrol the road."

"But—" Tor's fists were clenched, his black and red tattoos rippling as he folded his arms.

Tristan stood, giving him no time to continue. "Yes, sir. That's all you say. Do it now."

"Yes, sir, Captain, sir." Tor's reply was rich with sarcasm.

"No." Nim's voice was clear and firm as she rose to her feet. "Don't send him away. What's the point of this stupid game? Is it making you feel better to act all friendly before you condemn an innocent woman? Is this to lull me into some false sense of security before you—"

She cleared her throat, and Tristan braced himself, but she didn't finish the thought.

Instead, she stood, back straight, chin up, and slowly spread her wings. For the first time, he could see the deep gashes and angry, blistered burns. Her right wing hung slightly low, and he realized that she had flown miles with internal damage. It must have been agony.

Her head only just reached the top of his chin—she was tiny compared to him, or any one of the men, broken and exhausted, but she stared them down, unflinching.

The men in the clearing were absolutely silent, watching her as she stepped up to Tor and held out her arms, wrists together, palms up. Like a supplicant. Or a slave.

She continued, her voice only just loud enough for everyone to hear. "Do it. You know you want to."

Tor didn't move. No one did.

"So full of judgment," her voice was low and mocking, "you didn't even need to ask one single question before you condemned me. Do it. Here, I'll help." She shoved her bruised wrists toward Tor's chest. "First you take my wrists and pull, drag me to those trees over there." She tilted her head toward a small thicket surrounded by blackthorn. "That's right," she murmured as they all looked distrustfully into the darkness of the forest.

She lifted a trembling hand and pulled her jerkin collar wider, exposing her slender neck. "Then you wrap your hand around my throat and throw me to the ground, climb over me, pin me down, make sure I'm truly afraid. Then you whisper in my ear, nice and slowly, all the things you do to traitors."

A look of shocked horror crossed Tor's face. All the men were silent, watching with stunned faces while Tristan's beast went insane, emerald scales flickering in slow waves up his arms. "Stop it. No one is going to hurt you."

Nim spun toward him and laughed. But the sound held no joy, only grief and rage. "So you say. But you're the worst hypocrite of them all. You knew exactly who I was and came after me anyway. Don't pretend you're not here to drag me back to Grendel. What do you think Grendel will do when he gets his hands on me? Why not take a turn? No one will be surprised. Especially not after what you did to Val."

"What *I* did?" He couldn't help the harsh growl, ignoring the rest of her horrific accusation to deal with later.

"Yes. You. He loved you like a brother, trusted you, and you abandoned him when he needed you most."

"No. He betrayed us, led us into an ambush, and then ran, leaving good men to die. The king to die."

"That's not what happened." She was emphatic. "Val would never—"

Tristan cut her off, so enraged it was all he could do to get the words out. "You. Weren't. There."

"I wasn't at Ravenstone, but I was there when he came home a few weeks before. Silent and depressed, worrying himself sick. I was there when he told me of his fears that nothing could prevent another war. Val told me never to trust the king. And to make sure that I never, ever spent any time alone with Ballanor or Grendel." She slowly lifted her purple wrists once more. "And he was right."

"No," Tristan began, "he fled with Princess Alanna, leaving us all—"

"He was her personal guard, yes? His job was to take her to safety, yes?" Her voice was thick with outrage.

"Yes, but—"

"He did what any soldier with honor would do. He got the princess away from danger. And you condemned him for it. Used that as an excuse to accuse Val of treachery. You, his best friend, left him, without even once asking him what had happened."

Nim looked slowly around the silent clearing, meeting each man's eyes. "When Val came home, that last time, he said goodbye to Papa. Such a long, careful goodbye. As if he knew something bad was coming. I begged him not to go back, and do you know what he said? He told me that if good men refused their duty, however hard it might be, then evil men will be allowed to rule."

She wiped her shaking hand down her face, her eyes bright with grief and horror. "Val told me that everything I had ever heard about Princess Alanna was a lie and that he was the only person who could protect her. That he had to do his duty to her, or he couldn't live with himself. He told me to start preparing for war. And then he went back. Now you all want to tell me that a man who puts honor before everything would betray his own people. The men he saw as brothers. It doesn't make any sense."

Tristan clasped his hands behind his back, trying to control the roiling emotions churning through him. Confusion, anger, and the first nasty prickles of doubt.

"No." He shook his head, remembering everything Ballanor and Grendel had said. The proof they'd offered. "Val and Alanna were having an affair. He betrayed his brothers for her."

Nim laughed again, the sound deep with scorn. "Val? Seduce a married woman? You know him even less than I thought."

Tristan glanced at his men. When she said it like that, it didn't make a lot of sense. Val had been obstinate about never fucking a married woman, even when they threw themselves at them. Out of respect for Tristan. For what adultery had done to his childhood.

Was it possible that he had made a mistake? Had he truly abandoned his friend like she thought he had?

No.

She was wrong. People changed. Val certainly had. And he wouldn't be the first man who went insane over a woman. Tristan's father was an excellent example.

Around him there were multiple frowns and scowls. Everyone was thinking back, trying to decide if they had missed something crucial.

But they didn't need to wonder. King Ballanor had been certain. Lord Grendel too. The two highest-ranking men in the kingdom—the men they owed their loyalty to. They had evidence, eyewitnesses to Val and Alanna's affair. No one would accuse a princess of adultery without fucking good reason. And then there were those Verturian arrows. It was impossible to deny.

It was going to be terrible for Nim, but the truth was that her brother was a traitor.

He rubbed his forehead, wishing he could reach to the stabbing pain starting behind his eye. He couldn't think clearly about any of this. And making it even worse was the look on Nim's face. The way she bit her trembling lip. The tear streaks down her face as she showed them her neck.

But he did know one thing deep in his gut—this was not a woman who was party to some great deception. Whatever Val had done, she had no part in it.

Instead, someone had hurt her. Badly. Someone had done the things she accused Tor of planning.

He hadn't wanted to believe the old cook, but he couldn't deny it anymore. And now the Hawks were party to it too. Looking at her, he knew the truth. They had hunted down an innocent, wounded woman.

The thought sent his scales flickering along his arms in horror. Guilt churned, bitter at the back of his throat.

Nim's wings fluttered as she wrapped them around her body like a protective blanket, and he wished he could do something, anything, to take that look off her pale face. The look that said she'd judged them and found them lacking.

"Fine," she said, her voice soft and tired. Her shoulders slumped low in her exhaustion. "Hang me with Val. That's where I wanted to go anyway."

Chapter Seven

NIM PICKED up her cloak from where it had fallen on the ground and pulled it on, lifting the hood so that her face was covered. She was exhausted, and she wanted to cry. But the last thing she planned to do was show any more weakness in front of these men. In front of Tristan.

She walked a little way from the campfire and lowered herself to sitting, knees bent, back against a moss-covered rock. Her wing was throbbing again, but she didn't want to nurse it while the Hawks were watching.

After a few minutes, the man who'd smiled at her earlier —Mathos, Tristan had called him—brought her a plate covered in bread and eggs. His smile was gone, and he had a pensive, worried look about him.

She knew she should eat, so she forced down a few mouthfuls before her stomach rebelled and she pushed it away. Then she lowered her head to her knees and closed her eyes, trying not to give in to the wave of hopeless despair that threatened to engulf her.

She heard the squad finish eating and then Tristan

giving quiet commands. Gods, she still remembered when he was Tris. The skinny boy with dark hair and shadowed green eyes. Not anymore—now he was Tristan, Captain of the Guard, through and through, even while wearing the black.

It wouldn't be long before they were on the road. Well, what she'd said earlier was nothing but the truth; if they took her to Val, she would have achieved exactly what she wanted.

A soft jingle of buckles and the tread of boots walking away told her that they were moving out, and she thought about getting up before someone hauled her up. Tor most likely. Bastard.

But before she could move, Tristan sat down next to her. Somehow, she knew it was him before she even opened her eyes.

She lifted her head and glanced around, noting, to her surprise, that they were alone.

Tristan was sitting with his back to her rock, knees bent like hers, watching her with a strange, uncertain look. The look of a man facing battle, knowing he was unprepared. He cleared his throat twice before he spoke. "Jeremiel says you're telling the truth."

She stiffened. "Did you think I was lying?"

"No. I… no. Honestly, I'm not sure what to think anymore, but if there's one thing I'm sure of, it's that you don't lie. You never did, even as a child."

She let herself relax slightly. "What do you want, Captain Tristan?" She knew her voice had a mocking edge to it, but she couldn't stop it.

She could see his jaw clenching and unclenching as a sheen of forest green and pewter scales rippled up along the back of his neck, and she knew he must be deeply affected to be showing such a strong reaction. Since she'd known him, he had always worked hard to keep his cool. Kept his beast locked down. Almost silent. Other Tarasque had whole conversations with their beasts, but never Tristan. He kept his firmly under control. Gods knew that displays of emotion had never been accepted in his father's house.

His voice was rough as he spoke. "Nim, I have to know, did he… Grendel, I mean, did he…." His eyes flicked to the bruises at her throat and settled there as he searched for the right words.

She let the silence hang between them, but only for a moment before she replied quietly, "No."

The air left his body in a rush, the scales smoothing down his neck in a wave, and then rising again to hard armor as she continued, "But not for lack of trying."

His clear green eyes found hers. "Please tell me what happened."

It was the please that got to her, she didn't think she'd ever heard him use the word before, and she found herself answering. "Grendel came to the house. Told me that Val was dead. That he had died alone, abandoned by his squad. And that they were looking for his fellow conspirators. That we were all traitors. But now, I think… I think Val's alive and they wanted to punish him by hurting us."

Tristan grunted, a low sound, maybe agreement, maybe not, and she continued slowly, "Anyway, Papa was already dead, and that made him angry. So he took it out on me. At first, he just swore and ranted. Told me all about how Val had died, screaming and begging. All alone. But I didn't believe him. There's plenty of things Val would do but screaming and begging aren't among them. That just made him angrier. He wanted to punish someone. Immediately.

And I think….” She took a deep breath. “I think he likes pain. Other people's pain.”

Her hands started to tremble where they rested on her knees and she clasped them together to hold them still. To her surprise, Tristan covered them with his big fingers.

His quiet support helped her to keep speaking. She tried to be quick, professional almost, like giving someone a difficult diagnosis. Just say it, and then deal with the consequences. “He dragged me into the house, alone. To the kitchen. Then he threw me onto the table, held me there by my wrists and throat. Told me what would happen. How he was going to hurt me. Exactly what he could do with his knives. And how, afterward, he would drag me back to the capital for everyone to see.”

She was helpless to prevent her slow tears from burning paths down her cheeks as she relived the terror of that horrendous day. Grendel's foul breath against her face. His armor digging into her body. His repulsive weight as he ground himself into her. The gleam in his eyes as he described the exact size of his dagger blades and how slowly he planned to cut her. How the men would watch. How she had fought and begged, but it just excited him more.

Tristan was rigid beside her, his scales flickering all the way up onto his cheeks. Somehow his distress settled her, made it possible to finish, and the poisonous words poured out. “He let go of my wrists to undo his belt. It was only a second, but he was distracted, and I kicked him. He fell forward, but I was screaming and kicking so hard that I rolled off the table before he could reach me.

“I crawled into the stillroom. Most of my bottles were smashed, but there were a few left. One in a dark clay bottle, they wouldn't have recognized. Naphtha. Papa had it for something. I don't know…. Anyway, I threw it and it smashed into a pot boiling on the fire. It exploded in a huge fireball that took out half the rafters, flames pouring down the walls, an instant inferno. I was already running when I threw it, so all I did was launch myself up behind the fire, follow its path out the roof and fly away."

Tristan cursed and muttered viciously almost under his breath, just loud enough for her to hear. "I'll kill him myself." But, despite the murderous look on his face, his hand was soft and careful as he reached over and gently wiped her tears away.

He cupped her chin and turned her head to face him as he murmured, "He will never touch you again, I promise."

Nim shivered, confused. His words sounded genuine. Caring, almost. And she wanted to lean into his strength. This strange man that she had once known so well. She wanted to believe him, to not be so alone. She wanted him to be the man she'd wished for all her life.

But he wasn't that man. She couldn't trust him. She hated him for the way he'd treated Val, for hunting her down, for planning to hand her back to Grendel.

A small voice inside her whispered that he hadn't known the truth. Somehow, he'd been lied to. That maybe, just maybe, she could genuinely convince him. And, at that moment, sitting next to his big warm body, feeling his fingers sweep so very gently down her face, she felt safe for the first time in weeks. More than safe. She was with Tristan. And for the first time ever, he was genuinely, truly looking at her.

"How did you find me, anyway?" she asked softly, curious and wanting to change the subject, to shake off the confusing mix of emotions he was causing.

Tristan gave the kind of grunt that she was starting to recognize as reluctant amusement. "Sheer luck. We lost your trail over the forest in the middle of nowhere. We had no idea which way to go, but one of the men remembered a town a few hours' ride away, so we thought we might as well start there. At the very least, we might find somewhere warm to sleep. We got there late evening and showed your picture around after dinner. A woman in a pawn shop remembered you."

"Bloody broker," Nim muttered. "I knew I couldn't trust her."

His chuckle sounded genuine. "We didn't find you in the town, so we took a chance and spread out along the road. We were told that you were conspiring with Val, so we assumed you'd head north toward Kaerlud. Mathos calculated how far he expected you to get and then predicted you'd sleep, and that we'd easily spot you on the empty road in the morning. He was right."

Sheer luck for them, maybe. The worst kind of luck for her.

"I'm glad we found you, Nim. That you're not out here alone anymore," he admitted quietly.

Gods. He sounded so genuine. Tristan was sitting with her, listening to her, promising to protect her. His half-grin reminding her so much of the boy she'd known that it physically hurt.

She was about to ask him what he was going to do with her when he sat up to reach into his pocket. He opened her fingers gently and placed something warm and heavy in the center of her palm.

She looked down and let out a strangled sob. It was Val's signet ring.

"Oh, gods." Tristan looked deeply unsettled. "Now I made you cry again."

"No," she tried to explain, clutching Val's ring tightly

against her chest, "I'm crying because I thought it was gone forever, along with everything else. Everyone else. Thank you."

A thought struck her. "But it must have cost you a lot. I'll pay you back, I promise. As soon as I can."

Tristan looked even more uncomfortable, shifting where he sat. "Please, don't. It's yours. Your family's. It should never have been taken from you."

He looked so serious and honorable, so much like she remembered him. And she was so relieved, so glad to have Val's ring back in her hand, that she acted without thinking. Simply leaned over and wrapped her arms around his neck, burying her face into the warm skin at his throat where his pulse beat strong and steady.

His whole body went stiff, and she felt her face blaze with embarrassment. She started to pull away, wishing she hadn't done such a stupid thing. But before she could, his arms enclosed her in a tight band, holding her firmly.

She froze, confused and unsettled, but he just held her patiently. Slowly, she relaxed again, enjoying his scent of warm leather and male skin, the sound of his heartbeat thudding in her ear. Enjoying being cared for in a way that she had thought she may never feel again.

He turned, then, using his strong arms to lift her sideways and onto his lap, where her head could nestle against his chest, her body surrounded and protected by his, sheltered and safe.

Slowly, she let go of all the thoughts of Grendel, of being hunted and alone, of whether or not she could trust Tristan or any of his squad, slipping into the peace of knowing that he was holding her.

They stayed like that, breathing quietly in the dappled sunlight as birds called and sang around them. She felt a soft pressure on her hair and wondered if he had kissed her.

Eventually she looked up to see him staring down at her, eyes intent. She couldn't help her answering smile or the tiny thrill as his eyes flickered to her lips.

How many times had she dreamed of exactly this moment?

"Thank you," she whispered.

"What for?" His voice rumbled against her ear.

"For believing me. For making me feel safe."

"Mmm." The rumble felt soft and contented.

She felt the same. But that didn't change how little time they had.

"So," she asked against his chest, "what do you think would be the best way to rescue Val?"

"What?" he asked roughly, his face going hard.

She pulled away so that she could see him clearly. His eyes were narrowed, his shoulders bunched, scales flickering once more, and her heart dropped. "We are going to rescue Val, aren't we?"

"Well," he started and then paused.

"What do you mean, 'well'?" she hissed, scrambling off his lap and standing, rigid with outrage.

He rose too, looking down at her but not answering. His angry frown was back. Gods, how much she hated that closed-off look of bitterness and cynicism. He'd been quiet and reserved as a boy—with everyone except Val—but not hard and mistrusting like he was now.

"I thought you believed me!" Her voice had risen, and she hated how much it sounded like a child wailing.

"I do," he answered curtly. "I believe that you genuinely think—"

She didn't give him a chance to continue. "Gods. I've

gone from being a treacherous liar to a complete idiot. Too stupid to know whether my brother is a traitor. Too brainless to compare Val's behavior to Grendel's."

His frown deepened, but he still didn't answer, just looked down at her, jaw clenched. She refused to be intimidated by the way he was standing over her.

That woman, the one that played safe and tried to be good for everyone else, was gone. She had died in the flames that destroyed her home. The long night alone on the pier had only reinforced it. Now she would fight. Fight Tristan. Fight Ballanor. Fight them all if she had to.

She crossed her arms and glared back up at him. "I won't leave Val to die. You have to make a choice—trust me, or hand me back to Grendel."

Tristan clasped his hands behind his back, his scales flickering angrily up his neck once more as he replied in a controlled voice, "Nim, you don't understand—"

Gods. She did understand. She understood completely. How could she have been so stupid as to think that he felt anything for her? That he would genuinely want to help her.

She stepped backward, horrified and betrayed, wanting nothing more than to get away from him.

She caught her foot on a tangled root and almost fell, would have fallen if Tristan hadn't put out a strong hand and caught her. But she shook him off, snarling, "Don't touch me!"

He jerked his hand back as if burned, and she took the opportunity to turn her back on him and walk away. Chin in the air, shutting her anguish away under a thick layer of rage.

Chapter Eight

HOW THE FUCK had he gone, in less than a minute, from sitting quietly with his arms full of lovely, soft woman to this?

He couldn't remember the last time he'd held a woman like that. Maybe he never had. Her body had been so delicate and trusting against his, her breath warm against his skin. For the first time in weeks, longer maybe, he'd felt something move against the brittle shell over his soul.

The need to hold her there, protect her and keep her safe, had risen in a rush that almost overwhelmed him. His beast has been completely focused on her, convinced that it had found… something… as it urged him to hold her. To get as close to her as possible.

He had told himself not to touch her, not to give in to that blinding need to feel her skin against his—and then he'd found himself lifting her into his lap anyway. And for a minute, it had been perfect. Exactly what he had been missing without even knowing it.

And yet, somehow, it had only taken a few seconds to all

go to shit. Now he watched as Nim stalked out of the woods in front of him, her furious hurt battering him in waves.

He followed more slowly, keeping an eye out for any danger, angry with himself, but also with her. She was being bloody fucking unreasonable.

It was obvious that she was innocent—there was no way he would hand her back to Grendel now. But how could he keep her safe if she rushed straight back to Kaerlud and into the arms of the Blues that filled the capital? All for a man who might well deserve to be exactly where he was.

Nim was convinced of Val's innocence; but she was a good, loyal person who would never abandon her brother. And she was protected enough to think that everyone was like her. She didn't know what living through a war did to people. Fuck, she hardly even knew her brother after all the years he'd been away.

Still, there was a tiny, horrified voice inside him that wondered. What if he had been wrong all this time? If he had not left the palace too quickly to speak to Val after the king's death, might he have learned something that could have explained what had happened that day?

He was disrupted from following the thought any further by the sound of Nim shouting. He broke into the dappled sunlight of the road to see her standing belligerently in front of Tor.

The only Apollyon in the Hawks, Tor was not quite as tall as the rest of the squad, but he was still at least four inches taller than Nim. And significantly broader. His arms, as thick as her thighs, were currently folded over his chest so that the red and black tattoos marking his family heritage stood stark against his black uniform.

Nim was loudly insisting that Tor follow up on his threat and take her to her brother, with graphic reference to the size of Tor's manhood if he failed to do as he'd promised. Thimbles were mentioned. As was honor.

Tristan had honestly never seen Tor look so disconcerted. Around him, the men were not even trying to conceal their smirks, and a strange feeling filled him. A feeling of pride in this fierce woman. Of genuine amusement as he watched her intimidate his grumpiest soldier.

He felt his lips twitch but carefully controlled himself. He had a good idea that laughing would not go down well —even though it was Tor he was laughing at.

Instead, he stepped up, closed his hands on her hips, and lifted Nim away, enjoying her outraged gasp as he settled her a few steps further down the road, away from Tor.

"No one is taking you to be hanged. And no one is taking you to Grendel," he said, giving her a look that would have sent the soldiers under his command running but just made her tip her chin up and narrow her eyes.

He let some of his frustration leak into his voice. "Don't say it again."

He turned to look at the squad clustered around them and raised his voice. "Hawks, we have a problem. This is not a democracy. You do what you're told. And I do what I'm told. But not today. I will not hand this woman back to Lord Grendel."

"Nim," Nim said loudly.

He turned to her, annoyed at being interrupted, and glared. "What?"

"I'm not 'this woman,' I'm Nim. Val's sister. Morgan's daughter. Apothecary. I'm a person."

Tristan had to work hard not to bark at her in

frustration, especially when he turned back to see that his men were now laughing at him instead of Tor.

He ignored them and continued, "I cannot and will not hand *Nim* to Grendel. This puts us in direct insubordination of our orders. Anyone who disagrees with this decision is welcome to say so now."

The men grew serious, each looking around at his brother soldiers. One by one they all met his eyes and dipped their chins. They stood with him.

Tristan turned to Tor. He'd nodded, but Tristan needed the words. "Do you agree?"

"Yes, I agree." Tor's voice was strong as he replied. "She can't go back. I would never, not ever…." He seemed to lose the words, as if remembering Nim's earlier outburst.

"I think I speak for everyone," Jeremiel added, purple-blue eyes flashing, "when I say that our duty is to protect, not to harm. None of us would hand an innocent woman over to a monster." Then he turned to Nim, his purple-blue eyes serious. "You are innocent, aren't you?"

Her reply was outraged. "Of course!" But then she had to go and add a reluctant, "Except…."

Every single man stiffened, and Tristan took an instinctive step closer to Nim.

She continued softly, "Except if you consider me going to free my brother as a conspiracy to treason. Because you have to know that I don't plan to just leave him there."

Fuck. This woman. She was utterly incapable of lying.

Jeremiel nodded, confirming what Tristan already knew, that she was telling the truth. The entire squad relaxed, a few even grinning. Tristan pointedly ignored their knowing looks at how quickly he'd moved to guard her.

"You believe me?" she asked the men hopefully.

"We believe that you are telling the truth," Tristan

answered for them, carefully not adding that she could still be wrong about Val.

"Thank you," she said softly, a hint of color returning to her cheeks. "So you'll let me go?"

"Fuck, no." The words were out before he could stop them, and she whirled around, fists clenched. She opened her mouth for what would no doubt be a vicious analysis of him, his intelligence, and probably his prowess in bed, and he spoke quickly, hoping to explain. "Nim, please, I can't send you out alone to get hurt!"

"Oh." Her surprised gasp and sudden look of vulnerability at his words stung. Had she really thought he would just walk away and leave her to fend for herself? Or worse?

Maybe she had. And could he blame her?

"But what about Val?" she asked, looking up at him with those big blue eyes.

"I can't pretend that I'm convinced of his innocence like you are," he said, watching as she bristled. He kept going. "But I can concede that there is a chance that not everything was as it appeared."

"You'll help me?" she asked tentatively.

"I'm not sure how, but give us a chance to understand what happened. If, and I do mean if, it turns out that Val is innocent, I'll help you."

"Really?"

"Really." He meant it. He wanted proof. Wanted to know that he hadn't been terribly wrong about what happened at Ravenstone.

"Thank you." She smiled at him, a slow spread of joy that lit up her whole face, and he realized it was the first real smile she'd given. The kind of smile that made you want to get up in the morning. To do great things. To go down on your knees just to beg for one more chance to put that look on her face. The kind of smile he absolutely didn't deserve when he had every intention of proving her wrong about Val.

And yet... he would like to see that smile again. Fuck. He'd like to go down on his knees in front of her. He felt his cock twitch at the idea as his beast and body both stirred.

Nim had somehow gone from his best friend's baby sister to being entirely grown-up. A woman now. A woman that a small, faintly stirring part of his soul saw as *his*.

"If he's innocent, I'll help too," Jeremiel agreed, followed by mumbled agreement from all the men.

"It would be an honor to help such a pretty lady," Mathos added while wrapping his arm around Nim and flashing a smug grin as he did it. One more second and Tristan would have thrown him into a tree, but thankfully Nim shrugged Mathos off with a snort.

He nodded his head toward Rafael, the other Nephilim in the squad. Where Jeremiel had a gift for hearing truth, his brother's skill lay in healing. "Check her wing, please, Rafe."

"It's fine." The steel was back in her voice.

Gods, one hint of sweetness and then she was straight back to stubborn. But now he knew her weakness. She wouldn't lie.

He looked her in the eyes and asked, "Can you fly?"

"What? I... um...."

"So that's a no then?"

She didn't reply, and he knew he had her.

He nodded again to Rafael and watched as the tall red-haired man quietly moved her to one side and started asking her quiet questions. She looked so small and vulnerable, her wing trembling as she held it out, that he ached to take her into his arms.

Instead, he moved the men away to give her some privacy—not because he couldn't control himself—and began planning.

By the time Nim and Rafael had rejoined the squad, they were ready to leave. Scouts placed on rotation, two front riders, two at the back, and the two Mabin in the air. Nim would use the horse of one of whichever soldiers were in the air, swapping from time to time to keep everyone fresh for as long as possible.

They would reach the outskirts of Kaerlud before nightfall and find somewhere safe to stay. That would give them one day to try and get to the bottom of what had happened to Val. Not nearly enough time. And probably pointless anyway, since it was highly unlikely that they would find anything good.

He hated to imagine what it would do to Nim when she realized the truth about her brother. When she finally understood that Val was going to die in two days' time, no matter how much she believed in him.

He shook the thoughts away, glad that she couldn't read his mind, and helped her onto Garet's destrier.

He was pleased to see that her wing was positioned better where it lay folded, and that the fine lines of tension at the sides of her eyes seemed to have eased.

For the first hour of trotting down the dusty road, Nim and Rafe rode close to each other discussing different herbs and treatments. Nim wanted to know what he'd done to cause the warmth and relaxation inside her wing, but the Nephilim had just shrugged, either unable or unwilling to tell her. She didn't push the deeply private soldier, simply looked at him quietly, her face understanding, then she'd turned the conversation to her favorite ointments. Soon they were comparing notes on difficult cases and sharing amusing anecdotes.

Tristan knew nothing about healing, but he knew a lot about competence, and Nim had grown into a confident and capable apothecary. It struck him that he had been living his life, never really thinking about Nim, never wondering what she was doing, never considering that she might grow up and leave them all behind.

Occasionally, Val would mention different men interested in his sister. But the whole idea had seemed hypothetical. In his head, she was too young to be bothering with relationships. And he hadn't been all that interested anyway. But now he had the reality right in his face. She was not only entirely grown up, but highly skilled, and deeply desirable—from her big eyes all the way down her strong, softly curved body; in her innate strength and kindness. Even her complete inability to lie.

Suddenly those other men didn't seem nearly so hypothetical. And his beast didn't like thinking of them. Not at all.

The miles passed, and the sun reached its peak. Nim and Rafe's chatter faded away, and they rode silently except for the jingle of harnesses and belt buckles, the thudding of the horses' hooves on the long road.

They left the forest behind and traveled past farmers' fields, always taking the long way around any small villages they passed. Eventually he called a stop for a brief rest and to eat some cold rations while sitting at the side of a field that seemed to be filled with late carrots waiting for harvest.

Nim sat quietly to the side of the squad, alone, chewing her bread slowly as she ate. She had withdrawn into herself and looked worryingly pale. He was tempted to go and sit with her, check on her, but the smug, knowing look that Mathos gave him made him pause.

He didn't like how attracted he felt to her. And he really didn't like that his men knew it. Worse, she might not even want him with her. So, he stayed where he was and watched her from a distance.

He was grumpy and annoyed by the time everyone was back on the move. Nim changed to Jos's horse, and he used the opportunity to position himself a little behind her, scowling at Mathos when he grinned.

They'd been on the road for an hour, with the men bantering in low voices—mostly Mathos telling rude jokes and Tor trying to make him shut up—when something made Tristan focus on Nim.

At first, he wasn't sure what he'd noticed. She had become more slumped during the afternoon, her head bowed. But something had made her seem even less steady. A spike of concern from his beast made him nudge Altair closer.

A moment before he reached her, she started to slide. Her body simply tipped to the side and she lost balance in a smooth, helpless glide toward the distant ground.

He pushed himself forward and over in one rapid swoop, leaning precariously in his saddle to scoop her up. She startled awake, half held in his arms, her body stretched between the two horses with her foot tangled in the stirrup.

He had her at a horrible angle, but he held her tight, forcing the horses close together as Rafael dashed forward and freed her.

Finally, she was loose and he could settle back into his saddle, heart still beating hard from the sudden burst of fear and speed, and the effort of holding her safe across the two horses.

He held her firmly in his arms as she stared up at him, shocked into wakefulness, silver-flecked blue eyes wide and startled, and he forced himself to curb his first impulse—to shout at her for riding half asleep, for frightening him like that—and managed a surly grunt instead. She felt his ire anyway, because her eyes narrowed, and she immediately started to twist and squirm to be put down.

He clamped his arms around her and gave her his most ferocious glare, but all she did was roll her eyes and redouble her effort. Gods, if she didn't stop wiggling that rounded leather-clad bottom in his lap, they were both going to have a problem.

He frowned at her. "Will you kindly stop."

"No. I want to get off."

He raised an eyebrow. "Why? So you can go to sleep in the saddle again?"

She turned to stare at him, nose in the air. "That was a mistake. I'm awake now."

He turned and looked at Rafe, who gave him a quick shake of his head. As he'd suspected.

"No. It's not safe. You'll just go back to sleep. You can ride with me, or you can walk."

She huffed out an enraged breath. "You are so bloody frustrating! You know walking would take too long!"

His lips twitch as he suppressed the desire to grin. No one else ever challenged him.

She sighed again and then changed tack. "Anyway, it would be bad for your horse to carry the extra weight."

He considered the massive stallion and the tiny woman in his arms and surprised them both by grinning. "He's a warhorse. I think he can manage an hour or two."

She mumbled something vicious under her breath, but she turned and lifted her leg over the high front saddle horn, then wiggled that torturous bottom closer so that they fitted together.

He gritted his teeth and took a few deep breaths, grateful that his heavy leather breeches would disguise just how much she was affecting him.

Slowly, she started to relax between his arms. The stiffness of her spine softened, and she leaned her back against him, her head tucked under his chin. The men's voices lowered, as if they too wanted her to rest as they rode on through the weak afternoon sunshine.

He noticed the moment that her weight fell completely against him, but he was reassured by the slow rise and fall of her chest as she nestled against him. His beast stirred again, filled with a deep sense of connection.

She was so beautiful. And the first woman that he and his beast had ever agreed on wanting. He felt it down to the most primal parts of himself, how right it was to hold her in his arms. How badly he needed to protect her and keep her close.

How badly he wanted to slowly strip her out of those tight breeches and hold her against him with nothing between them.

Gods.

"Should we worry that she's passed out?" he asked Rafe in a whisper, too low to disturb her.

The other man looked serious as he replied carefully, after a moment of consideration, "No, I think it's just exhaustion. I don't think she's slept much, if at all, over the last three days. And she's been hurting the entire time…." Rafe let his sentence hang.

Tristan looked at his friend's grave, concerned face, and prompted, "And?"

Rafe looked at him, mouth turned down. But his eyes

were resigned. Like his brother, he never held back from a difficult truth. "You have to remember that she just lost her father, her brother, and her home as well as being attacked. She's very vulnerable right now. You need to be careful."

Tristan tried not to let his annoyance show. A day ago, the whole squad wanted to hunt her down and hand her over to Grendel. Now they were protecting her from *him*.

"You think I'd hurt her?" he asked in a tight voice.

Rafe looked away and then back again. "Not intentionally."

Nim turned restlessly against him, frowning in her sleep, and he forced himself to relax until she settled again.

The healer was right. Fuck it. He needed to protect her, and that included protecting her from himself.

Nim was much better off far away from a bitter, disgraced captain and his motley squad of almost mercenaries. There was no future for them. She would be on the run, and then hopefully settle down somewhere safe and pretty. Somewhere she could grow her herbs and make her ointments. While he was bound to service. Sent to the worst places in the country, even when they weren't in active combat. Living in tents. Eating what they killed.

She was everything good and innocent. A soldier's woman's life was not for her. And there was no way he could have her for just one day. His beast, worryingly, already considered her his.

Not forgetting that once she'd learned the unpalatable truth about her brother, there was very little chance she'd want anything to do with him anyway.

Hell. It would have been so much easier if they'd never found her. If she'd simply disappeared.

The most he could offer her was protection for a couple

of days and then he'd help her to do just that. Disappear. So she could have that perfect life.

And he would go far away, where this disconcerting blend of lust and protectiveness would fade, and he could get on with his life. Gods knew, the last thing he needed was to get tangled up with a woman. Especially Val's sister.

Chapter Nine

NIM WOKE UP DISORIENTED, her head foggy.

They had stopped traveling, and someone was carrying her. Tris. She could smell the slightly spicy masculine scent she knew was his. Feel the leather of his armor against her cheek, the warm strength of his arms around her.

It was almost like a dream, after being so afraid for so long, to find herself safely held. By Tristan. The boy she had fallen in love with so many years ago. Who she had never managed to let go of, despite everything. Who had caught her when she fell and held her safely while she slept.

Maybe she had overreacted earlier. Tristan had said that he would protect her, and everything he'd done had proven he was true to his word.

It wasn't surprising that he still had doubts, but he'd agreed to help her to see Val in spite of them, and she was certain that he would be convinced of the truth when they finally had a chance to speak to her brother. Val was a good man, she knew it in every cell of her body. And not just because he was her brother; it was in everything he did. And he had always spoken of Tristan and the Hawks as if they were heroes, even in those dark days leading up to Ravenstone.

Tristan tightened his arms as he walked, and she wished that she could stay like that forever, but she could feel him slowing. Soon he would realize that she had woken.

She knew, in her heart, that the Hawks were certain they were going to prove she was wrong about Val. They needed to prove it to themselves as much as to her. But she would take their help. It gave her the chance she needed to show them the truth. And if it came with time in Tristan's arms, a dream she had never imagined could come true, she would take that too.

She opened her eyes and took in where they were. They had stopped in a damp meadow, fragrant with dill and swept with long afternoon shadows. A small, abandoned shepherds' hut squatted next to a tiny pond, and all around it, the men were rubbing down their mounts and setting up camp.

She wiggled, and Tristan looked down, saw that she was awake, then lowered her gently to the ground.

"Thank you," she said, mostly to him, but loud enough to include the whole squad.

She took a few steps forward and looked inside the rough hut. It was empty except for a rickety stool, a swath of autumn leaves littering the hard floor, and a pile of blankets in a corner that she was sure would be so full of lice that they could move by themselves.

She snorted and turned to Tristan with a grin. "Remind you of anything?"

He scowled at her, face blank, and she couldn't resist needling him. "Come on, you must remember! The old hut in the hills that you and Val made into a fort and protected against all the vicious sheep. Don't you remember stealing pies for feasts and holding battles? You spent hours playing up there!"

He took a small step backward, not saying anything, but his scowl deepened, and she found herself stepping forward, placing her hand on his arm, desperate to remind him. "At the very least, you must remember that time I ran away from home and you and Val hunted all over the hills before finally realizing I'd been staying there all the time. It felt like forever, but it wasn't even one day."

She remembered it so clearly. They had been teasing her, calling her a baby. The two boys were seventeen and already soldiers, home for a few days' leave. They had been so confident and sure of themselves. Almost men.

She, on the other hand, had been just a few weeks past her thirteenth birthday. Mama had been lost only the summer before, and she'd been so sad and angry.

And so very desperate for Tristan to see her. To see that she was growing up.

It had seemed like a good way to shut them all up. Show them just how comfortable they'd be when the "baby" didn't turn up to bake their bread and run their home. So, she'd left.

She spent the afternoon collecting herbs and then she'd set up a camp in the old hut. She ate her sandwich and amused herself by imagining their faces when they realized that they had to cook their own dinner.

Of course, by the time the sun went down, it had occurred to her that the herbs were useless without her stillroom. That she was thirsty and couldn't go back to the river in the dark. That it was terribly lonely and cold all by herself in a strange hut surrounded by the evening calls of the local wildlife. And that it was too late to leave.

She had been so relieved when Val and Tris had turned up with lanterns, like heroes from the stories. She hadn't even minded the long lecture she'd had from her brother all the way home. Or the even longer lecture from Papa when they got there.

But now Tristan was staring at her, still silent, with the exact same look of frustrated annoyance he'd had that day, and she felt her cheeks heat.

She let her hand drop and stepped back, regretting the stupid story and regretting even more that she'd thought he would remember.

Gods, was she going to spend her whole life aching after a man who didn't want her? No. She was not.

She lifted her chin and pushed past him to join the men as they started a fire. By the prickling of the skin between her wings, Tristan was still staring at her, no doubt with the same exasperated scowl.

"How can I help?" she asked, wanting something, anything, to do.

"Why don't you help with the vegetables?" Jos suggested. She washed her hands in the pond, pleased to find the water fresh and clear, and then sat quietly, peeling and chopping the slightly withered carrots and potatoes. Soon she had a good pile to throw into the pot, already simmering with pieces of dried beef and herbs.

Job done, she leaned back as Jos sat down next to her, his wings folded neatly behind him. He gave her a kind smile, and she smiled back, glad for the small welcome.

"Now, I like to think I know a bit about women," he said, breaking into a wide grin as the other men snorted. Nim couldn't help but snort too, especially when Mathos chimed in, "The only women you know are your sisters!" but Jos simply winked at her and continued undeterred, "and I'm guessing that you would like a wash before dinner."

Gods. A wash! Just the idea made her conscious of how dirty and sticky she was. Her clothes and hair were caked in blood and dirt and still stank of soot.

"There it is!" He grinned at the look of longing she couldn't hide and continued, "I've warmed some water and put it into the hut for you."

"Oh! Thank you!" Warm water sounded like heaven.

He offered her a hand to pull her up, and she put her hand in his, breaking into a laugh when he pulled her up so quickly that she stumbled and would have fallen if he hadn't steadied her.

He offered her his arm and she took it, still smiling, as he led her formally toward the hut like a gentleman taking a lady to a dance.

Before she could reach the door, Reece called out in a loud voice, "Hey, pretty lady, do you need anyone to help you wash your back?"

She was about to respond when Tristan beat her to it with a bad-tempered growl from the other side of the camp. "All of you, leave her alone. Nim, be quick."

She let go of Jos's arm and rolled her eyes as she turned to drop Tristan a mocking curtsey, not bothering to wait for his reaction before spinning around and going into the hut. The door was too rickety, or she would have given it a good slam.

He'd been so kind and protective, promising that he would keep her safe, holding her close on the long ride. And she had known, without a doubt, that his body had reacted just as much as hers had responded to his. She had gone to sleep in his arms, feeling the heat between them, imagining what his hands would feel like on her skin. His lips.

But now he was back to his surly, frowning self.

She gave herself a shake. Her focus had to be on Val anyway. He was the most important thing.

Someone had done a reasonable job of clearing away the leaves and rotting blankets in the hut and, in their stead, a leather bucket filled with warm water sat on the small stool.

Gods, warm water. She could cry just at the idea of being clean.

She undid the stiff ties and breathed a sigh of relief as she took off the tight jerkin for the first time in days, letting her soft cotton blouse fall loose. She unlaced her long boots and yanked them off with a groan. She was about to pull down her breeches when she heard a quiet knock at the door.

"Who's there?" she called, damping down her sudden nerves. The noise had startled her, but if someone wanted to hurt her, they wouldn't have bothered knocking.

"Tristan."

She didn't want to face him again. Didn't want to be reminded of her lonely teenage years as she slowly realized that what she wanted from him was never going to happen, that no matter how many times he visited, he never, really, saw her. Her even lonelier years as an adult, knowing that he didn't want her and she didn't want anyone else.

"What is it?" she asked, wishing he would go away.

His annoyed grunt was loud enough that she could hear it through the door. "I brought you some fresh clothes."

She padded over and opened the door a few inches.

"Here." He thrust a small bundle at her, no doubt his spare shirt and socks.

She hovered for a moment, uncertain. She didn't want

to take anything more from him, but she really wanted to rinse out her clothes.

He pushed it toward her. "Just take it."

She reached out and took the bundle, glancing up at him as she did. As soon as he noticed that she was looking at him, the shutters came down and his face blanked, but what she'd seen in the moment before rocked her.

Just for a second, he had looked so much younger. Almost his old self. His eyes filled with a deep, complicated expression. Need. And uncertainty. And something like yearning.

But whatever it was, he hadn't wanted her to see it.

"Why are you doing this, Tris?" she asked him carefully.

"Jos said you'd like fresh clothes."

"No, not the clothes." She waved her arm around the hut, indicating herself. "This. Bringing me here, helping me with Val."

He looked confused for a moment, as if he didn't understand the question, before replying, "It's the right thing to do."

"No," she said, "it's not. You are obliged to follow orders. That would be the right thing for you to do. Not this."

She realized that she was clutching his shirt as if it could somehow save her from the dark look on his face and loosened her fingers.

She squared her shoulders and said what she had to. "You can leave me here. I don't mind. I thank you, genuinely thank you, for bringing me all this way. I understand that this is against your orders and that it would be better for you to go."

He strode into the hut and pushed the door closed

behind him with an irritated click. "What the fuck are you talking about?"

She stayed exactly where she was, determined not to be intimidated. "I'm not that little girl anymore, Tris, the one that annoyed you so much. I don't need another big brother bossing me around, and I'm very tired of you looking at me like you wish you'd never found me. I understand that you don't want to be here with me, so just go."

He stared at her for a moment before replying, his voice rough, "You're right."

"Okay." She took a breath and let it out slowly, determined not to show how much that hurt.

"But not how you think."

He stepped closer, and that time she did step back. He stepped closer again, and she tried to step back again, but realized she had her back to the stone wall of the hut.

He pressed one hand upon the wall behind her and leaned down, hard masculine body towering over her, lips against her ear, hot breath on her skin. "You're right. You're not a little girl anymore."

He pushed himself a few inches away. Just enough that he could watch her, his eyes clear and completely focused on her. She felt herself flush, her breath coming quicker as a deep longing pooled inside her.

His eyes flicked to the open neck of her blouse, and he lifted a huge hand and ran the back of his knuckles ever so slowly just under the cotton, along the top of her breasts as he whispered, "And the last thing I feel toward you is brotherly."

She couldn't help it, she arched her back. He turned his hand in response, cupping her breast as his thumb ran maddening circles around her nipple. The fabric of her blouse caught and tugged against the tightening bud, heat pulsing through her belly, and she let out a soft whimper as he lowered his head and sealed his lips over hers.

It was everything she had ever dreamed of and so much more. His lips were firm and smooth, his mouth hot and demanding. He was still thrumming her nipple through the cotton of her blouse as his other hand fisted her hair and angled her head so that he could take complete ownership of her mouth.

She went up on her toes, pushing into him, completely lost in the heady intensity of their kiss, the hot feeling of his body pressed against hers, the aching pull low in her core as he ran his tongue along hers and nibbled at her lower lip.

She forgot how angry she was with him. How frustrated his surly mood changes made her. She finally had what she'd wanted all her life. And Tristan. Gods. Tristan wanted it too.

She tugged his shirt up and ran her hands up the taut muscles of his abdomen, losing herself in the onslaught of sensations. Warm skin, hot mouth, her breasts heavy and aching. The heated wetness between her legs as she pushed herself into his body, desperate for more.

They were both panting by the time he pulled away and leaned his forehead down on hers, still caging her against the wall.

This was the moment. Now he would finally see her.

The hand that had been on her breast moved up to cradle her face as he closed his eyes and spoke in a gruff voice. "I want you. You're a beautiful woman. I want you more than I've wanted anything for years. Maybe in my whole life. But I don't want… this. It's too much, and I can't…."

He gave a harsh shake of his head, then opened his eyes and looked right at her. "You're right, I do wish we'd never found you. It would have been better for everyone. But that doesn't change anything. I will not send you out into danger on your own. Don't ask me to."

Nim leaned back against the wall, flustered and cold as he let her go. Her body still ached for him, while her heart wept with confusion. And hurt. A deeper hurt than she could have imagined.

His words played themselves over in her head. *I don't want this. I wish we'd never found you.*

Her throat closed over any response she might have made, and she watched in stunned silence as he turned away, never looking back. He walked out the hut and closed the door quietly, leaving her alone.

He wanted her, but not enough to be with her. Kissed her, made her ache for him, and then dropped her brutally back to earth.

Without even once asking what she wanted, he had broken through her defenses and then dismissed her like it meant nothing.

And then walked away, without a single glance back.

If she had thought those teenage tears had hurt, she had known nothing. Those had been tears of unfulfilled childish hope. This was complete and utter rejection.

She stood, frozen, as she heard him calling for his horse and commanding the men to guard her. Then the clatter of hooves on hard ground as he fled as fast as he could away from her.

She'd thought she had lost everything before, but it was only now, as he rode away, that she realized there had been more to lose.

Only when she knew he was gone did she sink to the ground and let the tears come.

Chapter Ten

THE MOON WAS HIGH, a bright crescent against the flowing silver clouds, by the time that Tristan made his way back to camp.

He let Altair pick his way carefully in the darkness and gave him an apologetic pat for keeping him out so late. He had ridden hard, hoping to burn off the swirling maelstrom of emotions burning through him, and he knew it wasn't fair on the loyal stallion after he'd already done a full day's work.

He was about five minutes from the hut when the first sentry stopped him. Jos. With a look on his face that could sharpen knives. "What the fuck, Tristan?"

Tristan slid off Altair and walked up to the snarling guard, only too happy to get in his face, half hoping for a fight. "That's 'What the fuck, Sergeant,' to you, soldier."

But Jos didn't back down, just opened his wings wide and intimidating and sneered, "You know, we put up with a lot of your crap, *Sergeant* Tristan, but when you start making innocent women cry, I think you'll find the squad takes exception."

"What do you mean?" All the air was sucked out of Tristan, along with a fair portion of his self-righteous rage.

Jos didn't bother to explain. Instead, he reached out a hand and pushed Tristan in the chest as he demanded, "What did you do to her?"

"Nothing!" Tristan growled, tempted to grab that hand and start ripping off fingers.

Nothing except lose his mind in the best kiss of his entire life. Nothing except force himself to walk away while his soul screamed and his inner beast rebelled, scales flickering all the way to his throat. Nothing other than try to do the right thing before he forgot himself completely.

Jos shook his head. "Bullshit. Nothing doesn't make a woman sob for ten minutes by herself. Nothing doesn't make her push her food around without eating it and then take herself off to a freezing cold hut, where she fucking cried again. We could all hear her."

Tristan took a step back and scrubbed his hand tiredly down his face. The rest of his rage drained away, leaving only hollow guilt. Fuck. He hadn't planned to make her cry. Hadn't even imagined that she would. He'd told her that he wanted her. That she was beautiful. Explained that he would protect her and help her with Val.

Hadn't he?

He thought back over the exact words he'd used, the words he'd done his best to forget as he pushed himself and Altair to their limit.

He remembered the stunned look on her face, the hurt, and had to recognize that he'd been lying to himself the entire time he was with her. And every moment since.

He'd pushed her away brutally. Somehow hoping that if

he was callous enough, it would make her stay away from him. He didn't want to see her. Look into those big eyes. If he did, he would have stayed.

Instead, he'd hurt her enough that she would be the one to keep them apart.

He couldn't blame Jos. He was only doing what Tristan would have done had the situation been reversed. They had a code. Sister to one was sister to all. Even Val's sister. It helped that she was brave and kind and pretty and all of them liked her.

He had no good answer to give his friend, so he didn't bother to try, simply walked on, past Jos and up to the fire. A few men were sleeping. The rest looked at him with the same disgust as Jos had.

Rafael flicked his eyes over him with the sternest judgment of all. And his indignation flickered back to life.

"I was following your fucking advice!" he hissed, not wanting to wake Nim.

"As I recall," Rafe said in a dark voice, "I specifically told you not to hurt her."

Tristan shook his head sharply. "You told me to leave her alone."

Rafe stood and glared at him, the firelight gleaming on his auburn hair and pale skin. "No. I did not. I reminded you that she's been badly hurt so you would treat her gently. Not so you would go barging in like an enraged bull and rip apart whatever small amount of remaining pride she had holding her together."

"And," Mathos said, rising from the far side of the fire, his face drawn into an unusually severe and disapproving mask, his burgundy and gold scales glinting at his wrists, "we've been discussing Val. None of us saw his famous betrayal. Only you. We trusted you in this—you were our captain, and we could see how badly it had hurt you. But now… we're not so sure."

His beast growled menacingly, and Tristan could feel his scales rising in a wave up both arms and over his shoulders as he replied, "The king himself said that Alanna was responsible and that Val was working with her. The Lord High Chancellor told me that they were having an affair. That there were witnesses in the Blues. You all saw those arrows. And you know how much Val had changed. You did see all of that. I suggested that we leave, yes, but you could have refused."

"We trusted you," Mathos replied.

Fuck that. Trusted. Were. Like it was all past tense. His beast snarled loud enough that they could all hear it. "And I trusted the king, who is my supreme commander, and his Lord High Chancellor."

There was a brief silence, eventually broken by Rafael. "Is this the same king who, when he was prince, newly arrived at court and playing at leader of the Blues, was a vicious and sadistic bastard that we all hated? The same king that not only became king because of this supposed treachery, but also used it as an excuse to break a treaty he'd been against from the very beginning. That king?"

"Gods, man," Tristan spat, "shut the fuck up! Do you have any idea what would happen if someone heard you?"

"Yes," Mathos said with vicious irony. "Exactly what happened to Val."

They all looked at each other, unsettled and slightly shocked.

Until a small whimper broke the heavy silence, and Tristan spun toward the hut. Another whimper echoed in the quiet, followed by an unmistakable gasp of feminine fear.

Family legend said that the Tarasque clans were descended from dragons eons before, and for the first time in his life, Tristan felt the truth of it. His scales flooded every inch of his skin and hardened into rigid green and pewter armor as the deep primitive voice inside him howled for action.

He had felt himself tear apart with every step he took away from her, and now his inner beast would not be denied for one more second. He would get back to his woman and defend her from whatever was hurting her, no matter what or who stood in his way.

But no one did. Every one of them stood back as he strode up and ripped open the hut door.

It was dark and freezing inside. Why the fuck wasn't she at the fire?

Someone handed him a lantern, and he stepped inside.

Nim was curled into a tight ball up against the far wall. Somehow her cloak had fallen or been kicked away, and she shivered in his spare shirt and socks, thrashing and mumbling in her sleep. Caught in a nightmare.

He couldn't bear it.

Within seconds he had her wrapped in her cloak and lifted into his arms. She jerked, gasping in fright, but he held her gently and shushed her as she settled back, still dreaming, into deeper sleep.

The men had laid out his bedroll next to the fire and covered it with blankets—a little way from where they had set their own bedrolls—and he lowered her gently into the warm refuge.

He glared at the tight faces watching him. "I'm not discussing Val now. We need the truth, and that is what we are going to Kaerlud to find."

There was a quiet ripple of agreement. Frankly, he didn't care, so long as they kept quiet. His priority was Nim.

After a moment's consideration, he unstrapped his sword and knives and placed them carefully to one side. He stripped off his armor and then, with a final look at his men, almost defying them to stop him, lowered himself to the ground beside her. Close enough to keep her sheltered from the wind. Close enough to protect her. Not close enough for his beast.

It was a long night. Every time she whimpered or lashed out, he soothed her gently, stroking her hair and telling her she was safe until she settled again. The guard changed, and changed again, and the hours passed.

And slowly he realized that he couldn't walk away again. It had cost him. And he couldn't bear that it had cost her. Now, he would fight for the chance to be with her.

And, after everything he'd said and done, that fight was likely to start as soon as she opened her eyes.

Eventually, the sun began to rise, and he stretched his legs one at a time, trying to ease the kinks from spending the night awake, lying on the hard ground.

The movement disturbed her, and she rolled toward him, her eyes wide and shocked as she noticed where she was. Such a deep blue, silver flecks glimmering. Like staring into the night sky. He felt as if he could fall into them forever.

But she blinked and, as he watched, he saw her withdraw, closing her thoughts to him as her face set in a cold mask.

"No, please," he whispered as he ran his thumb under her eye, along her cheekbone, "don't do that."

"Do what?" Her voice had that soft huskiness that drove

him insane. And a touch of acidity that he knew he'd more than earned.

"Pull away from me like that."

"I think you'll find," she replied in a harsh whisper, "that I learned how to do it from you."

"I know," he agreed solemnly. "I'm very sorry."

He'd surprised her into silence. She hadn't been expecting him to apologize, and her eyes were back to clear and wide. It was his opportunity. Probably the only one he'd get.

"I'm sorry that I was such an asshole. I don't have any excuse; it's just you… you make me feel… things."

"Things?" she repeated skeptically.

"Yes. Things I haven't felt for a long time. Things I didn't expect to feel." He paused for a moment before admitting, "I remember playing in the shepherds' hut."

He looked away, trying to find the words before facing her again. "Your mama died loving you. Mine ran away when I was four and left me with a father who hated her for her betrayal. A betrayal that no one ever saw coming. And he hated me for being part of her. I had nothing at home but beatings."

Her face softened, just a tiny bit. But it wasn't pity he wanted; he wanted her to understand.

"At your house, with Val and you, I had a home. It was the only time I was happy. And that day that you ran away, gods. You have to know that searching for you wasn't some kind of obligation. We weren't angry with you. We were desperate to find you."

She wrinkled her nose at him. "You were angry, I remember—"

He cut her off with a gentle finger over her soft lips. "Not at all. We both knew that we had taken it too far. That you'd run away because of our teasing. When we couldn't find you all day, we started to worry that you were hurt. Really worry. That's all Val could talk about, how he was going to have to go back to your papa only a few months after losing your mama and explain that he had lost his precious daughter too. And that we were responsible."

"I'm sorry," she whispered.

He was still stroking her cheek, his thumb rough against her velvet skin. "Please don't be sorry. I'm trying to explain. I didn't want to ever feel like that again, knowing that you were in danger because of me. That my actions had hurt you. I thought it would be better to stay away."

She snorted sadly. "You thought it would be better to walk away and leave me alone and vulnerable? That it made sense to hurt me so that you could avoid hurting me?"

When she put it like that, it made it sound even worse. He grunted. "It was stupid, I'll give you that."

Her lips tilted up in a small smile. She hadn't yet pushed him away. Not yet. It gave him hope. "Will you forgive me?"

The silence stretched uncomfortably as she stared intently into his face, looking for something. He didn't know what.

Eventually she lifted her small hand and rested it against his cheek. "Yes, I forgive you."

He let out a sigh of relief, his beast unwinding for the first time in hours. She was too good. Too kind. But he couldn't bring himself to say anything that might make her change her mind.

He was suddenly acutely aware of her warm, soft body beside his. The way her breasts rose and fell as she breathed. The memory of her hot mouth and gentle curves. And the flush rising over her neck told him that she knew exactly what he was thinking.

A throat cleared loudly on the other side of the fire, and Nim startled and then grinned as he looked up and growled.

He pushed himself up to standing and then growled even louder when he saw that Nim was standing next to him wearing nothing but his spare shirt and socks, with a long expanse of creamy leg between them.

It took him a second to find the words to bark out, "Turn around! Now."

Either the men were acting on their own honor or his threat was dire enough, but they turned their backs so fast that Nim started giggling again. A throaty chuckle of pure joy that reached all the way into his soul.

He spun her into his arms and started carrying her back to the hut to change but stalled when she reached up and ran her fingers carefully over his lips.

"You should smile more," she observed quietly, just for his ears, and without even thinking, he lifted her higher and pressed his mouth to hers.

It was only a moment, standing in the early morning sunshine with the squad waiting, backs turned, a few yards away. But she let out a soft sigh and kissed him back.

And he knew, without any doubt, there was nothing he wouldn't do, that his beast wouldn't do, to protect her. Somehow, they had crossed some kind of line, and he could never go back.

He broke the kiss and deposited her safely into the hut before he lost his mind and joined her. He grunted a rough command allowing the men to continue their duties, doing his best to ignore their grins and, in Mathos's case, a ridiculous wink.

By the time Nim was dressed, a breakfast of bread and cheese had been arranged, and the men were sitting together talking softly. She walked over and sat beside him on the ground, accepting a plate from Jos with thanks.

He'd never met a woman who would sit cross-legged in the dirt without complaining before, and by the bemused looks around him, neither had anyone else.

"So," she said eventually, "where did you go? Last night, I mean."

"I rode down to a pub in the nearest village. We're about five miles out of Kaerlud here, and I wanted to get a sense of what's happening."

"What did you discover?" she asked, her wings quivering behind her ever so slightly.

It was the question he didn't want to answer. But he didn't have a choice; he had to give her the truth. Everyone fell silent and focused on him. He kept his eyes on Nim.

He put down his plate and took her hand, wishing he didn't have to be the cause of the tremor he felt in her fingers. "Honestly," he said, looking down at her, "I don't want to tell you."

She sat quietly, gripping his hand, and waited, trusting him to continue.

He sighed. "Rumor is that Val is scheduled to be hanged tomorrow. There's a big spectacle planned just before the legions ready to march north."

"And?"

This was the part he particularly didn't want to tell her.

He let go of her hand, but only so he could wrap an arm around her shoulders. "They're saying that the king is holding him inside the castle. He's... uh... been chained to the wall inside the great hall."

The men around him bristled. Enemies were killed in battle. Or tried and hanged. Even traitors. Not displayed like trophies on a wall. It went against any kind of honor. It made so little sense that Tristan wondered if it was a mistake, a rumor that was out of control, growing ever larger in the telling.

Nim closed her eyes and leaned into him. "They're torturing him." It wasn't a question.

"If it's true," Tristan admitted carefully.

"Okay," She took a shaky breath. Then another. And he watched as she visibly pulled herself together, perhaps reassured by his skepticism, shook off her horror, and focused.

She turned those wide eyes back to him and asked clearly, "So, what's the plan?"

He raised an eyebrow, slightly unsettled by her certainty that he had one.

Chapter Eleven

NIM UNFURLED her wings and tested them carefully, stretching gently and lifting them in different directions. Whatever Rafe had done when he'd worked on her injuries had made an immense difference. Enough that she was confident she could fly if she needed to. Although, from the look that Tris was giving her, he clearly thought she should be resting.

She was almost tempted to have a little flight around the pond just to annoy him. Gods, it was hard to believe how much had changed between them. He had genuinely seen her—for the first time in their long history. And he felt something. Not the love that she had held for him for so many years, she knew that. But something.

Maybe she should have been slower to forgive him—especially after how he'd left Val, how angry she had been, and deep inside her, still was—but in that moment, seeing the vulnerability in his eyes as he apologized, she hadn't been able to hold herself back.

For the first time in weeks, she had hope. Together, they

might just stand a chance of saving Val. And, whatever happened, she would have had this time with the man she'd always loved.

She grinned to herself and focused on folding his spare shirt and socks together to return to him. She was looking down, distracted, and didn't notice that Tor had walked up beside her until he was right next to her.

The sudden appearance of his powerful arms, swathed in swirling red and black tattoos, right beside her, startled her, and she was flooded by an uncontrollable panicky fear that Grendel had found her. She gasped and flinched back, heart pounding, taking a few seconds to realize that it wasn't Grendel beside her.

And then Tris was there, his warm body pressed against her back, his arm wrapped around her middle, and she knew she was safe. Her pulse gradually slowed as she recovered from her shock.

"What the fuck, Tor?" Tristan snarled behind her, and a deeper sound, almost a growl, rumbled through his body, so low that she wondered if he even knew that he was doing it.

Glancing up at Tor, she saw a flash of hurt across his face, quickly hidden, replaced by a blank and stony glare. She had created this problem, and she had to fix it.

"No, no, it wasn't Tor's fault, it was mine." She made to step toward Tor, but Tristan's arm was locked around her waist, so she settled for reaching out and taking Tor's hand in hers. "Tor was just standing there, and I wasn't concentrating and I…" She took a deep breath knowing that only the truth would help. "I thought I saw Grendel. That he'd found me. I'm so sorry, Tor. I know you're nothing alike."

Tor's face softened as she spoke, but behind her, Tristan's grumbling growl was even deeper and more aggressive. Whether it was because she was still holding Tor's hand or because she'd been frightened, she didn't know.

She let go of Tor and spun slowly within Tristan's arm so she could lean against his chest and soak up his warm strength. All the men had shaved that morning in preparation for the city, and she couldn't resist running her nose along his smooth jaw and giving him a small kiss before nestling herself under his chin. "I'm fine, really," she whispered.

The rumbling changed pitch, ever so slightly, until it was almost a purr. She wrapped her arms around him and held him, uncaring of the other men nearby. Just knowing, somehow, that he needed her to hold him as much as she needed him.

Eventually his hold loosened, and she smiled up at him until he gently let her go.

"Tor, you can help Nim with her arms," Tris ordered with a nod, and Nim grinned and winked at Tor. He frowned back at her, but she thought the crinkles at the sides of his eyes were his version of a smile. They both knew that Tristan had meant it to be a compliment.

Nim sat on a tree stump and held out her arms while Tor used ink to draw swirling designs in a flowing pattern of reds and blacks all the way up her arms. They had decided that she would travel as his sister to enter the city, so he was marking her with his family tattoos, representing his unique heritage.

She had been so frightened by Grendel that Tor's tattoos had seemed ominous and threatening, reminding her of being held down, terrified, whenever she glimpsed them. But now, as she watched the evocative patterns slowly developing over her arms—each with its own meaning

reflecting Tor's family history, values, and beliefs—she
started to appreciate them for what they truly were.

Nim smiled at the still scowling soldier as he finished the
last few markings. "Thank you, Tor. These are truly
beautiful. I'm honored to wear the marks of your heritage."

He looked at her for a moment, face serious as a brief
flash of sorrow flickered in his eyes.

Slowly, as if uncertain, he touched his fist to his heart in
his people's traditional greeting. She touched her fist to her
heart in reply, acknowledging the solemnity of the moment.

They walked back to the group, where Jos handed her a
paste of ash and water to smear through her hair. She left
the men and went into the hut alone to gray her hair and
strap down her wings before completely covering herself
with her cloak. With a bit of luck, no one would be looking
for a gray-haired Apollyon spinster with a pronounced
hunch traveling with her brother.

She rolled her shoulders a few times, not used to the
constraints on her wings, and stepped out into the pale
morning sunshine to see most of the men already mounted
and ready to move out.

Tristan was waiting for her at Reece's horse, her satchel
already tied securely on behind the saddle, and she did her
best to look relaxed and confident as she walked over to
him, despite the churning mix of hope and fear in her belly
—this was their only chance to save her brother.

But he wasn't fooled.

He ran a gentle hand under her jaw, tilting her chin up
for her to look at him as he spoke. "We'll find him."

She nodded, not trusting her voice.

His face was set as he continued. "Listen to me, Nim.
Every man here will protect you. We will investigate what
truly happened to Val and do everything we can to make

this situation right. But we won't sacrifice you. Do you understand?"

She nodded again but felt herself frown at the same time. Val was her priority. She had accepted days ago that neither of them might survive the fight to end his captivity.

But now, looking into Tristan's solemn green eyes, for the first time in weeks, she wanted to live. Desperately.

"If it looks like you are in danger, I will take you away. When we are in the city, I'm in charge, and you will do what I say. Either accept it now, or we don't go. Promise me."

She nodded again, more confidently. Tristan had been the Captain of the Palace Guard; it made complete sense for him to take control while they were in the city. Once everyone was safe, well, that was a different matter.

Still, she couldn't resist teasing him a little. "Yes, Captain Tristan, sir!"

"Sergeant," he replied by rote before realizing what he'd said, and she giggled when the rest of the squad snorted. Tristan merely glared at them all.

He turned back to her and tucked a grayed lock of hair behind her ear. "I'm being serious, Nim."

She lifted his hand and brought it to her mouth in a soft kiss, then rested it against her cheek. "I know. I promise to do as you say while we're in danger."

He gave a rough grunt that sounded like agreement and then brought his other hand up to hold her face cradled between his palms while he leaned down and kissed her.

His lips owned hers, hot and smooth and firm. And she went up onto her toes to meet him. It was a kiss of longing and worry, of the heat growing between them. A kiss that acknowledged the danger they were riding toward and how much they hadn't said. And then it was over.

He pulled away and immediately swung her up onto the

large bay destrier, hardly looking at her. Not, she realized, because he didn't want to, but because he was holding himself in tight control.

He spun and walked off, and she wished she could call him back, but the emerald and pewter scales glittering along his arms stopped her. Accompanying her into danger was taking a toll on him, and she didn't want to make it worse.

Within seconds, Tristan was mounted on Altair and riding out with Jeremiel to form the front line. Jos and Garet were already in the air, scouting ahead, while Mathos and Rafe would follow a few minutes later to form the rear guard. Once they were safely through the city gates, they would separate to tackle their different tasks, avoiding being seen together in a conspicuous group.

Nim turned to Tor. "Shall we go then, brother?"

He didn't answer, simply kicked his stallion into a sharp trot, and she clicked to hers to follow.

It took a little less than an hour to reach the city, with the roads becoming increasingly busy with every mile they traveled. Farmers going to market, porters, peddlers, even a few ornate coaches, gilded and trimmed, surrounded by footmen and burly guards.

Tristan had learned that there was to be a huge banquet at the palace that night, and many of the wealthy nobility were making their way into Kaerlud to join the amusements, showing their allegiance and hoping for favors in the last days before the troops were gathered to travel north.

The plan was for Tristan and Nim to attend—and hopefully to find Val, or at least find the truth of what had happened to him.

Thinking about what Val was enduring made her heart race nauseatingly, so Nim chatted and asked Tor questions to distract them both. Gradually he started to reply with answers longer than one word. Once or twice, she was sure he almost smiled.

By the time they approached the gates, the road was thronged with people of every race, some with tattoos, some with wings, several with scales. Even the occasional Pythic Seer, eyes bound, being led slowly by the hand.

And through it all a heavy presence of uniformed soldiers, rough and loud, making coarse jokes and dominating the passing travelers with aggressive stares.

A subtle, but disturbing, space was left around the troops as people hurried past them, avoiding eye contact. In a way it helped; keeping her hood up and her eyes lowered fitted in with everyone else around them.

A glance at Tor showed that he had noticed it too. A muscle ticked in the corner of his jaw as he guided their mounts forward into the middle of the road—as far from the soldiers manning either side of the gates as possible.

The cavalry soldiers passing through their local country village had been increasingly belligerent. Ever since Ballanor had taken over as Supreme Commander, his soldiers had grown more arrogant, prone to making unreasonable requests and demanding overblown respect. But this was even worse. And by the look on Tor's face, not something he had expected either.

And the worst of it was that not all these soldiers wore the black uniform of the cavalry—soldiers the Hawks would have spent little time with. Some of them were Blues, the new group of guards that had been recruited after their ranks were decimated at Ravenstone. Damn, it was going to hurt the Hawks when they realized what had happened to the company they had been so proud to serve with.

Nim stared at her saddle, taking care to let her sleeves

fall back enough that anyone watching would catch glimpses of the swirling ink on her arms. She could feel her heart thumping in her chest, her hands sweating as she concentrated on keeping her breaths even and her shoulders relaxed as they walked the horses slowly into the city.

And then they were through.

Relief flooded her, and she had to hold in a giggle that she knew would sound slightly hysterical. She glanced at Tor again, and he gave her a subtle nod, eyes flicking back to the latest group of soldiers following a few yards behind them making rude comments at the expense of their fellow travelers.

Eventually they emerged into wider streets, and the crowds dispersed about their business, and, finally, Nim was able to take a long breath.

Before they could go to meet the rest of the squad, they had to make a few stops at the market. Tristan planned for them to join Ballanor's banquet as minor nobles, which meant that Nim would need something to wear.

Jos had promised that one of his sisters would have a dress she could borrow, something in gray or silver, but she would need to alter it before it would pass as rich enough for the palace. She also needed stockings, drawers, and a chemise for underneath her dress. There was no way she could get away with her leather breeches.

Tor knew the city well from his time as a Blue, and he led them down a winding path of cobbled roads. Some were so narrow that the windows of the flats above were close enough to almost touch, others wide and airy, bordered by high walls and hedges enclosing private gardens.

Eventually they turned the corner into a large avenue flanked by a multitude of shops with colorful awnings, displaying an array of every kind of clothing, haberdashery, and fabric, from bolts of homespun brown cotton through to shimmering silver silks. One storefront held only ribbons in a rainbow of different shades, another only shawls.

Costermongers had set up their stalls and carts down the middle of the avenue, some laden with secondhand clothes or pieces of used fabric, too cheap for the fancier stores. On one end of there was an area dedicated to meat and produce, carts selling hot food and autumn harvest fruit and vegetables.

All around was a great swath of people and noise as customers haggled over prices and sellers cried their wares.

Nim and Tor dismounted, and Tor took the horses so that Nim could wander slightly ahead and look for what she needed.

It didn't take long before she found a gleaming silk offcut in deepest midnight blue, a color that she had always loved, and she imagined that she might drape it over the skirts of the dress Jos brought her. Sparkling paste earrings followed, good enough quality to withstand a cursory glance, as did silk gloves and a used but serviceable pair of deep blue velvet slippers. Nim passed each purchase back to Tor, who dutifully packed them away into the saddlebags.

At last she only needed underwear, and she grinned at the stricken look on Tor's face when she pointed toward a discreet store tucked away to the side of the market.

She took pity on the poor man and told him that she would go in and he could wait outside, all while chuckling at the relief on his face.

It didn't take long to find what she needed, although each new purchase left even fewer coins in her rapidly diminishing purse. Well. She wouldn't worry about it. First, they had to survive the night, then they could think about money.

She stepped out of the store and looked around for Tor. He was down the road a little way, where the fabrics gave way to food sellers, buying what looked like several large meat pasties.

Her tummy rumbled, and she realized that she was starving. A hot pasty, thick with meat and gravy, was exactly what she wanted. Perhaps followed by one of the gleaming apples being inspected by a mother and her little boy at the next cart over.

She was just stepping onto the street when a commotion a little farther down brought her attention to a trio of soldiers dressed in the uniform of the Palace Blues. Tarasque, like Tristan, but more arrogant somehow, meaner looking.

They were coming down the street directly between her and Tor.

She pulled her hood further forward and stepped back, shrinking against the wall near an alley entrance, keeping far away from the light.

Around her, she noticed the banter and jostling had fallen away as an oppressive, fearful atmosphere washed over the crowd. Many people, like her, had quietly moved to the edges of the street, giving the soldiers a wide berth until the soldiers' rough laughter was the loudest sound on the streets.

Nim risked a glance up through her eyelashes, hoping to see how far away they were, and froze. They had stopped at the apple cart where she could see the mother, pale-faced, pushing her son, maybe five years old and dressed in threadbare browns, behind her back and stepping carefully away.

But the costermonger stopped her with a rough bark. "Oy! You'd better pay for that!"

The mother looked around confused, only to realize that her son still held an apple. She gave him a firm nudge, and the child, clearly reluctantly, started to hand it back.

Whether it was simply that he desperately wanted that apple or because of all the threatening grown-ups watching him, the boy fumbled.

Nim watched the whole thing as if in slow motion, the moment the apple started to fall. The child's frantic attempt to catch it, the mother trying to help, and the inevitable crash to the muddy cobbles, where the apple smashed and sprayed mud and juice over the nearby soldiers' boots.

There was a horrified hush as the lead soldier slowly looked down and then back up, filled with rage.

Before the mother could stop it, the soldier had her son by the collar, lifting him in the air and shaking him like a dog would shake a rabbit, while the boy wailed and sobbed.

"Please! Please, sir! It was an accident! Please!" the terrified mother begged.

The soldier just laughed and threw the boy to his friend, who caught him just over the ground and swung him back again as he wept for his mother.

She fell to her knees and desperately wiped the soldiers' boots with her sleeves, trying to fix the mess as he held her son high up by his ankle, upside down, head toward the cobbles.

"What would you say the price is for new boots, lads?" the soldier asked with a vicious gleam in his eyes, his arms rippling with orange and burgundy scales.

The mother rocked back on her heels, face pale as bone. "Not new boots, sir, please, it's just some dust——"

Before she could finish, the soldier opened his hand and dropped the boy, and she launched herself forward, only just managing to grab him before his head hit the hard cobbles. She was off-balance, on her hands and knees, head bowed as she frantically reassured her son.

"Do you know," the soldier turned to his friends with a grin, "I think I'll just take my payment now. Brastius, hold her."

Nim's heart thudded heavily in remembered panic and the horrified realization that this new breed of Blue Guards truly believed that they could do anything they wanted. Ballanor and Grendel had taught them that.

Before the woman could think to move, the second soldier stepped forward and dropped a knee onto her shoulders, shoving her face into the cobbles. She started to scream, a high-pitched, breathless sound of pure panic, as the first soldier slowly undid his belt.

Around them the streets were silent except for the mother's distraught screaming. Most people cleared quickly away; those with no choice but to remain turned away their faces.

But Nim would not turn away.

She launched herself toward the woman at the same instant as Tor leaped forward, the horrified outrage that she felt, mirrored on his face.

Tor landed a solid punch to the jaw of the soldier holding down the mother before the man had even completely understood the danger he was in.

The soldier stumbled back, and Nim was able to pull the woman into her arms. She was breathing in short, panicked gasps, her whole body shaking as she cried out desperately for her son. Nim reached across to the boy and pulled him in against her body and held them both as the fight raged around them.

She could hear grunts and swearing as Tor, weaponless

and dressed in casual clothes, battled the three heavily armed soldiers.

Sparks flew nearby as a sword hit the cobbles. Someone snarled a curse, and a different voice gave a sharp groan of pain. Nim ignored it all as she tried to pull the mother and her son away, but the woman was almost incoherent with her fear and seemed unable to stand, and Nim couldn't carry both her and the child.

Suddenly, the sounds stopped, and she lifted her head to see Tor ringed by the three soldiers, all with their swords drawn and pointed at him.

All were covered in sweat and blood. The soldier Tor had punched, the youngest-looking, had a split lip beginning to swell. The soldier with the dirtied boots had a steady trickle of blood seeping from his nose. And Tor himself stood with blood running down his face from a cut over his eye and a viciously long gash threading down his arm.

There was nothing more Tor could do; he was surrounded, empty-handed and alone.

The first soldier stepped up to the women where they huddled together and grabbed the mother by her hair, pulling her up out of Nim's arms and thrusting her face toward Tor as she whimpered and begged. "This. This is what you will die for," he growled out before throwing her back to the ground where she curled into a ball around her son and wept.

"And as for you…." He spun toward Nim where she knelt, and she shrank back into her cloak and ducked her head into her chest.

He stepped forward and let fly with a savage kick toward her side. She saw him lift his foot and flung herself away but not quick enough to escape entirely, and she felt fire as the toe of his boot scraped viciously along her ribs.

Beside her, Tor shouted in horror and fought to reach her, but the other two soldiers held him back.

"Get up," the soldier growled to the women. "We'll deal with you when we get to Gatehouse."

Nim ignored the burning agony down her side as she rose slowly to her feet, trying not to panic.

Gatehouse Prison was the worst possible place they could go. Filled with murderers and thieves. Policed via a brutal hierarchy of thugs and gangsters. Even she knew of it, despite having lived all her life in a distant village. And it filled her with terror.

They were alone. Unlikely to live through the next hours. Her brother didn't even know she had tried to reach him. And Tristan….

Her heart ached. What would Tristan think when he found out what had happened? Gods, she wished they'd had more time.

She kept her face down as she helped the other woman and her son to their feet and wrapped her arm around them, thoughts rushing desperately as she tried to think of something, anything that she could do to fix this. And came up blank.

Chapter Twelve

TRISTAN FOLDED his arms and tried not to glare at the third innkeeper they'd seen that morning.

The man was short and wiry with a shiny bald head and flushed face. His Tarasque scales were a dull gray and he had a disconcerting nervous habit of wringing his hand through his apron, all while darting glances toward the kitchen at the back of the room where Tristan had seen two pretty, blond-haired young women disappear as soon as they arrived.

The Cup seemed clean and well run, with a few locals sitting in a corner enjoying a rich-smelling stew. But, much like the other inns he'd tried, it seemed that the rooms that would normally house merchants, wealthy farmers, and other travelers were surprisingly quiet. A glance around the stables had shown empty stalls and a daydreaming groom.

And yet the innkeeper had taken one look at him, Jeremiel, and Garet and, just like the two before him, insisted that they were full.

Once they had seen Nim and Tor safely through the city

gates, they had separated to their different tasks. Tristan had thought their job would be quick and easy. Get lodgings, ideally spread across several nearby inns or taverns so that they didn't form too obvious a squad, and then get back to Nim.

And yet, here he stood. Making no progress whatsoever. And the delay was riling the primal part of him. The part that had claimed Nim and wanted to know where she was. Right now.

"I have been past your stables. I can see for myself, man, you're not full. Surely you want the coin?"

The man mumbled something vague about guests arriving later. Tristan looked at Jeremiel over his shoulder, who shook his head briefly. Lie.

Tristan scrubbed his hands down his face. "I don't understand the problem. We know that you're empty. We need rooms. At least one, for my, uh…."

He was going to say sister, but that just sounded wrong. He cast around for a better option, aware that the innkeeper was watching him closely.

"Wife," he settled on eventually, ignoring the quiet snort from Garet behind him.

"Your wife?" the innkeeper asked suspiciously.

"Yes. My wife. And her brother," he added. It was a good thing he hadn't said sister if Nim was going to arrive with her arms inked.

"You need a room for you and your wife? And another for her brother?" the innkeeper asked, looking uncertain.

"Yes." Tristan took out a gold coin and offered it to the man. "This should cover two rooms for the next two days, including meals and hot water, with stabling for our horses."

It was way more than the room was worth, but they had to have somewhere to stay.

The innkeeper eyed the coin as he let go of his apron and wiped his palm down the cloth a few times before replying slowly, "I just remembered that we had a cancellation this morning. Two rooms are free after all. One for you and your wife. One for her brother. But," his lips pinched as he eyed Jeremiel and Garet, "there are no other rooms. At all. Whatsoever."

Tristan sighed and glanced over at the two other men. Jeremiel shook his head slightly, while Garet shrugged. Another lie. But nothing they said was going to change the man's mind.

"Fine," Tristan agreed, "we'll take the two rooms. We'll be back later this afternoon. Please get them cleaned and prepared in the meantime."

The innkeeper took a step forward, and Tristan noticed his hands shaking. "Money first."

Tristan bristled. "Gods, man. I'm not paying you now and then coming back later to find the rooms are gone."

"No, no." He shook his head violently. "I would never. The rooms will be ready, I swear. Money first."

Tristan sighed and reluctantly handed over the coin before stalking back out to the dusty street. He was getting bloody tired of the way everyone they came across reacted to their uniforms. He had been so proud, worked so hard for the honor of wearing one.

They started to make their way down to the nearby market where they would find Nim and Tor, and he turned to the other two men as they walked. "What the fuck has happened to this city?"

"Did you see the way he looked at us?" Garet replied, equally unsettled.

Jeremiel nodded, his jaw clenched. "Yes. It's the same as

the other inns we tried. No one wants soldiers. They're afraid."

Tristan grunted. That was exactly what he had thought too. And he didn't like it.

"Where does that leave us for tonight? I want everyone well rested before we try this insane plan. Any thoughts?" Tristan asked.

"Jos and I can stay with his family, and maybe the rest of you can try the barracks?" Garet suggested.

"No," Tristan replied. "That would mean four of you turning up without the rest of the squad. Someone would ask questions."

"There are a few Temples nearby that offer hostels. We could try that," Jeremiel suggested, and Tristan grunted his agreement.

They walked in silence, each lost in their own thoughts, and it took a moment for Tristan to notice that there suddenly seemed to be a lot of people streaming toward them.

People hurrying, heads down. Almost as if they were trying to get away from something, all while trying to look inconspicuous.

A few noticed him, Garet, and Jeremiel and immediately shied away.

The heavy prickling in his chest ramped up a thousand levels, merging with an uneasy, roiling feeling of danger deep inside his gut as his beast began to growl. Where was Nim?

He lengthened his stride and picked up speed, pushing against the oncoming crowd as it broke and cleared around him.

Everyone seemed to be moving out his way impossibly slowly, and the dark part inside him flickered, wanting nothing more than for him to draw his sword and hack his way through the mass of streaming humanity.

With every passing second, he became more certain that Nim was in danger.

He turned the corner into the avenue they'd been looking for, his eyes instantly settling on the small group at the far end of the street, near the food stalls.

A brute of a soldier, arms rippling with red and yellow scales, had just let fly with a vicious kick that sent a small, cloaked woman flying into the dirt.

He knew that cloak. Knew that woman.

For an instant, he felt as if he'd been flooded with ice, but just as fast, it was replaced by a molten volcanic fury toward the men who had hurt her. Again.

Tristan threw himself forward without thinking, briefly registering Tor as he struggled against his captors. He only vaguely heard the soldier's threat to Nim as she pushed herself off the ground and wrapped her arms around some unknown woman and child.

She had her back to him, and he dimly realized that she hadn't seen him. A small part of him, the part that stayed cold and detached however bloody the battle, reminded him that he couldn't give them away. If he did anything to reveal who she was or his connection to her, it would all be over. The next few minutes would determine whether or not Nim survived the day.

He reached the group in seconds, and before the soldiers had even noticed he was there, he was already roaring, "Attention! Right face!"

The three soldiers turned and snapped to attention by rote, but then they saw who had commanded them and blinked in confusion, not sure whether he was someone they had to answer to.

Tristan was wearing the black uniform of the cavalry divisions, compared to their Palace Guard Blues. Which put them above him. But he was a sergeant, while they were corporals. They were new to the palace guard, while Tristan carried himself like a commander.

Tristan gave them no time to consider their options and instead stood in front of them, legs spread wide, arms behind his back as he bellowed, "What the fuck is happening here? Corporal, report!"

The three soldiers exchanged smug glances despite their blood and bruises. "Just a little cleanup, sir."

His scales flickered over his face, all the way to his eyes, and he knew that his rage was written over his body for all to see.

He ached to rush to Nim. To pull her into his arms and carry her away. She had startled, whirling round to see him when he first spoke, and now she stood, eyes wide in her pale face, one arm wrapped around her ribs.

The other was held in front of her as if she had started to reach for him, recognized that it would be a bad idea, and stopped herself. But her eyes were soft with relief.

A deeply unsettling feeling filled him. The feeling that she was his, and she was hurt, and that he would tear down the world to save her. And that if he showed one iota of that, she would die.

He turned his back on her before he lost control and grabbed her, and arched an eyebrow at the soldier, face carefully blank.

The soldier continued with a sneer, "A few more to sleep at Gatehouse tonight. Thought we might take them now, maybe even take our payment while we're there, if you know what I mean. You can join us if you like."

Tristan hadn't known that it was possible to reach a

point of rage so potent that merely killing someone would never be enough. Or that it would be possible to stand still while the desire for violence raged through him and keep his voice calm enough to reply. "What the fuck did you just say, Corporal? Be very clear about what it is you think we're going to do together."

"I, uh…," the soldier spluttered uncertainly.

Tristan took one threatening step forward, enjoying the way the soldiers flinched back.

"We didn't mean nothing," the man who'd kicked Nim said sullenly.

"Keep. Quiet." Tristan lowered his voice to a menacing rumble, gratified to see the soldiers glancing at each other, smug looks morphing into uncertainty.

"And you?" Tristan turned his attention to the woman clutching a small child. "What is this all about?"

The woman whimpered and shook her head, refusing to speak.

He turned to Nim, wondering what she could read in his face, and demanded, "You, girl. What's going on here?"

Her eyes narrowed, and he knew he would pay for the "girl" later. But she obviously understood what he was trying to do, because she answered in a soft, terrified voice that struck him to the core, "Please, sir. It was an accident, sir. Just a little dust on his boots when the boy dropped his apple, and he… he…." Her eyes darted down to where the loudest soldier's belt still hung open, genuine fear in her eyes, and the iron control holding Tristan together almost cracked.

He took another step toward the three soldiers, now huddling together for support against the death showing in his eyes.

"What the fuck were you thinking?" he asked again,

voice so soft they had to strain to hear him. Garet and Jeremiel stepped up closer. They knew what that quiet voice meant.

"They got to learn respect. Captain says to keep them in line, show them who's in charge," the soldier with the bleeding nose answered in a surly voice.

Gods.

Tristan had known, intellectually, that after the Blues were decimated at the massacre of Ravenstone—and his small remaining squad was banished to the ass-end of nowhere—the entire company would be replaced.

And, if he'd thought about it, he might have considered the consequences of the new captain of the Palace Guard being one of King Ballanor's cronies. Or what might happen if the new company was entirely filled with men who were only there as political favors and in recognition of the years that they'd spent carousing with the prince and Grendel. All under the leadership of two men who loved to play at sword-fighting but who had never spent even one day on campaign.

But he had been far away, licking his wounds, consumed with rage at how they'd been betrayed, and had never, not until that exact moment, truly imagined what would happen when men like Grendel were in charge.

"What's he got to do with this?" He nodded toward Tor.

"I'm her brother, sir. It's true, sir, what my sister said," Tor answered, nodding toward Nim.

Tristan winced at Tor's attempt to sound harmless not five minutes after he'd been beating three armed soldiers bloody. Hopefully, the assholes in front of him didn't notice how ridiculous the massive Apollyon sounded.

Tristan looked around the silent, empty street. Shutters were down, stores had locked their doors, their owners watching warily from upstairs windows and behind curtains. This was what it had come to.

He turned to the shivering mother cuddling her son. "You learned respect today?"

"Yes. Sir. Please." Her words were almost impossible to understand through her sniveling.

He gave her a brief nod. "Off with you."

The soldiers twitched but stayed silent as she grabbed her son by the hand and the two ran as fast as they could, never looking back.

As soon as they were gone, he motioned to Tor. "Take your sister. You can go."

Tor took a step forward, but the youngest of the three soldiers, the one with a swollen and bloodied lip, stuck his hand out to stop him. "No. He struck an officer. The penalty is death."

Tristan let out a slow breath. He was stuck. Either he killed all three soldiers now, here in the middle of the market with a hundred hidden witnesses. Or he had to let them take Tor.

He watched his friend, who stared back, impassive. And then Tor gave a tiny, almost imperceptible nod.

Nim looked between them frantically and shook her head repeatedly before whispering in a broken voice, "No. No. You can't."

Tristan firmed his voice. "Say goodbye to your brother, miss."

Nim glared at him with eyes filled with horrified fury before surprising them all by flinging herself into Tor's arms.

Tor caught her, more shocked than anyone, and stroked her hair softly while she clung to him and cried.

Tristan could do nothing except stand and watch,

listening to her quiet sobs while Tor whispered something too low to hear.

One of the Blues sniggered, and Nim spun away from Tor, tear-streaked face filled with hatred, and opened her mouth. He couldn't let her do it. One word, and she would be going with Tor. He clamped his hand over her mouth, ignoring her muffled screech of rage, and wrapped an arm around her waist as he pulled her away.

Her flinch as he touched her ribs was almost more than he could bear, but he kept a firm grip on her as he passed her over to Jeremiel and Garet and muttered, loud enough to send a clear message to the three soldiers, "See that she gets home safely, I'll assist here."

He didn't dare look at her as he spun on his heel and gestured for the soldiers to lead the way to Gatehouse.

Chapter Thirteen

NIM DIDN'T KNOW whether to scream or rage as she watched the soldiers lead Tor away. She still had tears lodged in her throat, but they were joined by a vicious fury more potent than anything she had ever experienced.

And the person she most wanted to kill at that moment was Tristan. How could he do it? To his friend. To her.

She took a step, meaning to run after them, to stop them, to argue, scream, grab Tor. Something. Anything.

But Jeremiel was suddenly in front of her, his tall lean frame blocking her view, stopping her.

His voice was harsh as he muttered a single word. "Don't."

"But—"

"No. Anything you do now will make it worse. Do you want all of us thrown in Gatehouse with Tor?"

She settled back onto her heels, trying to calm her raging emotions and just think. She was desperate to get Tor back, but she didn't know how to do that without risking Tristan and the others.

She didn't regret one second of helping the other woman. There was no way she could have lived with herself if she hadn't. And she had known that there would be repercussions. But she hadn't expected the horror of feeling like she was losing another brother—her fear for Val was too raw to allow her to be rational about Tor.

And, if she was being completely honest, at least some of her rage was because of how completely unaffected Tristan had been by her. How little he seemed to care. He'd just pushed her away without even looking at her. Again.

A stray tear ran down her cheek, and she swiped it away with the back of her hand.

Jeremiel's face softened. "Oh, little Mabin, don't cry. We will get him back. And Tristan… Let's just say that I've never seen the captain like that before."

She wiped her nose. "Surely you've seen him blank-faced and walking away before."

Garet snorted at her side as Jeremiel replied, "We obviously saw something different. From where I was standing, he looked like he was about to rain hell down on the world. When he came around the corner and saw you on the ground, gods, I thought we might finally see what happens when the captain loses his mind."

"Really?" she asked softly, wishing she had seen even a flicker of emotion in Tristan's eyes.

Jeremiel guided her to start walking as he led their horses out of the market and frowned down at her. "He couldn't give you away. What do you think would happen to you if those Blues figured out who you are?"

She would have argued, but he carried on before she could, and this time went straight for the jugular. "What exactly do you think would happen to Tor and the captain if they were found protecting Lanval's sister?"

Her anger drained away, replaced by a nauseating thrum of guilt.

She knew that Tor was only her pretend brother, but she had grown to adulthood hearing Val's stories. He had spoken often of these men, had loved them like a family. And that was before she had spent time with all of them, got to know each of them.

Her hands felt cold and clammy as she realized the truth. In her desperate focus on Val, she hadn't properly considered just how risky it was for them to help her. And now they were all in danger.

The last thing she wanted was for any of them to be hurt, particularly because of her.

She slowed, letting Jeremiel and Garet pull ahead as they walked the horses down the cobbled lane toward the inn, considering her options.

The Hawks would be better off without her. They could go back to the barracks and report in. Say they couldn't find her. Grendel would never have to know. They would remain exiles, but at least they'd be alive.

She slowed down even further and considered slipping away. Jeremiel and Garet were deep in a serious conversation and wouldn't expect it. She could let herself drop farther back and then quietly turn into an alley and away.

It was so tempting.

But she knew in her heart that she couldn't do it. She couldn't leave them without saying goodbye. She couldn't leave Tor, in the Gatehouse because of her. She definitely couldn't leave Tristan without seeing him one last time. And she knew that leaving on her own would most likely result in her dying in the near future—which wouldn't help anybody.

She walked a little faster and caught up to the others just

as they arrived at a friendly-looking inn with a freshly painted sign showing an ornately jeweled silver chalice.

Just before they reached the entrance, Jeremiel stopped her and pulled her to one side, a small frown wrinkling his forehead. "Before we go in, you should know, the captain told the innkeeper that you and he... well, that you're married."

"Married?" she repeated, confused.

"Yes. They wouldn't give us a room. Not that I can blame them after.... Anyway, the captain told them you were his wife and got a room for you. Ah... I mean, you and him. And one for your brother. Um, Tor."

Jeremiel looked so flustered that she couldn't help a small chuckle despite her boiling emotions. "His wife, huh? Isn't that just typical Tristan? Marries me without bothering to ask or buy me a ring."

"Well, strictly," Jeremiel started, clearly having been with Tristan when he bought back Val's ring, but Nim glared at him until he gave an embarrassed shrug and opened the door.

She liked the Cup immediately. It was warm and inviting, the wooden tables shone, and the air was rich with the mouthwatering aroma of roasting lamb and rosemary. She wished that she could have visited at any other time.

The innkeeper came bustling out when they arrived, his eyes narrowed under a concerned frown. Nim turned on her most charming bedside manner to greet him, smiling and complimenting him, all while hoping he didn't think it weird that she kept her hood up and her sleeves held tightly down.

Eventually she was able to escape to her bedroom while the men took the horses to the stables. She hung her coat behind the door, dropped her satchel down next to it, and looked around.

The room had a row of small windows letting in the autumn light that gleamed over polished wood floors. Several cheerful rugs softened the room, and a small fire crackled in the hearth. The bed was wide and built up with a surrounding step, a carved wooden headboard, and draped with dark green velvet curtains, bundled to the sides for the daytime. The matching green and white quilt looked soft and warm.

Next to the bed was a small seating area with two comfortable-looking armchairs and a low table.

A back corner had been partitioned with a screen, and when she peered around it, she found a small table with a basin and a jug of water. She washed her face and hands, scrubbing away the sand and dirt on her palms, cleaning out the grazes from where she'd fallen in the market. There was nothing she could do about her ribs, but at least nothing felt broken.

There was no longer any need to try and maintain the pretense of being related to Tor, he would not be joining them in the inn. So she soaped her arms and, with a pang of sorrow, washed away the smudged swirls of ink.

Then she turned and rinsed her hair as best as she could, running a fine comb through the thick strands until all the ash was out and the smell of smoke was washed away. She rubbed it dry with the small towel and then plaited it into a long braid.

Finally, clean and dry, she sank into the closest armchair and let her head drop into her hands.

Thoughts of Tristan, Tor, and Val swirled through her head, and she considered and discarded a million different crazy schemes to save them. Ideas of drugging the guards, distracting them while the others freed Tor, even breaking in herself, were all contemplated and abandoned.

She felt helpless, unable to avoid imagining what Val was going through, chained to a wall in the palace. Now Tor, too. Hurting and alone. She hated it.

She stood and started to pace. Waiting around in her room like a good little girl was killing her. She had to do something.

It occurred to her that she could go down to the prison and look around, at least get some sense of where they were keeping Tor, perhaps even learn something about what would happen to him in the morning.

If she went to Gatehouse as Tor's sister, she could probably learn more than the men would, maybe even get to see him.

She could also check that Tristan hadn't somehow become caught up in Tor's imprisonment. He had been gone for so long. Too long. The thought of him locked in a dark cell beside Tor played vividly in her mind.

She looked out the window. The sun was sinking down the sky, afternoon shadows lengthening across the street.

She couldn't waste any more time. She had to go. Immediately.

She looked all over the room but couldn't find any way to leave a note, but she didn't want Tristan to arrive and think she'd simply left. She took Val's ring from her pocket and put it on one of the pillows, hoping that he would see it there and know that she would be coming back soon. If she could.

She wasn't going to think about any of the things that could go wrong. She pulled on her cloak, lifted the hood to cover her face, and took a few breaths. She was ready.

Then she ripped open the door, about to fly down the stairs, and almost screamed in shock. Standing right in front of her, hand lifted to knock, was Tristan.

And he did not look pleased.

He took in her traveling cloak with a glance, his frown deepening. His eyes swept the room and rested for a moment, probably on Val's ring, as pewter and green scales joined the furrowed lines on his forehead. Gods. That was bad.

He stepped forward, pushing her back, slammed the door behind him, and asked in a rough voice, "Going somewhere?"

She considered explaining that, yes, she had places to be. That she was busy. That it wasn't up to him whether she left or not. And that she didn't care to be bossed around.

But she could feel the tension vibrating through him, the strain from the catastrophe in the market and his distress about his friend, all pushed down deep within him. Held so tight that she wondered if he even knew how badly affected he was.

The low rumble was back in his chest as his scales flickered in a gleaming wave from his hands and up his arms, all the way to the short leather sleeves of his jerkin, reappearing over his neck and jaw and up to his temples.

All her thoughts of fighting him fell away. He might not realize it, but he needed her.

She went up onto her toes and ran her nose along his jaw, along those magnificent, primal greens and smoky-grays, and then pressed her lips against his neck, where his pulse beat a hard rhythm.

His body was so stiff that, for a moment, she wondered if he would push her away, and she hesitated. But then he wrapped his hand into her hair and tipped her head back, staring down at her with fierce green eyes. And a second later, he sealed his mouth over hers.

Heat poured into her as he ran his tongue over her lips,

and she opened for him, almost whimpering as he surged inside. Owning her, dominating her, until she lost herself in the fever of his mouth on hers.

He spun, lifting her, and pressed her into the door, one heavy leg sliding between hers so that she was balanced, riding his hard thigh as he kissed and nibbled his way down her throat, his breath searing against her bare skin, and she ran her hands up his shoulders and around his neck as he lifted his head and took her mouth once more.

His hands moved to her breasts, thumbs sliding in through the sides of her leather jerkin to graze roughly over her nipples, callouses catching against the cotton of her blouse in torturous tugs. Her whole body responded, as if there was an electric connection between her nipples and her clit.

She ground herself against his leg, but her leather breeches were in the way, and she couldn't get the friction that she desperately needed. Couldn't relieve the ache spreading through her core. She moaned into his mouth, trying to get closer, to drown herself in his body.

He responded by stepping back and swinging her into his arms. In two huge strides he was at the bed. He threw her down onto the covers, her back across the bed, her legs folded down the side, and she immediately pushed herself up onto her elbows, watching him as he watched her.

His legs were braced, his face severe, his eyes almost glowing, their green was so intense. She was close enough to see a ring of smoky silver around each iris, leaking into the green, and she knew that his inner beast was right at the surface, driving him.

If she ran now, he would be on her in a second. But she had no desire to run. She let her legs fall open, and he stepped between them, towering over her in a way that should have made her feel small and vulnerable. Instead, she felt power running through her in sensuous waves.

Better than the first time she'd leaped off a high cliff into the waiting air currents. Better than soaring through the air and then diving into a cold mountain river. Better than anything she'd ever felt before.

She sat up fully, bringing her face to the massive bulge in his breeches. He didn't move, but his eyes narrowed, watching her. She lifted a hand and ran her nails languidly over his cock, loving the way the dark silver bled further across his eyes.

Moving just as slowly, she lifted her hands away and tugged at the string of her jerkin and pulled the laces, shrugging until she was free. Slowly, carefully, she unwound the leather bindings that had strapped her wings down over her blouse, his eyes glittering as he watched her every movement.

Her breasts fell loose, heavy beneath the soft cotton, and her wings unfurled behind her in a sensuous glide over the bed, tingling as the blood returned.

She turned her attention to her breeches, lifting her hips so that she could start to pull them down. The movement broke Tristan's heavy stare, and he growled as he pushed her hands aside and pulled them down himself.

She lay back and let him tug off her boots and then slowly pull her breeches the rest of the way. He dropped her clothes to the floor and then pulled her down the bed until her bottom was hovering right at the edge and she was completely open in front of him.

Her wings fluttered at her sides as she fought to stay still, locked beneath the intensity of his gaze.

He dropped to his knees on the raised step beside the bed and then put his hard hands on the inside of her legs and pushed them wider, holding her open as he ran his mouth up the soft flesh of her thigh, pausing at the join between her thigh and hip to run his teeth across the straining tendon.

She could feel her legs starting to tremble, her breath coming in rough pants, but he held her still as he ran his chin over her mound, his beard tangling with the curly hairs, tugging with sharp, teasing bursts. He moved to the other side, nibbling and sucking the join of her thigh, his face nudging against her folds but never quite touching.

She closed her eyes, clutching the bedcovers as she whispered, desperate, "Gods. Please. Tris. Please."

She tried to push herself closer, but he held her down with one arm over her belly, still sucking the inside of her thigh as he slowly ran his free hand all the way from her knee to her groin.

Finally, finally, he reached her entrance, his fingers dancing around her in a torturous circle, then just the tip of one finger entering her before retreating. Then entering her again. Then retreating.

He moved his mouth over her, hot, humid air touching her in delicate puffs as his fingers entered her and retreated yet again.

She squirmed, panting, but he was ruthless. His tongue flicked out in concert with his torturing finger, licking her clit in short bursts while he thrust a second finger inside her entrance.

Her whole body was flooded with molten need, and the world narrowed down, falling away until nothing was left except him. It was too much. It was not enough. She needed more.

He lifted his head for a moment, fingers still inside her, curled forward, but not moving, and she nearly wept with desperation until he rumbled, "Lift your shirt." She pulled the blouse up over her flushed breasts as he watched from between her legs.

"Show me."

She lay back and pushed her breasts together, feeling his rumble turn into a deep, animal purr. "Pinch your nipples."

She closed her fingers over her nipples, letting her eyes flutter closed as she tugged and pulled, feeling his hot breath right over her clit as she throbbed around his fingers.

Then he was everywhere. Moving, gliding. Pressure and heat and relentless strokes ratcheting her higher.

He closed his lips on her pulsing clit and sucked. The heated suction pushed her over, and her whole body clenched in a devastating orgasm.

Waves of exquisite sensual pleasure flooded through her as she writhed against him, pushing herself into his scorching mouth. Closer to him than she had ever been to any other person.

He stayed with her, still kneeling between her legs, as she came back to herself, until she lay, flushed and soft, eyes half-closed, watching him. Then he finally stood, stripped and laid his clothes aside.

He was magnificent. Layers of muscle overlaid with emerald-green and pewter scales that gleamed from his neck, down his arms, wrapping around his abdomen to highlight the ripples of his muscles, then fading into smooth brown skin in a hard, muscular V, leading to his straining cock, rigid against his belly and weeping with his need for her.

He was mesmerizing.

Tristan crawled over her, pulling her up with him to lie fully across the bed, and nestled his hips between her legs as he held himself over her.

She ran her hands up his arms, glorying in the warmth of his skin, the masculine scent of his body, his strength surrounding her. He brushed his cock through her slick folds, and she shuddered and wrapped her hands around his flexing arms, lifting herself to meet him.

He paused, the head of his cock notched just at her entrance, and looked down at her, his eyes almost completely silver, his voice rasping. "Tell me you want this, Nim."

She had no doubt at all. There was nothing she wanted more. "Yes. I want this."

"I haven't got a sheath, sweetheart, but I'll do my best to make sure there's no babe."

"I trust you," she murmured as she wrapped her legs around him and pulled him slowly into her body, reveling in the exquisite glide of his flesh into hers. A little uncomfortable, foreign, but she was so wet and swollen and ready, all she wanted, needed, was his body inside hers.

Until he paused, forehead furrowed, a sudden question in his eyes. "Nim, are you…?"

She didn't want to answer, didn't want to say or do anything to take away from the magic of the moment with him.

But he wouldn't move. She sighed and gave him a small smile. "Technically… not anymore."

"But… I don't understand. Val said that men were visiting. Interested. Surely you can't have been alone all this time?" He looked so uncertain. He had no idea.

She wanted to howl.

None of them were you! I waited, and you never came back.

She couldn't tell him the truth. He wasn't ready. She didn't want to see those shutters come down if she told him how she felt. How she had always felt.

And none of it made any difference anyway, given the danger she would soon be in. She couldn't even be certain she would be alive in the morning.

But she was entirely certain that she wanted him. Wanted *this*.

And equally certain that he was about to run.

Chapter Fourteen

TRISTAN FROZE, his body trembling while his dark, primal center railed against him, howling to plunge deeper, take her. Own her.

She had been so hot, so tight, clenched around him like a vise. And he'd been lost in her. In her scent, all warm woman and something softly sweet that was uniquely Nim. Lost in her taste—still in his mouth—and the way her body undulated beneath his.

It had taken him a moment, seeing the flicker of discomfort cross her face, to properly understand.

He had had many women. From the moment he became a soldier, they had thrown themselves at him. And it only got worse when he was made Captain of the Blues. They had chased him with fervor. A game where everybody won. And he had loved playing it, not hesitating to take what was offered. Right up until the squad was relegated to the forty-ninth.

But every single one of those women had been experienced. He had always made sure of it. Worldly, knowing, clear on what he was offering. Which was nothing. He had been completely honest upfront, scrupulously careful to always use a sheath.

And he had done none of those things with Nim.

Gods. What would Val say? She was his baby sister. His friend would kill him, and he probably deserved it.

He had to get off her. He knew. He had to make this right, somehow. Talk to her. Ask her forgiveness.

But just as the thoughts flashed through his mind, he saw her walls go up. His muscles bunched, about to pull away, but she beat him to it.

She dropped her legs to his sides, her hands falling off his arms as she turned her face away.

And the beast inside him roared to life. She was *his*. She belonged to *him*. And he would have her.

He moved his weight onto one arm so that he could free a hand to cup her chin and pull her back to face him as he growled, "What the fuck did I say about pulling away from me?"

Her eyes flew open, startled, suspiciously wet, and he knew that she had somehow known everything he'd been thinking. She'd expected him to run.

And he also knew with no doubt whatsoever that he would never run again.

His cock was still hard inside her. The only woman who had ever made him feel anything. And he wanted her more than he wanted to live.

"Tell me now, Nim, do you want this or not?"

"Yes." Her voice was a whisper. "I want this. I want you." Her eyes were wide and gleaming, still uncertain of him, silver flecks dancing like stars over the ocean.

He rolled them to their sides, holding her as if she were infinitely precious, then lifted her leg over his hip so that he could slowly nudge deeper inside her, watching her carefully the whole time.

Finally, once he was seated fully inside her, he lowered his head and took her mouth, kissing her with long, luscious strokes. All while running his hand slowly down her side, taking his time on her smooth skin, dragging his fingers over her breast, circling her nipple with his thumb as she slowly relaxed beside him, around him.

The tension in her slight frame melted back into languorous heat as tiny goose bumps chased along her smooth skin. He dragged his fingers over her, touching her, molding over her ribs, careful to avoid where she'd been hurt, circling her puckered nipple, following the heavy thump of her pulse along her neck as her breathing deepened.

Her wing came around and over them, encasing them in a heavy cocoon, and his skin beaded with sweat as he held himself still, concentrating entirely on her pleasure. Running his tongue inside her mouth in time with his fingers as he tugged her nipple, his cock pulsing inside her as her walls fluttered.

She moaned, tightening her leg, pushing herself down, and he dragged his fingers over her breast, down her belly and onto her swollen clit. His thumb drew lazy circles through her folds, where they joined, around the swollen nub as she started to pant, her hips thrusting toward him, seeking more.

Slowly, finally, he began to move. Pumping into her in time with his stroking fingers, adding pressure with each circle of her clit as she pushed further into him, her breath coming in short gasps as she moaned against his mouth.

He lifted her leg higher, changing the angle, knowing he had reached exactly the right position when she shuddered, clenching around him as he stroked her, pumping more firmly deep inside her.

He maintained that relentless, steady, rhythm, the pressure in his fingers, his mouth on hers, until she arched, moaning, her nails digging into his arm, and shattered around him with a half sob, clinging to him as her inner walls milked and sucked him until he couldn't hold himself for one more second.

He thrust into her, hard, needing to feel her, once, twice, and then, almost too late, he pulled out and came in huge spurts all over her belly and breasts.

She opened her eyes slowly, looking at him, completely focused on him despite the slowly receding haze of release. Waiting, he knew, to see what he would do.

It was an easy decision. He leaned down and touched his lips to hers, almost overwhelmed by the sensations flooding through him. Light. Air. Joy.

Gods, when last had he felt joy?

And then she smiled, a look of such wonder on her face that he felt himself smile back. She laughed, a glorious throaty sound of delight that reached into his soul. And saved it.

He ran his thumb over her lips, wanting to feel her laughter in every part of him, and then leaned down to press another gentle kiss onto her softly smiling mouth.

He lifted himself off the bed and found a small towel, which he used to clean her body and between her legs. There was a small amount of blood on the inside of her thighs, and he pressed another kiss onto her creamy skin, overwhelmed with what she had given him.

Once she was clean, he lay back down beside her and pulled her against him before reaching down and taking hold of a blanket to cover them both.

The dark voice deep inside him was clear: Nim was his. And, for the first time in his life, he felt all the parts of himself align, his inner beast settling as he wrapped himself around her, surrounding himself in her scent.

They lay quietly together, and he listened to her heartbeat thumping slowly as she relaxed, gently falling asleep in his arms.

His smooth arms. He looked down and noticed that his scales were completely gone, flattened down to clear, tanned skin for the first time in days. Weeks even. The first time since Ravenstone.

And it was because of the beautiful, brave woman cuddling against him in a cocoon of warmth.

The minutes ticked by as he held her, let her rest. He wished that they could lie there forever. But he knew they couldn't. It was time.

"Nim, sweetheart, we have to get up."

"Mm-hm." She snuggled deeper into his side, covering him with her wing.

He groaned. "I don't want to either, but Jos will be here with your dress any minute now, and if he sees you like this, I'll have to kill him."

She chuckled sleepily and opened her eyes, blinking a few times as she tried to wake up before replying in a husky voice, "Don't do that. I like Jos."

He frowned at her, and she chuckled again and ran a soft finger down his jaw as she whispered, "Not how I like you."

He turned his face into her hand and kissed her fingers gently, still frowning. "You're mine now, Nim." He said it quietly, but even he could hear the deep rumble beneath his words.

"And you're mine," she agreed immediately, and he

almost smiled, until she finished, "Now we just have to survive."

Fuck. He didn't want to think about her in danger. He definitely didn't want her anywhere near the palace. But he also knew that if he tried to forbid her, she'd just go anyway, without him.

He sat up and swung his legs around and out of the bed, still holding her hand, and turned sideways to look at her.

She lay in a disheveled tangle of blankets. Her hair had come loose from its tie and lay in waves the color of rich cocoa spread across the cotton sheets, and she watched him with clear eyes.

Never before had he imagined having something so perfect. Or that he would feel so utterly unworthy.

He let go of her hand so that he could tuck a curl behind her ear, wondering how it was that he had known her nearly all his life but only truly found her when there might be so little of it left.

His thoughts must have shown on his face, because she sat up beside him and tucked herself under his arm before wrapping her arms around his waist. "Tell me what happened."

"We took Tor to Gatehouse, found the guards there, and paid them for a solitary cell and a doctor to see to his wounds." He sighed, thinking about how horrific it had been. If the city was cowering under a state of constant fear, the prison was fifty times worse.

A powerful wave of guilt washed over him. How had he left his friend among those killers and torturers? How could he have been losing himself in Nim's body when who knew what the fuck was happening to Tor?

His scales were back, rippling up his arms in a long slide of disquieting remorse as he realized how wrong it was for him to take such pleasure, and he started to push himself off the bed. But Nim held him even tighter and threw her leg over his thigh. He would have to bodily remove her to stand, and a low rumble started in his belly.

But she was having none of it. "Stop that. If anyone is to blame, it's me."

His attention snapped back to her. "What the——"

"No," she interrupted in a rough voice. "Where do you think I was going when you arrived? Out to look for you and Tor. And why? Because I have spent the whole afternoon coming to terms with the fact that none of you would be in this position if it weren't for me."

He was speechless for a moment as his brain raced through the implications of what she was saying. What, exactly, Nim might do if she thought she was personally responsible for an entire squad's safety.

It was his turn to clamp her tight to his body as he rasped out the words, "Hell, no."

She squirmed against him, trying to get free, but he held her too tightly for her to escape, and eventually she softened against him.

Her voice was firm, but he heard the vulnerability beneath her words as she spoke into his chest. "Don't ask me to regret this, Tris. I won't. It meant something to me. I understand that you have probably done this hundreds of times, but it was important to me."

His scales rippled over his back and up his neck as he tried to control himself. He wanted to fling her onto the bed and prove to her, again and again, how important it was to him. How important *she* was to him.

He settled for pulling her around to straddle him, her beautiful naked body pressed against his cock as it hardened painfully between them.

He wrapped a heavy hand around the back of her neck and pulled her down until her forehead rested against his and her wings fluttered closed behind him. "Never tell me that you don't mean anything to me. Never again. I told you that you're mine; did you think I said that lightly?"

She shook her head slowly, but he could see she wasn't convinced. He needed to show her.

He tangled his fingers in her hair and kissed her. Kissed her like she meant everything in the world to him.

Because she did.

He didn't deserve her. Everything about him was a mess of scars and cynicism where she was beauty and light. But he would take whatever she would give, for however long she gave it.

By the time he broke away, they were both panting, her nipples hard points against his chest. He was about to give in and throw her onto her back when a loud knock on the door startled them both.

Nim curled in against him at the sound, and he tightened his arm around her, holding her close as he growled, "Go away."

"It's Jos. I've got Nim's dress," came the muffled reply.

"Leave it outside."

"It needs altering."

"Go away and sort it out."

A few seconds passed as footsteps faded and new ones returned, and the knocking resumed.

"Get up. We have to talk." It was Mathos. "They've taken your recommendation and run with it. Tor's being moved tonight."

Nim raised an eyebrow, and he answered her unspoken question. "I suggested that it would be a good idea to move him to the cells in the palace. That the king might want to hang him tomorrow as part of the celebrations."

Nim blinked, stunned for a moment, before understanding lit her eyes and she replied, "We can get them at the same time."

Gods, he hoped so.

He raised his voice again. "Fine. We'll be there in five minutes."

He heard Mathos make a rude comment about captains who could only last five minutes and then laugh loudly at his own joke, as his footsteps faded away.

He buried his face in Nim's neck and closed his eyes, his arms wrapped tightly around her. Trying to inhale her, to memorize her scent, memorize the feeling of her pressed against him.

Just in case.

Chapter Fifteen

Nim and Tristan dressed quickly and made their way downstairs to find that Mathos had organized a small private reception room for the Hawks. The large wooden table in the center of the cozy room was already set, covered in platters of hot roast lamb with minted peas and steaming baked potatoes, loaves of bread, and rounds of yellow butter.

Mathos grinned as he told them how the innkeeper had wrung his hands and twisted his apron at the idea of the whole squad arriving for an early dinner, but had eventually been convinced that they were celebrating Nim and Tristan's new marriage and reluctantly allowed them in.

Tristan grunted grumpily while the men laughed, but Nim held her breath, wondering how he'd take the focus on their relationship. His scales were down, his eyes crinkled at the corners in an almost smile, and she slowly relaxed.

She hadn't eaten all day and the food was delicious, the room warm and peaceful as the men concentrated on their dinner. Tristan's thigh pressed reassuringly against hers, and she felt genuinely accepted by the Hawks. But she still couldn't settle.

Her thoughts were in a blur, her emotions a strange swirling combination of fluttering butterflies every time she looked up and saw Tristan watching her, the hot pulse of remembering what they'd done, and a cold underlay of fear for her brother, Tor, and the men around her. Trepidation about the night ahead. And a strange, painful uncertainty.

Tristan was like a dream, a beautiful dream that she had longed for all her life but had also known could never really come true. She'd heard what he'd said—that she was his— but she also knew that every time things had turned difficult, his first instinct was to walk away.

And who could blame him? His own mother had abandoned him, leaving him with an abusive bastard of a father. The king had banished him without a second thought. He had never trusted anyone except Val… and look how that had turned out.

And, on top of that, just a few short days ago, she had been building herself up to hate Tristan for how he'd abandoned her brother.

Val. Gods. Did he imagine anyone would come for him? Or did he think he was completely alone? It had been weeks since he'd been taken prisoner; she couldn't even imagine what it had done to him.

Her appetite fled, and she pushed away her plate. Tristan glared at her and pushed it closer again. She scowled and pushed it away once more. His glare deepened, and he leaned over and put his lips against her ear. "Eat. We don't know what will happen or when there will be food again."

She shook her head. "I'm not hungry."

"Please. It… does something to me. I need you to try."

She sighed and put a forkful of meat into her mouth, chewing dramatically while he watched with one raised eyebrow.

She managed a few more bites and then really couldn't stomach any more. She pushed the plate away to the other side of the table, daring him to try and get it back. He just shook his head and then glared at Jos when he sniggered.

She didn't want to eat. She wanted to get to Val.

Finally, the food was finished and the plates cleared. Everyone leaned back in their chairs while Jeremiel walked over and locked the door to the rest of the inn.

Tristan turned to Mathos. "Report."

"Tor is being moved to inside the palace walls tonight. I've bribed the guards with a promise of more coin tomorrow if he gets there in one piece."

"Do we know anything about exactly where in the palace he'll be going?" Garet asked.

"Most likely the new cells."

Tristan looked to Reece, the squad's engineer. "Tell me about the changes to the layout."

"I've taken a walk around and spoken to some of the local builders," Reece explained. "Ballanor has had teams working on defenses round the clock since we left. Two rings of walls are being added, with the old towers at their corners. He used the Tamasa to flood the gardens, which are now completely underwater, forming a massive moat. Tower Gate was submerged when they built the moat, so now the only access is through Court Gate."

Jos whistled. "That's not a palace; it's a fortress."

"And where are the cells?" Tristan asked.

"The Constable's Tower has been fortified and cells added. That's where we expect them to take Tor."

"And is that where Val is?" Nim asked, working hard to keep the worry out of her voice.

Mathos shook his head, giving her a sympathetic look. "Sorry, Nim. I asked around, and Tristan was right, Val is shackled to the wall inside the great hall."

"How long?" she tried to ask, but it came out as a rasp. Somehow, she had convinced herself that it wasn't real. That no one, however depraved, would genuinely hang another person on a wall. She cleared her throat and tried again, "How long has he been there?"

Mathos looked away, like he didn't want to answer, but she stared at him, resolute, until he turned back and faced her. "Several days."

Her mind flooded with images of Val. Playing together in the stream next to their house. Val teaching her how to fly. Collecting blackberries in the autumn and carrying them back for their Mama. Val lifting her onto horseback. Val's face, pale and drawn, his spine stiff, as he stood beside Mama's bed and said goodbye to her for the last time. A boy trying to be a man.

Val leaving after his last visit, his face as grim and bleak as if he was going back to war. Val insisting that he had to return to the palace, that his honor demanded it.

Val shackled to a wall. Val starving. Being tortured. In pain and all alone.

She pushed her chair back and stood, suddenly overwhelmed.

There were too many people and not enough air. Her ears were ringing, and she couldn't take a breath because of the tight band of pain around her ribs. The thickness in her throat.

She had to get out of the room. Get away from everyone.

She took a step toward the door, but Tristan was there before her, blocking her way. His arms came around her, and he pulled her into his chest, wrapping her in his warmth and strength. "Take a breath, sweetheart."

His chest moved beneath hers, and she took a breath with him, almost on instinct. And then another. Everyone else faded from her mind. They might as well have not existed. It was only her and Tris, breathing slowly together.

The ringing noise faded gradually, but he didn't move. Just held her firmly in his arms, not bothered that his men were watching.

Eventually he leaned back and tipped her chin up to look her in the eye as he spoke. "You can do this. And I'll help you. Whatever it takes."

She clenched her fists in the front of his shirt, wanting to shake him. Her fear swirled with helplessness and bled into rage. Into the furious need to blame someone. And, in her deepest heart, she already blamed Tristan. Despite everything they'd shared, she hadn't let go of the deep kernel of anger at him, and all the Hawks.

"You left him!" she whispered harshly. "He's there because of you!"

Tristan took a slow breath, his eyes not wavering from hers as he replied sincerely, "I regret that. More than you can know. But I can't go back and change it now; I can only go forward. Whatever happens, we will free Val."

"Why?" Her eyes burned with the tears that she was too angry to shed.

"Because we need the truth. None of this makes sense to me, and I want to hear what Val says—like I should have right in the beginning. Because, if he has committed a crime, he should have been tried by the Nephilim Justices and executed, not hung on a wall. Because coming here and seeing what has become of the Blues has been... horrifying. And because Val was my closest friend. But, mostly, more than any of that, because they came after you, Nim. And because he's your brother and you love him."

She wanted to stay angry with him. To rail against everything that he had said. To hold onto the righteous fury and the strength it gave her. But Tristan looked so grim and worried, his voice deep with conviction as he kept his eyes locked on hers, the emerald and pewter of his scales rippling up his arms and the deep rumbling back in his belly.

He lifted his hand to her cheek, his eyes deep with sorrow and sincerity, and she clasped her own hand over the top, holding him there.

She had been angry, so very angry with all of them. But she had come to realize that the Hawks—Tristan—had made a terrible mistake, and that they were as determined to find the truth as she was. That they were equally horrified by what was happening to her brother, and that they were risking everything to make it right.

In his last awful goodbye, Val had told her that no matter what, she should trust Tristan. He had told her that there were things she didn't know and that he wouldn't, couldn't, share. And lastly, that if anything were to happen to him, she should go to the Hawks.

When they'd abandoned him, she'd thought he was wrong, and had disregarded that advice, but now she knew that Val had been right—she should have gone straight to the Hawks and made them understand. But, even as she recognized their genuine commitment to finding the truth, her heart still beat a heavy rhythm in her throat. What would happen if they were forced to choose between Val and the new king?

The king was their supreme commander, and Tristan and Val had always believed that that they owed their obedience directly to him. It wasn't surprising that when the king condemned Val, it would have seemed unquestionable to Tristan. He was a loyal, honorable man who could never imagine lying about such a thing. Who would never dream that his king would deceive him.

She leaned her head against his chest and whispered, "I believe you, but I'm afraid."

Tristan growled deep in his belly. "You should be afraid. What we're doing is dangerous. And if anyone ever finds out, we're all going to die. Slowly and screaming."

She knew that already. And she'd made some peace with it. What she didn't want was for her actions to endanger anyone else. To put them in a position where they had to make an impossible choice. However angry she had been, she didn't want anyone to die because of her.

As her rage subsided, exhaustion crept in. And guilt. Who was she to expect these men to give up everything?

Nim turned in Tristan's arms and looked around the room, meeting each man's eyes. "I'm so sorry I got you into this. I understand if you don't want to be part of any of it."

Tristan's muscles went rigid under her hands, but then slowly relaxed as the men called out their commitment, one after the other.

"You can't get rid of us, darlin'," Mathos said quietly, "This is our fight now. It was our fight the moment we stepped into the city and realized what these new Blues have done to our people. And I think I speak for everyone when I say that we would never have left Val if we'd understood that there was any doubt of his guilt. And I'm including the captain in that."

"I should never have left Val without first trying to speak

to him," Tristan agreed, "and there's absolutely no way we're leaving Tor. Or you." His voice lowered. "Whatever you think of me personally."

She turned back, resting her hands on his arms, and looked at him. His face was carefully stoic, but she had known him all her life. And now she knew his soul.

The look of yearning was back, no longer hidden. Alongside resignation and... was that sadness? Loss? Silvery streaks bled across the green of his eyes as his jaw clenched.

He took a tiny step back, loosening his hold on her, and she suddenly realized that he expected her to push him away. And that he would let her do it, in front of all his men, and then help her to rescue Val anyway.

It was all she needed to settle her last lingering concerns. Tristan had already made his choice between her and Ballanor. And, despite his doubts about Val, he had chosen her.

When she was a little girl, her mama used to say *the heart sees what the eyes cannot*. She had never understood it before, not truly. But now she did. Her heart had known him all her life. Either she trusted that now or she had to leave him forever. And leaving him was not an option. She had trusted him with her body, she would trust him with her life.

She stepped forward, closing that small distance between them, not caring that the others were watching as she lifted onto her toes so she could look him in the eye. "I trust you."

He tipped his chin in a single nod of acceptance, but she could see that the look of loss was gone from his face, replaced with surprise. Wonder even. A small half-smile lifted his mouth at the corners as he ran his hands over her cheeks, tucking her hair behind her ears.

"I hate to break up... whatever this is," Jos interrupted,

"but we need to get moving. Nim, your dress is with Melandra—"

"Who the hell is Melandra?" Tristan asked, still looking down at Nim.

"The innkeeper's lovely daughter, of course," Reece replied. "Apparently she's particularly skilled at dressmaking. Among other things."

"Gods, Reece," Tristan complained, "how did you manage to find a woman here?"

"Who, me?" Reece replied with a smirk. "I merely referred to her other skills, like needlework and—"

"She'd need skill with needles if she's going to spend any time with you," Mathos quipped, earning a snort from everyone in the room.

Jos chuckled too before continuing, "Anyway, as you were, uh, busy earlier, I asked Melandra to sew on the silk overlay for you. She promised to hang your dress up in your room when she was finished."

"Good," Tristan agreed, "and while Nim changes, the rest of us need to shave, brush our uniforms, and polish our boots. I want us ready to move out in an hour."

Nim joined the chorus of *yes, sirs*, adding in a small salute, which earned her a glare. Somehow that stern look settled her. Teasing him and having him respond relieved some of the tension of the last half hour and gave her the reassurance she needed to let go, to some degree, of the jumbled mix of anger and fear that had been driving her and quickly climb the stairs to her room.

Everything had been set to rights, lamps lit, the bed made, and the jug filled with fresh warm water. And hanging on a hook on the wall was the most gorgeous dress she'd ever seen.

A floor-length velvet skirt in dark silver was now overlaid

with soft falls of the heavy blue silk from the market, everything gleaming in the firelight. The bodice was also silver, with a sweetheart neckline and silky off-the-shoulder sleeves, the front panels embroidered with silver vines adorned with tiny leaves and flowers that caught the light with a soft shimmer.

Gods, Melandra had done an amazing job.

Jos was Mabin, like Nim, and his sister's dress came with soft open panels at the back for her wings. She sighed with relief, thankful she could avoid the captive discomfort of binding her wings.

She stripped off her leathers and had a quick wash in the basin before sliding on the delicate stockings and silk chemise she'd found in the market store.

There was a gentle tap at the door, and she called a quiet, "Who's there?"

"Mel, I mean, Melandra, milady. Jos asked me to come and help you."

Gods, having someone watch her get dressed sounded terrible, but she needed the help. She opened the door to let the young woman inside, thanking her for the beautiful work she'd done on the dress and trying not to feel like an idiot standing there in her underwear.

They both smiled at each other a little uncertainly until Mel showed Nim the silk ribbons she'd brought with her, offcuts from the overskirt, and soon they were chatting about how best to use them.

Eventually, they decided to weave them into Nim's long hair in strands of delicate plaits. Mel helped her to brush her hair into long shining waves before winding the ribbons into a series of tiny braids that would fall among the soft natural curls of Nim's hair, adding a hint of shining blue, while leaving most of her hair tumbling down her back.

Next, Mel helped her to step into the dress. It was slightly too small, but she managed to squeeze into it, especially once Mel took charge of her new corset and laced her far more tightly than she ever would have laced herself.

It hugged her figure in a way that she wasn't used to, the velvet wrapping sensuously around her hips, with soft blue silk falling down the back and drawing attention to the swell of her bottom, while the corset pushed her breasts up until they strained in soft mounds against the embroidered neckline.

She hardly ever wore dresses in her old life, let alone anything so opulent and seductive. Maybe she could keep this one and wear it one day when she wasn't so terrified for her brother.

She smoothed down the luxurious skirts and slid her feet into the velvet slippers, adding the sparkling diamante earrings to complete her outfit.

There was a small mirror hanging on the wall next to the basin, and Mel took it down and held it for her while she twisted and stood on her toes, trying to see how she looked. It was impossible to see much in the small, slightly cloudy mirror, and eventually she gave up.

"Do you think it'll be okay?" she asked the younger woman instead.

"I think your husband will swallow his tongue!"

Nim chuckled with her. She couldn't imagine Tris swallowing his tongue. She could easily imagine him scowling darkly and perhaps asking her if she was cold.

She pulled on her dark blue gloves and then slipped Val's ring onto her thumb, took a deep breath, and let it out slowly, relaxing her shoulders.

She was ready.

Chapter Sixteen

TRISTAN FELT like an idiot in the formal wool coat that Jos had found for him.

It was much longer than he was used to, lined with silk and closed with a row of heavy silver buttons. Thank the gods he was able to wear his usual black leather breeches and jerkin underneath. Hopefully, nobody would notice his heavy boots, but nothing was going to induce him into heeled dancing shoes.

He would need to play the part of a minor noble to accompany Nim, while everyone else would wear their dress uniforms but stay outside as backup. They wouldn't be able to come inside wearing their black cavalry uniforms, and they certainly couldn't pull out their old Blues without being instantly spotted by the new palace guards.

Reece had disappeared for nearly an hour but finally returned with the invitations that they needed, and then he and the rest of the Hawks had left to tend to their respective tasks.

Which left Tristan in the room where they'd eaten dinner. Alone. Waiting.

Waiting and thinking about how little they knew, how vague their plan was, and imagining all the hideous things that could go wrong. What the consequences would be for Nim if it did.

He hated going into conflict without a firm plan and at least two backup plans. But they simply didn't have enough information. Val was hanging on the wall in the main hall; that was all they knew. If it was true.

And their plan was even more vague. Get in. Stay out of sight. Free Val and Tor. Somehow escape without dying. Keep Nim safe.

Fuck. He didn't know what he'd done to earn her trust, but it was the most precious gift anyone had ever given him. He wanted to throw her over his shoulder and drag her away, not lead her straight toward the very men that had set him to hunt her. He was taking her to the single most dangerous place she could go, and all without any kind of real strategy.

He paced the length of the room, then stuck his hands in his pockets and paced back again, scowling at the clock ticking loudly on the mantelpiece. Feeling the unhappy rumble of his beast vibrating in his bones.

How long could one woman possibly take to get ready? The longer he stood around, the more time he had to think about everything that could go wrong.

He glanced at the clock again. They needed to arrive at the palace with the crush, just when the guards at the gates were at their most overwhelmed and least likely to look at his face. He was wearing his formal court clothes and had let his too-long hair fall loose over his collar, but it was hardly a disguise.

He turned and paced the room once more, and then, finally, heard a noise on the stairs and turned to face the door. There was a gentle knock, and he called out a stern, "Come."

Nothing could have prepared him.

He had seen her naked just a few hours before, and he still wasn't prepared. Gods. Nim's dress seemed to glow softly in the lamplight as it caressed her sensuous curves and lifted her breasts in a way that made his mind immediately fill with a multitude of carnal images.

She tilted her chin up, and the light caught on her sparkling eardrops, making him want to pull the lobe into his mouth and worry it with his teeth while his hands ran up her thighs, lifting that sinful skirt. He wanted to devour her. He wanted to take her hand and pull her upstairs and lock the door.

The very last thing he wanted was to take her to the palace looking like that.

He could feel the tension in his jaw as he clamped his teeth together and tried to get his thoughts together.

The corners of her mouth tilted up as she watched him. Every other woman he'd ever known would have sulked that he hadn't complimented their dress, but Nim seemed to know exactly what he was thinking despite his silence. And she was amused.

She tilted her chin further. "How is your tongue?"

"What?" He had no idea what she was talking about.

Her smile widened. "Did you swallow it? Mel assured me you would."

"Uh... I...." He had no response, so he scowled at her instead.

And Nim, being Nim, merely laughed and gave him a mocking curtsey.

Jos had left a soft hooded velvet cloak for Nim—dark gray and lined with silk—and he helped her into it before holding out his arm.

He was grateful when she took it and pressed herself neatly against his side. His need to protect her was almost overwhelming, and having her close settled him just a little.

He led her through the back door to the stables, where Mathos and Rafe had finished preparing the borrowed carriage. It was a sturdy, comfortable-looking carriage with an open top and soft leather seats, suited to a prosperous innkeeper looking to advance his family.

It wasn't as ornate as he would have liked, but the men had polished the metalwork until it shone and littered the seat with plush gold damask cushions.

They had harnessed Altair with Mathos's stallion, Heracles, and the two powerful bays stood waiting impatiently, necks arched and black manes plaited, while Mathos and Rafe, both dressed as coachmen, did their final checks.

Before he could talk himself out of it, he lifted Nim into the seat, climbed up beside her, and ordered the men to drive on. The horses clattered forward over the cobbles and through the narrow alley that led to the street.

"Did Reece manage to get us invitations?" Nim asked as she settled herself against the cushions.

Tris took them out of his pocket and passed her the fine white cards, the delicate watermarks at odds with the two vicious boars locked in battle of the royal crest.

She ran a slim finger over the flourishing script. "And how exactly did he get hold of these?"

Tristan paused, wondering how best to answer, finally settling on vague truth. "He got them from a friend."

She looked up, one eyebrow arched delicately. "A friend?"

He cleared his throat. "Yes. A young widow who has decided not to go to the palace tonight. You're taking her place."

Nim's nose wrinkled. "Does Reece have a lot of 'friends'?"

Tristan heard Mathos snort from the box seat and settled for a grunt rather than a response. Reece had more "friends" than anyone he'd ever met.

But Nim wasn't giving up that easily. She turned her clear eyes on him and asked in a soft voice, "And how many 'friends' do you have?"

Mathos snorted again, and Tristan had to curb the overwhelming desire to reach across and haul his second-in-command bodily off his seat and throw him from the coach.

Nim merely settled back in her seat and waited.

Gods, why couldn't they have had this discussion in private? He leaned down, put his lips against the delicate skin of her ear right where he would like to bite it, and replied in a low voice so that only she could hear, "Only one."

Both of her eyebrows went up in a silent question.

He stared back.

She continued to watch him, not giving an inch.

Fine. "Women started coming to the barracks when I was seventeen," he admitted, "but none of them, not one, was my friend. Only one woman has ever been that close to me; a beautiful, courageous woman. I've known her all my life, but only now realize exactly what she means to me."

Nim blinked several times, a suspicious sheen in her eyes, and then asked in a low whisper, "What does she mean to you?"

"I told her already. She's mine."

Her eyes sparkled. "Maybe you're hers?"

"Yes," he agreed, "that too."

Nim turned at his side, wrapped her small hand around his neck, and tugged him down to press her lips to his in a hard kiss. It was over far too soon, but he knew what she felt. There was no time. No time to say all the things that should be said. To do the many things he wanted to do with her.

So many years alone, and now just a few hours together might be all they ever had.

She laced her fingers through his as she turned and watched the view. He could feel her tension rising as they made their way ever closer to the palace, but her grip on his hand was firm and steady.

They turned the corner into an area that he used to know well. When he'd left the palace, it had been a prosperous road of merchants. Tree-lined promenades had led up toward a picturesque market square dominated by a gorgeous gold filigreed astronomical clock and allowing glimpses of the palace.

Now, it looked like a war zone. Buildings had been destroyed, shops were closed, broken bricks and old wood littered the streets.

When he'd been sent away, Tristan had thought it was a terrible punishment. Looking at the new fortifications and the devastation that had accompanied their installation, he saw that it had been a gift.

Other coaches and carriages, many opulent with gold and velvet, some brand-new and gleaming, others showing the wear of many years of use, were all converging in an impatient queue. They made their way forward increasingly slowly, Nim's hand clasping his tighter with every passing minute.

The coaches in front of them moved forward with a cracking of whips, and suddenly the view ahead was clear.

The road opened into the wide square. No longer picturesque, it was now as shattered and litter-strewn as the road leading there. The last time he'd been there, the square had flanked a long, wrought iron fence that gave glimpses of the palace's luxurious gardens. Now, the fence had been replaced with an ugly blight of a wall—a huge, untidy structure of stones and bricks, built too quickly for any kind of elegance—and its forbidding pair of heavy black gates.

Along the new wall, near the gates, was a row of parked coaches, coachmen and footmen laughing and talking in the absence of their wealthy masters.

To their left stood a huge wooden platform. And on it, lit by flickering lanterns, gallows.

Fuck.

Next to him, Nim went completely still, and he wrapped his arm around her, pulling her against his body and nestling her head into his chest. He dipped his head and lowered his voice so that no one else could hear. "Look at me."

She tilted her head up and looked at him. Her face was pale and drawn, and he cupped her cheek, using his hand to keep her eyes pointed solely at him.

She gave a small, tremulous nod, and whispered, "I can do this." But she kept her gaze firmly on his as they drove slowly past.

Before they reached the end of the interminable square, he felt her fumbling with something. Looking down, he saw that she had pulled Val's ring off her thumb and was offering it to him. "Look after this for me? Please."

He didn't try and speak against the tension in his throat, simply put out his hand and let her drop the heavy signet ring into his palm before tucking it safely into the inner pocket of his breeches. There was no way he could put it on his own finger.

Eventually they reached the new Court Gate and were approached by a trio of harassed-looking guards. They were wearing the green uniform of the infantry, thank the gods, not cavalry, as were the additional soldiers spread out along the walkway at the top of the wall.

He held out the invitations as Nim smiled weakly at the soldiers, who made a big production of looking down their noses at the borrowed carriage and checking the watermarks on their cards while spending significantly more time staring at Nim's chest.

The beast inside him rumbled, a hairsbreadth from defending what was his.

Nim held his hand even tighter and he kept himself under iron control until they were waved through with a smirk from the soldiers.

"Where are the Blues?" Nim asked in a whisper once they were past.

Tristan cast an eye over the heavily guarded walls. "I guess the king has them arrayed through the palace for the banquet." He shook his head. "This amount of force is... excessive. He'll have called in reinforcements."

Nim nodded slowly, no doubt considering, just as he was, what such a huge display of power might mean for them when the time came to try and leave.

They passed the gate and drove out onto a low cobbled bridge, only just wide enough for the rows of carriages and coaches going to and from the palace. The bridge was flanked by tall wrought iron lamps, their light sparkling on the water that lapped noisily against the bridge.

Water. Gods. The bridge had once spanned a tiny stream that ran delicately through the manicured gardens that surrounded the palace.

Ballanor's mother had loved the gardens. She had spent many hours cultivating them into a vast array of formal beds of vibrant blooms and informal meadows filled with an array of pretty shades, all interlaced with walkways and dainty arbors.

They had been immaculately maintained after her death, a memorial to the lost queen, and the old king had used them for entertainments, filling them with music and dancing, balloon flights, even a menagerie.

Now they were gone. Flooded. Sacrificed to the moat.

And for what? The war in the north should have been over. And even if hostilities had resumed, they were hundreds of miles away. Tristan couldn't imagine the strategic benefit of the massive amount of destruction and cost the changes to the palace had caused.

It felt like the behavior of a spoilt child kicking down a sandcastle. Ballanor's juvenile revenge on the mother who had dared to die and leave him, and the father who had made no secret of how little he thought of him.

Was that what it was all about? Could Ballanor have ordered the attack at Ravenstone himself in some childish revenge? To one-up the king, end the treaty, and get back his war? His chance to prove himself the better strategist all while adding immeasurably to his coffers with pillaged wealth. Was that what all these shows of power were all about? Ballanor's feelings of inadequacy?

The thought was staggering, and Tristan felt a cold

ripple as his beast flicked scales all the way up his arms in horror.

He had never believed that the king, his supreme commander, would lie to him. But maybe he'd been wrong. Maybe Nim was right and it was Val he should have trusted all along.

Gods.

The crowd shuffled forward again, breaking into his thoughts, and he pushed away his traitorous musings to focus on the danger immediately ahead.

The bridge ended at a long line of scaffolding and piled stones where the inner wall wasn't yet finished. The stones were topped with flickering lanterns and, in some places, massive torches, their flames dancing and smoking in the evening breeze.

A wide-open space marked where the gates would eventually be installed and was currently filled with clusters of soldiers. More soldiers were positioned over the stones and scaffolding. And, more worryingly, they all wore black uniforms. Cavalry.

Coaches were being stopped at the gates so that their occupants could disembark, and then turned around to head back over the bridge to wait in the square until the end of the banquet.

While the soldiers were distracted by the carriage in front of them, Tristan hopped down and then lifted Nim down beside him. He could feel how tightly she was holding herself, and he felt a flood of pride at her resilience. The way she never gave up. Her deep loyalty to her family.

Mathos gave him a nod and then he and Reece spun the coach around before the guards could get a good look at them and clattered away over the bridge.

They were alone.

Tristan reached down and pulled Nim's cloak together to button it under her chin, covering her as much as possible until they were inside.

The gap left by their coach was quickly filled by a massively ornate carriage covered in scrollwork and gold leaf, and he paced their walk slow enough that they were quickly caught up by a loud party of older men and one heavy dowager.

Nim understood immediately and dropped a deep curtsey to the older woman before complimenting her effusively on her glittering peacock-styled green, blue, pink, and gold shawl.

Tristan thought it was hideous, but the woman was soon engaged in a long discussion of feathers and her favorite colors and was still talking loudly when they reached the soldiers.

These guards were far more vigilant, looking for weapons, rechecking invitations, and asking questions. Tristan stepped up close behind Nim, leaving his collar turned up and his face angled away from the torches.

"So then the downstairs maids had to wash all the feathers again!"

He had missed the rest of the story, but Nim laughed and patted the older woman's hand encouragingly, and they took another step forward, bringing them right in front of a pair of lieutenants.

Men he recognized. He didn't know them well, but he knew their faces. And they would know his.

He dipped his chin, keeping his cheek against Nim's hair, hoping he looked like a stupidly besotted husband as she handed over the invitations.

The soldier glanced at them and passed them back,

casting a cynical eye over the party. And then stopping at Tristan. "Step back, please."

Tristan stepped to the side and held his hands out, willfully misunderstanding, and turned around slowly, showing that he had no weapons on him while keeping his face turned away.

"Face this way and step into the light."

Tristan took a breath and began to turn, but Nim, acting as if the soldier was talking to her, immediately stepped between them and turned into the light.

"Like this, sir?" she asked in the sweetest, most girlish voice he'd ever heard her use.

"No. I want to see—"

"I'm so sorry. Of course you need to check me for weapons too." Nim dropped her cloak onto her arms and rolled her shoulders back, and the soldier immediately dropped his gaze to her cleavage.

"I don't have anything dangerous on me, I promise, sir." Nim giggled and then shrugged, making the smooth tops of her breasts rise invitingly as every single soldier's gaze fastened on her.

Shit. Didn't she know that they might have sketches of her? Anyone could recognize her. She was in infinitely more danger than he was, and she had just drawn everyone's attention.

It made perfect sense that he should throttle every single one of the men looking at her. To keep her out of danger. Obviously.

His fingers twitched as he held himself back. But his beast let out a long, rattling growl.

They were going to be having a long conversation about who handled danger in the future. But first, he had to get her through the gate. Tristan had no problem with playing the disgruntled husband. He snatched the invitations back and grabbed her hand, pulling her away. "Come along now. We're late."

The soldiers laughed, and someone behind them called out, "You need a real man, sweet thing. Let me show you what you're missing!" Tristan didn't dare turn around, or he might kill every single one of them.

He was walking too fast, Nim almost running next to him, but he couldn't stay there for one more second.

They sped down a short, open path through a large arch and into a wide cobbled courtyard before he finally slowed.

He drew her to the side, into the shadows of an archway, and paused there for a moment while he redid the button on her coat.

She leaned heavily against him, and he wrapped his arm around her shoulders, holding her against his side while he tried to think of the best way to explain that she should never. Ever. Under any circumstances. Do something like that again.

But she spoke first. "Gods." Her voice was shaky. "I think I want to be sick."

Hell. He hadn't thought of how bad that was for her, his head too full of images of what would happen if the soldiers recognized exactly who those tantalizing breasts belonged to. All while his gut was roaring that they belonged only to him.

It had been too fucking close.

But they were in.

Chapter Seventeen

Nᴉᴍ ʟᴇᴀɴᴇᴅ her head against Tristan's chest just for a moment, wishing she could somehow absorb some of his confidence, and then slowly lifted her head to look around.

The courtyard was lit by a multitude of lamps, their bright light glittering in the spray from a massive three-tiered marble fountain that dominated the area. The fountain was topped by a trio of rearing winged horses, their forelegs raised as if they might leap from the sparkling water and into the air at any moment.

On either side of the courtyard were long covered walkways, accessed by rows of pointed gothic arches. Thronging through the walkways and all around the fountain was a mass of guests, steadily making their way over toward a pair of heavy wooden doors set with iron bands that stood open to the great hall. And between the guests, the ever-present blue uniforms of the palace guards.

Rising from the hall was a deep rhythmic beat of bass drums accompanied by a tremulous vielle in an eerie tune that lingered almost on the edge of discordant. A melancholy female voice sang a soulful lament, contrasting compellingly with the heavy beat, and Nim felt as if she was suddenly back under the pier, bewitched by the music of the pleasure pavilion above while the dark waters churned below her.

A wave of goose bumps spread over her skin as she remembered the feeling of being hurt and alone. Hunted.

She was still hunted, still in danger, still searching for Val. But this time, she was not alone. Tristan was with her, his warm strength anchoring her. And, more than that, she had changed. She had begun to take control of her life.

She could do this.

Carefully sticking to the shadowy walkways, they made their way toward the great hall.

As they walked, she watched the crowds, a new apprehension simmering in her gut. "Where are all the women?"

Tristan shook his head briefly, his body radiating concern. There were a few older women, like the one that Nim had befriended at the gate, but otherwise there were hardly any young women. Those few that were there were in small clusters, surrounded by husbands, fathers, and brothers.

"Keep your cloak closed."

She nodded quickly, in complete agreement.

There was a crush at the doorway, too many hot bodies, too much sickly-sweet scent poured onto sweaty skin. Nim had to take deep, slow breaths, supremely grateful that it was Tristan's hard, clean-smelling chest that she was pushed up against.

And then they were through, into the great hall. Massive crystal chandeliers cast golden light over the ostentatious display of wealth and power and the seething, surging crowds while the music beat steadily on.

Huge tables lined both sides of the hall, covered with an array of every food imaginable, from aspic made from calf's heads, and peacocks roasted and presented in their feathers, to mincemeat pies and marzipan cakes.

Ale and wine flowed freely, and serving men moved amongst the masses, handing out crystal glasses of champagne.

The walls were covered with plush velvet drapes interspersed with detailed tapestries, while the back of the room was reserved for an ornate dais holding two heavy gold thrones in front of an opulent backdrop of Sasanian silk brocade.

The slightly smaller throne on the left stood empty. On the right sat a tall Apollyon, not quite as heavily muscled as Tor, more refined somehow, but still strong and stocky, with chestnut colored hair and a thin nose. He sprawled lazily across the throne as if it were a wooden chair in his local tavern.

He was dressed in a long burgundy tunic embellished in shimmering gold and silver, its short sleeves displaying his bulky arms, tanned beneath their mass of serpentine black and red tattoos. Unlike Tor's, whose markings told a story of honor and duty, even from a distance Nim could see that these were harshly barbed and malicious-looking. A heavy golden chain of office circled his chest, glittering with rubies and onyx.

The king.

Tristan stayed resolutely turned to the back of the room, and Nim could take her time in studying Ballanor over his shoulder. There was a wide space cleared in front of the throne, and now and then someone brave enough, stupid enough, or desperate enough approached him obsequiously, despite his sardonic sneer and tapping foot.

They were all dismissed with an annoyed flick of jeweled fingers and quickly scurried away again.

The room was hot and stuffy, overcrowded, and pungent with the smells of food, perfume, and too-warm humanity. Nim found herself repeatedly jostled as people pushed past to reach the food-laden tables and then pushed back again with platters covered in delicacies.

But no Val. She ran her eyes over the tapestries and velvet drapes lining the walls, frantically searching, but all of them lay flat.

They'd taken such a massive risk. For nothing. She looked up at Tristan's locked jaw, the scales flashing at his throat, and whispered, "He's not here."

Tristan shook his head. He didn't need to say anything. It had been extremely dangerous getting in, and it would look suspicious if they suddenly left. Still, it wouldn't hurt to start sidling toward the doors. If they got into the grounds, at least they could go and look for Tor. And perhaps Val had been moved to the cells.

They both took a step toward the door, and then another.

Before they could go any further, there was a disturbance from the courtyard. The musicians faltered and then, at a gesture from the king, stopped playing. The crowds elbowed and shoved, trying to see what was happening.

Tristan wrapped a solid arm around her waist and drew her back toward the wall, ducking his head down beside hers so that he could watch unobtrusively, as she stood on her toes looking between the people in front of them.

A small unit of Blues stepped into the door and

immediately spread out, clearing a wide space as the banquet guests pushed even further back.

Between them stood a small woman, her red-blond hair falling loose down to her waist. She was dressed in a short, sleeveless muslin shift that showed the green bands of stylized Verturian knots tattooed around her biceps—but nothing else.

Tristan bent closer to her ear and whispered almost too low to hear, "Keely, the queen's maid."

The crowd in front of her parted slightly, and Nim could see that Keely was barefoot on the cold stone. And that she had a long chain shackled to one ankle, the end gripped firmly by the lead soldier.

She must have been terrified, but Keely's back was straight, her eyes narrowed in a glare of such loathing that Nim could feel its fury all the way from where she stood at the back of the hall.

Nim turned her head to watch the king. For the first time, he'd lost his bored slouch and was sitting forward, his lips curled up in an arrogant smirk.

He held out a hand, his rings sparkling as he gestured the guards closer.

The group walked forward, the chain rattling along the floor in the ominously silent hall, and stopped in the clear space in front of the throne.

The king stood abruptly and stepped down from the dais to the floor, heels clicking on the marble as Keely took a stumbling step backward in a futile attempt to escape.

The lead guard chuckled and shoved her forward, hard enough that she tripped on the chains at her feet and fell heavily to her knees in front of King Ballanor.

Ballanor smirked down at the woman at his feet. He leaned forward and put his face against hers, his voice low but clearly audible in the frozen hall. "I told you you'd get on your knees for me eventually."

Keely pushed herself backward, her bare feet scrabbling on the slippery floor as she tried to stand, but the guard grabbed hold of her hair and held her still.

Ballanor simply watched in amusement before lifting his hands and clapping loudly. The doors were flung open once again, and a new set of guards stepped in. The first immediately stepped to the side and called in a loud voice, "Her Majesty, Queen Alanna of Brythoria."

A second later a tall, slim woman stepped into the hall, head bowed and arms clasped in front of her. She had long, golden hair lying loose in a soft fall down her back, held back from her face by a gleaming diadem, its intricate Verturian knotwork reflected the intertwining green tattoos around the tops of her bare arms. Her luxurious dress, the color of the deep forest, was cinched in at her tiny waist with a gold belt of the same weave as her diadem and the tattoos around her biceps.

She lifted her head, and the crowds nearest her gasped softly. She simply lifted her chin further and made slow eye contact with her mesmerized audience.

As she turned her head, Nim saw what had caused the onlookers' shock. One side of the queen's face was marred by a livid purple and green bruise. Her lip was split and her eye puffy and swollen.

Queen Alanna acted as if nothing was amiss, simply took one graceful step forward, followed by another, flanked by her guards as the crowd separated before her.

The woman her brother had returned to protect kept her spine straight and her posture elegant as she slowly scanned the mass of people in front of her.

Alanna's gaze traveled over Nim, passed, and then flew

back to her, their eyes meeting in a flash of something that seemed like recognition before the queen quickly swung her head away and stared at the king, resolutely ignoring Nim and the mass of gaping guests.

Nim had heard that Queen Alanna was cold and uncaring, proud and difficult. But Val had told her that everything she'd ever heard about the queen was a lie.

She watched her now, a young woman, not much older than Nim, alone in a foreign country, bruised and hurting. Standing with grace and poise despite the evidence of abuse all over her face, while her husband sneered maliciously down at her. A husband Nim already distrusted on every level.

She didn't look proud and difficult to Nim; she looked like a woman who had wrapped her armor around herself so tightly that she could barely carry the weight. But who was pushing forward nonetheless. A woman who had known who Nim was. Could easily have given her away. But who quickly averted her gaze instead, protecting her.

The guards walked the queen up to Ballanor, forcing her to stand before him.

And then Nim saw Grendel stepping away from the refreshment table closest to the dais to stand beside the king. He had been hidden by the crowds before, but now she couldn't miss him. Her breath caught in a reflexive flood of fear and horror, and she flinched, every nerve standing on end.

Tristan's hand wrapped around hers and gripped it tightly, and she clung to him, using his strong grasp to anchor her. Forcing herself to stay still and silent as they watched the king play out his macabre little act.

"Thank you for joining us, wife," Ballanor drawled as Queen Alanna dropped a rigid curtsey. He flicked his fingers toward the kneeling maid. "I seem to have found a little butterfly flitting about the palace."

Alanna lifted her chin. "Let her go. She hasn't done anything wrong."

"Oh, I beg to differ." The king's tone deepened to an ugly growl. "I think she let herself out of your rooms specifically to defy my orders. To collude with a traitor."

He whirled back to Keely and leaned over her threateningly. "Didn't you, little butterfly?"

Keely glared up at him, refusing to answer.

Ballanor spoke through a snarl. "Someone tried to take water to my prisoner; someone thought they could help him. Directly against my orders. And why would you do that, little butterfly, if not because he is conspiring with your mistress?"

"No. That's not—" Alanna began desperately in her soft Verturian accent, but she was cut off by the king's harsh voice.

"Let's see, shall we?"

He gestured to Grendel, who gave a curt nod and then stepped up toward the thrones. Against the wall was a small pulley, and he wound the lever in a quick series of turns that briskly tugged the opulent brocade to one side.

From the front, it had appeared flat, but now she could see there was a hollow behind the curtain. And there, in that close, dark space, chained naked against the wall, was Val.

Nim remembered being a young girl out fishing with Tris and Val, following the gurgling, rushing snowmelt up into the hills one spring. She had grown bored of waiting for a fish to bite and decided to play along the bank instead. She was jumping from rock to rock when she landed awkwardly on a large boulder, slick with moss and spray, and slipped.

She had only been underwater for a few seconds before Val had hauled her back up, but she still remembered that feeling of sudden icy cold, burning as it sucked the breath from her lungs. How the world had gone instantly silent as her ears filled with frigid snowmelt, her body shocked to stillness.

That was how she felt.

Val was hanging, almost unconscious, arms chained to a rafter above his head, legs spread-eagled in vicious iron shackles that Nim knew would be slowly siphoning out his life. His beard was rough and dirty, while multiple angry red welts and weeping lacerations marred his pallid skin. Which she could see, even from halfway across the hall, was sheened with an unhealthy sweat.

Val was here. Her big brother. Gods. What had they done to him?

Across the hall, Alanna's face went deathly pale beneath her bruises. Next to her, Tristan went from stiff to completely rigid, his tension pouring off him in dark waves, echoing her own, as his beast rattled menacingly just on the edge of hearing.

Even Tristan's firm calloused fingers gripping hers no longer helped. There was a dull roaring in her ears along with an icy trickle of sweat slithering down her neck, and she took a small, unconscious step forward.

Tristan's hand clamped onto her elbow, and she froze. What could she possibly do? What would flinging herself at him achieve other than her pointless death? Nothing.

"Get him up," ordered Ballanor, and Grendel stepped forward and punched Val hard in his exposed abdomen, raking his fist into the long bloody gashes already there. Her brother let out a groan of agony as Grendel grabbed his hair and pulled his head up to face the king.

"Stop it!" The queen took a step forward, only to have her guards grab her arms and hold her still.

Ballanor turned his cold eyes toward her. "You would think, wife, that you would be less protective of the man that killed our father, the king." Alanna stayed silent as Ballanor continued, "Unless his betrayal was at your bidding? Hmm?"

Ballanor jumped up onto the dais and prowled across to Val. Grendel still held her brother's head up by his hair as the king clamped a brutal hand around his throat. "Come now, Lanval, we have a room full of witnesses here, all arranged just for you. Tell everyone the truth."

The room was tomblike as Ballanor leaned even closer to Val's swollen face. "Let's start with how you've been fucking my wife."

Gods. He sounded so certain. So adamant. She flicked her eyes to Tristan, to the appalled shock written over his face. And then back to the horror playing itself out on the dais.

Val's voice was scratchy and rough, but his reply was easy to hear in the dead silence of the stunned hall. "I never… never touched her."

Ballanor smirked. "Then what, pray tell, were you doing all alone with her?"

"I was her personal guard. I was bringing her back to the palace." Val's broken voice faded. "We were attacked…."

The king gripped Val's throat tighter for a second and then thrust him backward, hard, smashing his head into the wall.

Ballanor spun and leaped off the dais down to the floor as guests scrambled to clear a space.

And then he smiled, looking out across the breathless crowd.

"The queen orchestrated the massacre at Ravenstone, and you helped her," Ballanor said over his shoulder in a soft, smooth, infinitely terrifying voice, playing to his audience. "Only someone with military knowledge could have done it. Tomorrow you'll be hanged for treason, but today… today you're going to confess, in front of all these people, so that everyone will know the truth."

"Not… not true," Val protested brokenly, his head sagging against the wall, blood dripping down his abdomen where his wounds had opened.

Ballanor chuckled darkly, still watching the courtiers and nobles that filled the hall. "Come now, Lanval, tell us what she promised you so that we can punish the woman who brought you so low. Help me to give her the justice that she deserves."

He turned back and smirked at Val. "Tell us how you worked together to murder your king, and we'll make sure that your deaths are quick. Or so help me, your execution will take days."

Val turned his head away in silence.

Ballanor watched him, arms folded, tapping his foot.

And then he smiled again. "It doesn't matter anymore, Lanval. I met with my council this morning and tried the northern whore for treason. We found her guilty." He shook his head in a mockery of disappointment. "All these weeks of pain, and we didn't need your confession after all."

"No!" Alanna's voice shuddered as she turned wide eyes toward the king. "How can you try me in my absence? You have no right! There is no evidence—"

Ballanor shrugged, interrupting her. "It's done. The arrows were Verturian. And you survived. Only one person could have told them where the meeting was, and that was clearly you. Everyone agrees."

"That's not evidence!" Alanna's voice rose in desperation. "I demand—"

The king turned on her, cutting her off with a malicious laugh. "You don't make demands." He turned to the men flanking her. "Guards, take the queen—"

Val lifted his head, stopping the king with one rough word. "Wait." It was only slightly louder than a whisper.

Ballanor folded his arms, eyebrows raised. "What now?"

Val ignored the king and looked directly at the queen instead, his battered face grim but resolute. He had a strange look of acceptance, peace almost, as if he had finally reached an impossible decision.

Nim saw Alanna take a deep breath and roll her shoulders back, but before the queen could say anything, Val was speaking, looking out over the crowd.

"I'm sorry," he whispered in his grating, broken voice.

It sounded as if he was apologizing to the crowd, but Nim saw that his eyes rested, just for a moment, directly on the queen.

Val turned to Ballanor, the weeks of his torture etched heavily across his face. He closed his eyes for a moment before opening them to gaze out at the crowd. "I confess. I did it. I wanted to be king. You were supposed to be there, to die alongside Geraint. I thought, when you were gone, she would turn to me for comfort…." The sentence seemed to have exhausted him, but he swallowed and continued, his voice almost too faint to hear. "But you must believe me, there is no reason for me to lie when I tell you, Queen Alanna had nothing to do with it."

"Hmm." The king sighed loudly. "You sound so very sincere, I almost do want to believe you. But someone had to contact the Verturians. Someone that they would trust. We have enough evidence to convict her, no matter what you say."

Val was sagging heavily against his chains, and Nim wondered whether he was going to pass out, but his rasping voice was resolute. "Queen Alanna did nothing wrong. No matter what you do to me, I'll keep telling you the same thing. She. Is. Innocent."

"She is a traitor!" Ballanor said loudly, his voice rising with annoyance. "Why not just be done with this tiresome game and admit the truth—she'll hang now, whatever you say."

The words seemed to suck the last remaining fight out of Val. Beside her, Tristan's scales flashed around his throat and up the sides of his face.

Her eyes prickled with hot tears of despair and rage. There was nothing anyone could do for either of them. Not against a king that convicted his subjects in their absence, without a justice.

"No." Keely's melodic voice was grim with determination as she climbed to her feet, shaking her head. "No."

The whole court focused on her as she continued. "I did it."

She turned and looked at Alanna as she finished, "Val is *my* lover. We planned it together. The queen never had anything to do with it."

Whispers and shocked conversations broke out across the room as Keely stood, trembling but defiant.

This changed everything. Ballanor couldn't find Alanna guilty after two public confessions exonerating her. If he went ahead with her execution, he would massively undermine his own rule while guaranteeing swift and violent reprisals from Verturia. And by the mottled red climbing his neck, he knew it.

"No!" Alanna's voice was too high, hysterical almost. "Please, no." The queen tried desperately to step toward her maid, but her guards held her firm.

Keely stood resolute. She lifted her chin, her voicing firming. "It was me. I hated this kingdom, and I hated this court. I've detested every minute of the time I've spent here." By the look of loathing she gave Ballanor as she spoke, Nim could easily believe that this, at the very least, was true.

And so could everyone else.

Ballanor took three big strides across the floor and slapped Keely hard across the face, whipping her head back with brutal force. "Shut up!" he roared at the small woman, his face twisting in rage as she sank back to the floor, her hands pressed against her cheek.

"And you," he waved at Alanna, "I'll deal with you later." He turned to her guards. "Take her back to her room."

"No, I—"

He didn't let her finish, merely waved an irritated hand at the guards, who stepped up to the queen and jostled her roughly out the door and away.

The king clasped his hands behind his back and cast his eyes over the crowd, his lips tight with rage. Eyes glittering.

Slowly he seemed to relax. To accept that he could not execute the queen.

Eventually he waved toward Val. "You all stand as witnesses. Captain Lanval and his lover, Keely, have confessed to treason. Now you'll all see how we deal with traitors."

Ballanor gestured for Grendel to step up next to him

and announced with a soft menace, "Traitors die. And their loved ones are purged from the earth. Lovers. Fathers… even sisters. Let this be a lesson to you all."

Nim felt her heart racing even harder as terror flooded through her. He couldn't possibly have recognized her hidden away in the crowds. Could he?

Ballanor nodded at Grendel, who smirked back and then waved toward the door leading to the courtyard.

A Blue Guard, resplendent in a brand-new palace uniform of dark blue tunic with its shining silver boars locked in embroidered battle, stepped through the door. His boots clicked on the marble as he made his way down the hall.

She didn't recognize him at first, it was so unexpected. But one second later, her horrified brain caught up to what she was seeing. Who she was seeing.

Tor.

Nim's heart stuttered and then sank, her gut clenching around acid as her mind galloped wildly through all the possible reasons he might be there, dressed in the Blue.

She considered running. But where? All the doors were blocked by soldiers. There was nowhere to hide. If she moved, she would be seen. Gods. Could she fly? A glance up at the roof promised fiery death in the chandeliers.

And then it was too late. He had stopped in front of her, staring right at her, his heavy hand falling to grip her shoulder.

He turned his head and smiled coldly back at Ballanor and Grendel. "This is Lanval's sister. Nim."

His face was blank, jaw clenched, dark eyes merciless.

Nothing remaining of the friendship that she had thought they were growing. Just cold-blooded betrayal. And then he made it infinitely worse. He gave Tristan a rough clap on his back and smiled ruthlessly. "You did it, brother."

"What? I don't...." Nim's whole stomach was in her throat. She couldn't get the words out. Couldn't understand.

Suddenly there were guards roughly pulling her away, hands digging painfully into her skin. A flurry of excited whispers rippled all around her as they marched her into the center of the room beside Keely.

Everything was hazy. Except one thing. Grendel walking over to Tristan and handing him a brand-new Royal Palace Guard blue tunic.

"Thank you, Captain." Grendel gave Tristan a small nod. "I'll be honest, I didn't think you'd get her here, but I keep my promises. Your squad is back in the Blues as agreed. Space is being made for them in the barracks as we speak."

What? The agreement for her capture had been to reinstate the Hawks? She was going to be sick.

Nim reached out a hand toward Tristan. She needed him. Needed him to choose her over the Blue tunic he was being offered.

Every visible inch of his skin was gleaming with green and pewter, scales covering his hands, the whole of his face, even to his cheekbones and across his forehead.

She couldn't get her throat clear, but she tried to call him anyway, his name just a dry whisper in her parched mouth. "Tristan!"

His hand gripped the tunic like a lifeline, but he didn't move.

The soldiers pulling her away grabbed her arms, and she fought against them, threw her weight wildly as she tried to escape. But their rigid grip didn't break.

"Please! Tristan!" She hated that everyone could hear her despair. But he still didn't reply.

Tristan turned away and focused on Grendel. "What will you do with her?"

"Ah." Grendel gave a slow, poisonous smile. "We wanted her as incentive for Lanval, to help him… remember. But when you had seemed to have failed, the king went ahead and tried the queen anyway. And now Lanval's confessed…."

Grendel sounded almost disappointed, but then he ran his eyes slowly over her, lingering on the exposed flesh where her cloak had been pulled open by the rough handling of the Blues. "Oh well, I'm sure we'll think of something to keep her occupied. Don't worry, she'll still hang with her brother tomorrow."

Chapter Eighteen

NOTHING HE HAD EVER SEEN or done, and there had been many brutal moments on battlefields and off them, had prepared Tristan for what it felt like to stand still and watch two thugs drag Nim away while she called for him. While she reached back for him. And he did nothing.

It slowly tore his soul in two. One part went with her, and the tattered remains stayed behind.

She would never forgive him. Not this time. Gods, he would never forgive himself.

Val was throwing himself against his chains, his face a rigid mask of anguish as he screamed at Grendel in his broken voice. It was a sound that burned into Tristan's brain forever.

He had failed his best friend in every possible way. Failed Nim, in every possible way.

He could feel the blue tunic in his hand, its smooth fabric burning his skin, and he wished he could throw it far away. But he was committed now.

He turned his gaze to Tor, hoping to see something,

anything, in his face. But it was completely blank. Was that what Nim saw? No emotion in either of them whatsoever? Fuck. Another agonizing shaft ripped through him. For a few beautiful hours, she had been his.

That was over now, but he would keep that memory forever. It would have to be enough.

A shudder ran down his back as his beast went insane within him, filled with the horror of standing still while every single muscle in his body screamed for action.

Tor's heavy hand came down on his shoulder, almost as if he was giving him the support he needed. Almost as if he understood. As if he hadn't just caused him to betray the most important person in his world.

Hardly moving his lips, Tor muttered the same two words that had started this disaster. "Trust me."

The soldiers hauled Nim to the middle of the room where they threw her into the cleared circle. Without even hesitating, she immediately placed herself between Keely and the king.

Gods. Why did she have to always be so fucking brave?

Her chin was up as she stared past all the men ogling her straight at her brother. Her voice was clear and loud, although he knew her well enough to hear the tremor she was trying to hide. "I love you, Val."

She pulled Keely to her feet and wrapped an arm around her. "I love you, and I will look after Keely. I promise. Please, don't hurt yourself, we'll be with you soon."

Val stopped throwing his body against his chains and hung, limp and desolate, his ravaged body shining with an unhealthy sweat, blood dripping down his arms where the iron cuffs had cut through the skin and seeping from the wounds in his abdomen.

Ballanor laughed, and it sounded deranged in the

appalled tension of the room. Every single person there was aware that one day it could be them on that wall.

The king laughed again and nodded toward Grendel. "Take them to my room and lock them in. But don't start without me. We still have a party to attend." He looked around at the frozen courtiers with a mocking smirk. "This is a party, isn't it?"

Grendel gave a brisk nod and then took hold of Nim's arm and Keely's chain, gestured to the same soldiers that had manhandled her earlier, and dragged them out a back door.

Tristan had already taken a step when Tor's voice pulled him back. "Don't do it. Not unless you want us all to die."

He stopped. And tried to focus through the pain pounding through his head as he overruled the most primal parts of himself and stood still.

The king waved, and the music started again, but it sounded discordant, the players missing notes in their shock. Ballanor flung himself back onto his throne, Val hanging behind him like a macabre canvas, and slowly, tentatively, a hushed whisper began around the room.

Finally, Val's head dropped to his chest, and Tristan wondered if he was unconscious. Gods, he hoped so. What was happening to Nim? He didn't think he could bear to imagine.

"One more minute," Tor's rough voice rumbled quietly.

Tristan stared at Val and counted the seconds. Nim was right; he was responsible for this. And, even though he'd lost her, he was still going to fix it. If it was the last fucking thing he ever did.

Finally, the minute was done. Tor gave a tiny nod, and they started to move slowly out of the room, doing their best to look relaxed and casual. Boring.

The king was deep in discussion with one of his ministers, and the crowd was starting to talk among themselves more freely. Servers moved around the room handing copious quantities of champagne to the suddenly parched guests. The music slowly returned to its previous heady beat, even if the laughter of the crowd now sounded suspiciously forced.

They cleared the doors and into the quiet courtyard, deserted except for patrolling Blues. The fresh air blowing cold on Tristan's skin made him realize, for the first time, that he was fully battle scaled. From his hip bones to his ankles, up his waist and chest, his back, along his arms to his fingers, over his face and around his eyes, he was covered. Ready for mortal battle. But with no one to fight.

Horror, rage, and grief coursed through his body as he strode past the fountain and through the arch.

As soon as they were on the narrow path, out of sight, Tor turned on him. "Put it on."

"No." Nim thought he'd betrayed her for that tunic. There was no way in any kind of hell that he was wearing it.

"Put it the fuck on."

He had trusted Tor this far. He ground out a rough, "Fuck you," but he reached for his stupid silver buttons anyway. Which was when he noticed that he had claws. Fuck. That had never happened before. The beast inside him was through rage and into incandescent, unthinking violence.

Anything to get back to the woman he had claimed. And it was taking everything he had to keep it in check.

He couldn't get the buttons open, so he settled for tearing them off so that he could shrug out of the coat and change into the loathsome blue tunic.

And then they were moving again. Down the path, past the scaffolding and unfinished inner wall.

The carriage was waiting for him, Mathos and Reece in the driver box, but both now wearing their blues. Both rigid with tension, burgundy scales flickering along Mathos's jaw as he and Tor hurled themselves up and onto the seat.

The infantry soldiers guarding the gate gave them a respectful nod. Gave their tunics a respectful nod, at any rate. And then they were on their way, over the bridge and back into the square, past the ominous shadow of the gallows and into a small side street.

And every second he got farther away, his mind played a reel of horrific images of what was happening to Nim at the palace.

As soon as they were out of sight, he turned to Mathos. "Stop. Right now."

Something in his face must have warned his second-in-command, because Mathos didn't hesitate; he simply pulled the carriage up to a wall and stopped.

"Out." He pointed at Tor.

And then they were both out, and he couldn't hold himself back for one more moment. He hauled his friend up and threw him against the wall. Flung himself forward and gripped Tor around his throat, pressed backward into the rough bricks, ready to kill him. Only vaguely aware of the blood running down Tor's neck where his claws had pierced the skin.

"What the fuck have you done?" He almost couldn't recognize the agonized rasp as his own.

Tor didn't answer, but Mathos was there, scales gleaming and flashing, pulling him away. "Hear him out."

He shook his head, unwilling, unable to let go of Tor's throat. But he loosened his grip slightly. "Speak."

Tor could have been an asshole. Fuck knew he had it in him. But something in his face softened, and without prevaricating, he spoke. "I'm trying to save her."

"By getting her locked in a room with Grendel? Are you insane?"

"No. Gods, man, no. I don't want her in a room with Grendel any more than you do."

Tristan growled and retightened his grip on Tor's neck, but the other man simply shook his head ruefully. "Fuck. You know what I mean."

"Hear him out," Mathos repeated, and Tristan knew it must be bloody serious when he didn't even bother to crack a joke.

"They knew who I was," Tor said, face grim.

"Who knew?"

"As soon as I got to the Constable's Tower, the guards recognized me. Within minutes, I had that fucking sadist, Grendel, there. Then the soldiers from the market were called back, and of course they mentioned Nim. And you. Grendel knew it all. What was I supposed to do?"

Tristan grunted. It was a disaster.

"But then I realized. You were never going to get me and Val out of there. Not ever. Not even if they didn't recognize you."

"We would—"

Tor cut him off. "This way, we get our uniforms back—"

Tristan started to growl, and Mathos grabbed his fist before he could swing. "What the fuck did I say?"

He took a step back and tried to stay calm. He could listen. He could force himself to do that much.

Tor shook himself off and stepped away from the wall.

"Not like that. I mean we can get back in. That's what our uniforms get us. The run of the whole damn palace."

Tristan froze as his mind swept over the implications of Tor's statement. It was true.

As soon as he'd seen Val hanging on that wall, he'd known that there was no way that they were going to get him out of there.

And that understanding had been followed swiftly by the terrible insight that Ballanor would never have hung a guilty man on his wall. The king would have marched Val in front of the Nephilim Justices, proven that he was a traitor before their Truth Seekers, and had him executed on the spot—the queen following him rapidly afterward.

Standing in the hall, watching Ballanor torture his friend, he had had to face the distinctly uncomfortable truth that he hadn't really expected to find Val at the palace—the rumor that his friend was chained to the king's wall had seemed impossible—and even as he had slowly realized how corrupt and dishonorable the Blues had become, a part of him had still rejected the idea that his king had looked him in the eye and lied.

He had still been hoping that he could take Nim into the palace and prove that Val had been correctly tried and found guilty, and then sneak her back out again.

Gods, he was an idiot.

There had never been a chance to get Val out of the great hall with Nim. But now, with the whole team inside, it just might be possible.

He looked at Tor and across to Mathos. Back to Tor. Fuck, he owed him. He met his friend's eyes. "Thank you."

Tor gave him a brisk nod. "We understand."

Tristan eyed them skeptically. The entire squad was

relentlessly committed to being single. How could they possibly understand the hell that he was in?

And just like that, his mind was back to playing a horrific reel of Grendel, Ballanor, and Nim.

And then Mathos was there, hard hand heavy on his shoulder. "Pull it together, Captain. Your woman needs you."

He grunted and tried to ignore the white-hot agony that stabbed his heart. She would never be his again.

But that didn't change that Mathos was right; she needed him.

He pulled himself together. "What's the plan?"

"It's just arriving." Mathos gave a bloodthirsty grin and turned toward a loud clattering of hooves. The rest of the squad had arrived, already wearing their Blues.

"Tor sent out a runner while you were making your way into the hall," Mathos supplied as the others climbed down and tied their warhorses up on the posts along the side of the square.

"Jeremiel and Garet, you're with the horses," Mathos commanded. "Rafe, take Reece, find us a safe house, somewhere downriver. That leaves four of us to go back in. Get your asses moving."

"Just a moment." Tristan's voice came out rougher than he intended, but everyone stopped in their tracks and turned toward him expectantly. "There's no going back after this. If we go into the palace in our uniforms and take Nim out of the king's bedroom, that's it. After this, we're outcasts. If we even survive." He met each man's eyes. "Be sure."

The men looked at each other silently, and back to him. Horses jostled each other, and a night watchman called in the far distance, but otherwise no one moved.

Of course. He couldn't expect them to do this. The risks were immense, and the chance of success negligible. It was only sensible that they should take this chance to get as far away from him as they could.

Just as he opened his mouth to tell them that it was alright, that he understood, Mathos spoke. "Hey, didn't we have to sit through this speech once already? Gods, you and Nim are exactly the same." A few people snorted as he continued, "Anyway, I've never liked this uniform. It pinches."

"True," Jos agreed with a sage nod. "And I'm sick to death of rations. Could do with some civilian food."

"Yes," Reece joined in. "I bet women would go mad for a mercenary. With the added bonus that they couldn't possibly expect one to stick around."

Everyone laughed.

And then grew somber again as Jeremiel added, "We don't leave a brother behind. Never again. And that includes sisters."

Fuck. These men.

Tristan cleared his throat. And then cleared it again.

Finally, he found the words. "Hawks—move out."

Chapter Nineteen

ALANNA LISTENED to the lock on her bedroom door sliding closed and allowed her shoulders to curl forward as she wrapped her arms around herself and shuddered. A hot tear tracked its way slowly down her face, stinging as it reached the broken skin of her lip.

She crossed the floor, her body aching as if she was a hundred years old, passing through the arch that led to her small bathing room to look at herself in the mirror. Her face looked hideous. She couldn't resist prodding the puffy, swollen flesh, wincing at the fiery burn.

It wasn't the first bruise he'd given her, not by any means. But it was the first one she was proud of. All the others had filled her with deep wracking shame. But this broken face, this she'd earned defending Val.

She poured a little cold water onto a cloth and wiped her face, soothing the swelling, then made her way to her closet and rifled through it.

She dropped her luxurious green dress on the floor carelessly, kicking it out the way, and left it there. Instead she pulled on a pair of old leather breeches and tied them tightly at the waist. She slipped into a cotton shirt and covered it with a soft leather vest, then took down a heavy black woolen dress, a mourning dress, and stepped into that as well. It had a row of tiny buttons—up the front, thank the Bard, or she couldn't have managed them on her own—and she tugged and wrestled them closed.

Usually Keely would have helped her. Usually her hands wouldn't be shaking.

No. That was a lie. Since she'd come to live here, her hands had been shaking most of the time.

She could still remember, as clear as looking in the mirror, the first day she'd arrived at the palace. Married in a hurried ceremony, no ball, no breakfast. Two witnesses, Keely and King Geraint, and it was done.

Ballanor had refused any kind of celebration. His father had forced him into the wedding, given him the choice between saying "I do" and leaving court to return to the country. He'd sucked it up and married her, but he was damn certain that he wasn't going to look like he was enjoying it.

Of course, then he'd told everyone at court that it was her fault. That she refused to honor their customs. That she had been the one who denied them their dancing and food and fireworks. And King Geraint had shrugged and done nothing.

The bleak little ceremony was barely over when her new husband had grabbed her arm and hustled her down through the freezing courtyard to the barracks, still wearing her wedding dress, where he'd shoved her in front of three of the burliest soldiers in the mess room.

"Now, wife," Ballanor had said with a smirk, "choose your personal guard." And then he had mock whispered, loud enough for everyone to hear, "Touch him and he'll die. If he sees you touch anyone else, they'll die. Consider him your keeper from today. Choose now."

Her heart had pulsed so heavily, she thought she might have an aneurysm right there in the barracks. She had realized that her fingers were trembling against her throat and slowly lowered her hand. How to possibly choose?

Two of the soldiers looked just like Ballanor. Smug. Supercilious. Arrogant. Brutal.

The third one just looked brutal.

She was tall, but he still towered over her, with arms almost the size of her thighs. His leathery wings were pulled back respectfully, but she was sure they'd be wide and intimidating if he chose to spread them. His black hair was slightly too long, brushing the top of his collar while his deep blue eyes sprinkled with silver flecks watched her closely. But something about him, something in the quiet way he stood, his hands clasped behind his back, reassured her.

She raised a shaking hand and pointed at him. "That one."

"Captain Lanval, you're now personal guard to the princess. See that she does as she's told."

Ballanor turned her around and marched her away, Lanval immediately falling into step behind them.

That split-second choice had cost him everything.

Everything that came after started in that one desperate instant. She wished she could go back in time and change it. She wished she could tell him how desperately sorry she was.

But instead, he had apologized to *her*. Bard.

The tears were falling heavily now, but she didn't bother

to wipe them away. And she didn't make a sound. She knew better.

She added a heavy shawl to her dress. She was much too hot. But she didn't care. She preferred to wear as many clothes as possible. Especially for sleeping.

She gave her room a quick, paranoid glance. She was alone. She pulled open the drawer she used for women's things and shoved her fingers to the back. There. A wrinkled paper packet filled with brown powder. She pulled it out and shook it.

Opium. And who knew what else. Keely had smuggled it in for her, to help when the pain was bad, but she had been too terrified to ever try to use it. She'd seen opium addicts in the market back home, and whatever moment of reprieve it might have offered hadn't seemed worth it.

But now? At the end? No Keely. No Val. And absolutely nothing she could do to save either of them. Now, it was different.

She sank down onto the side of the bed and held her head in her hands, her hair falling loose around her face. Bard. They had sacrificed themselves to save her. And all she could think of was how she could possibly survive without them.

She would try to escape in the morning. And if that didn't work... *when* that didn't work, she would try to get a message out. Somehow. She would keep trying—for as long as she could—but if it got too bad, she would take the powder. All of it. And chase it with the bottle of wine she had hidden behind the wardrobe.

At least that way she would be in control. She would choose how she died. And when. It wasn't what they wanted for her, but the hell she was living in wasn't what they'd wanted for her either.

She plucked along the seam of her mourning dress until she found the small blade she'd sewn into the hem. It had broken off Ballanor's razor one morning, and she had slipped it into her embroidery basket before anyone noticed. A shiver of relief fluttered down her arms. It was still there.

First the powder. Then the wine. Then the blade.

But not until she'd done everything she could to avenge their deaths.

She turned and lay quietly on the bed, curled onto her side facing the room—there was no way she could lie on her back—wondering how long it would take for the party to finish. And how drunk Ballanor would be when it did.

A door opened and then slammed closed in Ballanor's adjoining room. There was a connecting door, which only locked on his side, and through it she heard a muffled male voice giving orders.

Unusually, there were no answering giggles.

She always tried to warn the women away, but they just laughed at her. The cold, jealous queen. Not especially pretty. Frigid. Barren. Prone to tantrums and childish rages. They could so easily see why he didn't want her.

And then she was the one who had to listen to their weeping through the door.

Well, she still had to try. She tiptoed up to the door and put her ear to it just as the outer door slammed shut.

She decided to count to two hundred to be certain that the guards had definitely left, when there was a quiet tapping at the door.

She sprang back, heart thumping, and froze. That never happened.

There was another low knock. She didn't know what to do. Was it a trick? A trap? Then she heard a rough scrape of the bolt.

She looked around the room frantically. She couldn't get out, and there was nowhere to hide.

The bolt slid the rest of the way, and she knew that it would be opened at any second.

She couldn't just stand there waiting for whoever it was to burst into the room. She crept back to the door, wishing she was stronger, took a deep breath, and pulled the door open herself, ready to fight.

And immediately stifled a scream as Keely and Nim fell against her and all three of them collapsed to the floor in a rough tangle.

"Bollocks," said a quiet voice she didn't know. Nim, obviously.

"Yes. Bollocks," Keely agreed. Alanna agreed too, but couldn't find the words as Nim jumped up and set about pulling her and Keely back up.

Nim and Keely were both stripped down to their shifts, shoeless and wild-eyed. The chain that had been wrapped around Keely's ankle had been moved to her wrist and shackled to Nim's wrist too, joining them.

Keely looked as if she could commit a murder. Nim had the pale, shocked look of a woman whose life had just disintegrated around her.

But what she couldn't get her head around was what they were doing in Ballanor's room. "What's happening?" she asked softly, knowing that it was nothing good.

"Grendel brought us...," Nim started, and then, when she saw the look on Alanna's face and her instinctive step back, quickly added, "He's gone. The king told him he had to wait for after the banquet. He's gone back for now."

"I hate him," Keely added, her tone slightly stunned as she wiped her hands down her shift, trying to remove the dirt from the floor of the Great Hall.

Alanna hated him more than she'd ever imagined possible. "Why didn't they take you to the cells?" she asked carefully.

Nim shook her head, her face pale and drawn. "I think there's more to this punishment still to come."

Alanna felt the nausea rising, burning inside her throat. Nim was right. She ran the back of her hand over her mouth and tried to breathe through the need to throw up.

"I'm so sorry," she whispered. Knowing it was not, could never, ever be enough. How much had she cost these women? She leaned her hand against the wall and let her head drop to her arm in exhaustion.

But Nim didn't allow her to sink into her misery. Val's sister used her free hand to give her a shake, and Alanna gasped. No one except Keely ever touched her. But Nim didn't seem to care. She simply waited until Alanna made eye contact and said firmly, "None of that. This is on Grendel. I hate him too, by the way, and that asshole you're married to."

Alanna was so shocked that she let out a horrified giggling snort and then immediately shamed herself by bursting into tears.

She made a point of hiding behind her frozen walls and never showing any kind of weakness. And now here she was crying in front of the only two women whose opinion actually mattered to her. The constant relentless terror of the last weeks coming to a vicious crescendo in the great hall, Val and Keely's imminent deaths, Nim's too… it was suddenly too much for her, and she couldn't help her breathless sobs.

A pair of warm arms immediately circled her and held her close, which simply made her cry even harder. "Shush now," Nim whispered. And then Keely was there too, her arms around them both, the hideous chain clanking and rattling as they moved.

Eventually her tears slowed, and Alanna lifted her skirt and wiped her face.

"What the hell are you wearing?" Nim whispered, taking a good look at Alanna's breeches and mourning dress combination.

Alanna snorted again and then looked helplessly at Keely. She wasn't used to someone speaking to her. She wasn't used to people acknowledging her at all.

Keely's face was grim as she tried to say something to help but found nothing. In the end, Alanna gave a small shake of her head and looked away as she whispered, "It makes me feel safer."

Her gut tightened, waiting for pity. Or condemnation. But Nim merely nodded in understanding, wiped her eyes with the back of her hand, then nodded again. "Right. All three of us need to get out of here. And, on our way, we can pick up Val."

Alanna was in awe. She looked from Keely to Nim, and the words just slipped out. "You're everything I imagined."

"What?" Nim asked, confusion clear in her voice.

"Val. He spoke of you often," Alanna admitted.

"Did he?" Nim raised a quizzical eyebrow. "I wish I could say that he had spoken of either of you."

Alanna shook her head. She wished that too. "He couldn't. Not because he didn't trust you," she added quickly, seeing the hurt on Nim's face, "but because he loves you so much. He wanted to protect you from Ballanor and Grendel."

"Yes. Well. That was a great success," Nim said softly.

Alanna could feel tears building once more and pressed

into her eyes with the heels of her palms. What could she say? Nim was right.

Nim looked thoughtful, as if she were carefully considering her words before she spoke. "Okay. I'm trying to understand. I—" Nim's voice broke, and this time it was Alanna that reached out. It felt so strange to willingly touch another person, but this was Val's sister. She owed it to her. And more than that, she wanted to explain. "Val never betrayed the king," she admitted in a low voice.

"Of course not." Nim's reply was so instantaneous that it took her breath away. This was what loyalty looked like. What family should be like.

"And we're not lovers," Alanna added, wanting Nim to know the truth. And it was the truth, whatever she may have wished for in the most secret places in her heart.

Nim nodded slowly, looking curious but not surprised, her eyes flicking to Keely.

"Val didn't conspire with Keely either," Alanna said softly. And then she forced her spine straight and reached for the ice she was going to need when Nim's kindness turned to disgust. "Everything he's done, the reason he's been tortured, is because he knows the truth." She lowered her eyes. "And because he tried to save me."

"What truth?" Nim's voice held no condemnation, not yet.

Keely answered for her. "The only person who could have set up the massacre at Ravenstone was Ballanor. He chose that location. And he took the letter that Alanna wrote to her mother. He also complained of illness on the morning of Ravenstone and asked his father to go without him. Oh, he told everyone that it was Alanna's fault he wasn't going, but he did that so often that we didn't see how dangerous it was until later."

Keely gave them both a somber look before continuing. "Val knows all of this because he was Alanna's personal guard. His proximity to her means he is the only person who genuinely knows everything that happened. If he testifies before the Nephilim Justices, then everyone will know that the king murdered his father and blamed Alanna. Ballanor wants him dead before he can do that."

"But then why not just kill him? Why wait all this time? Why torture him?" Nim asked slowly in a low, pained voice.

"Too many questions would be asked if Ballanor simply executed the queen. Verturia would be compelled to declare war immediately and avenge a wrongful execution, and, since the Brythorian armies were all decommissioned by Geraint, Ballanor would lose. Ballanor needs her dead too, she's as much a risk if she goes before the justices as Val. More, even. But if Val confessed and blamed the queen, it would be enough to execute them both," Keely explained.

And there was more. Alanna didn't want to tell her, but she knew she must. "We heard Ballanor commanding Grendel to fetch Val's family. We think that, when Val refused to confess, Grendel went after you... to force him to say what they wanted."

"Well, they've got me now," Nim said quietly.

Keely sighed. "Now you're just the icing on the cake. Captain Lanval won't change his confession, but they can still hurt him by hurting you. Hell, they'd enjoy hurting you even if Val was already gone."

Alanna kept her eyes on the floor, waiting. Her mind supplied all the condemnation to come. What would Nim think of her, knowing that her brother was dying because of her? That she had been attacked, forced from her home, would soon be brutalized by two vicious sadists, and in the morning, she would be hanged. All because of Alanna.

But nothing happened. Silence filled the room.

Alanna glanced up, confused, and immediately wished she hadn't. Nim was looking up at the ceiling, her face set with pain. A silent tear wound its way down her cheek. The intensity of Nim's grief, resonating with her own, was almost too much for Alanna to bear.

"I'm sorry," she whispered again.

"No." Nim shook her head roughly. "None of this is your fault. Val would never stand by and let a woman be hurt. Especially not his queen, the person he'd sworn an oath to protect. His honor is everything to him."

She turned to look at Keely. "And you also confessed to save Alanna?"

Keely gave a curt nod, breaking Alanna's heart. "Oh, Bard, I wish you hadn't. Keely, my friend, I don't know what to do!"

Keely took hold of her hands, the chain tugging Nim closer too, and held them tightly. "Listen to me. They were going to kill me anyway. At least this way, one of us has a chance."

Alanna shook her head helplessly. She wasn't worth this. And she didn't have a chance. Not really. Not even now that her conviction was overturned.

Keely gave her a gentle shake. "Don't do that."

Alanna took a breath and tried to think of something, anything, to say.

Nim was visibly pulling herself together, and Alanna did her best to do the same. She didn't deserve any of Nim's kindness or Keely's sacrifice, but she wasn't going to degrade either of them by complaining.

She met their eyes, hoping they could see how much their compassion meant to her. "Thank you."

Nim gave her a tremulous smile. "Okay. Talk me

through what you've tried so far."

Alanna shook herself. Every single person, other than Keely, would have simply assumed she had walked away and left him to die. But not the woman suffering the most.

She felt utterly humbled.

She also had no desire whatsoever to admit to such a strong woman what had really happened. How useless she'd been.

Before she could think of a good reply, Keely was speaking. "The first time we tried to free him, we were seen sneaking out of Alanna's rooms by one of the Blues. The king and Grendel took turns beating the queen with a belt until she passed out. That's how she got that bruise. Her back is still bleeding."

Nim looked horrified, but Alanna shook it off. What were a few bruises compared to what Val had gone through?

Striving to look calm, she picked up the story. "The second time, I distracted the guard and Keely tried to take Val some water. That was when they captured her and accused her of being Val's accomplice. After that, Ballanor told me that the next time I tried anything he would walk into the market square and pick ten people at random to hang with Val. I… ah…." She was ashamed to admit the next part, but she lifted her chin and told the truth anyway. "Honestly, I probably would have risked it, but they've doubled the guard and kept me locked in my room by myself ever since. I've tried so hard, but I can't think of a single way out of this."

Nim's face was filled with horrified anguish, and Alanna wished desperately there was some kind of comfort she could offer.

But she had none. There was no way out.

Val, Keely, and Nim would die in the morning.

Chapter Twenty

NIM WATCHED Alanna with a mixture of powerful emotions warring inside her. She was still reeling from seeing Val. And then what had happened with Tristan. Never mind being frog-marched into the king's chamber and stripped.

She knew she was probably in shock. The tiny tremors wracking her body supported that diagnosis. And, for the first time after so many days crying over her losses, her eyes were dry. Was it a bad sign? Maybe. Or maybe she was finally discovering exactly how strong she really was.

Alanna waited. Waited for Nim to hold her responsible for everything that had happened. To blame her. Hate her.

But Nim honestly couldn't do it. Alanna winced every time she moved. She had the look about her of someone pushed so far past what they could endure that every breath was a battle. And yet she was still battling. For now, anyway. Nim had seen the look of hopelessness on her face when she considered the executions planned for the next day.

Nim found herself respecting her. And more than that, liking her quiet strength. Her self-deprecating humility. Her obvious loyalty to Val. And the close bond she had with Keely. Whatever else Alanna may be, she was most definitely not an ice queen with a tendency for tantrums.

It didn't surprise her at all that Val had sacrificed himself for the woman he had sworn an oath to protect, but she understood it better seeing how much he would have admired her too.

Keely was a surprise though. She was clearly very loyal to Queen Alanna. Not soft and sweet—but beautiful, a warrior woman, strong and lean. Not Val's usual type, but who knew what had happened between them?

At this point, none of it mattered; she could try and get her head around her brother's love life later. After they had survived.

For now, she had to clear her head and think.

Which was nearly impossible with the image of Tristan, knuckles white as he gripped his new uniform, blazoned into her mind.

She wondered if he'd realized that his fingertips were bleeding where claws had split the skin. Or that his scales had covered his whole face except for his eyes.

Gods.

Was that going to be the last time she ever saw him? With that look on his face. The look of abject devastation that he thought he was hiding behind his clenched jaw. The claws.

Her whole body ached with grief and loss. Seeing Val hanging on the wall was the hardest thing she'd ever done, but a close second was calling out to Tristan and watching him shut down completely in front of her. He'd looked as if the world had ended.

Maybe it had. She wanted to crawl away. Allow the shattered parts of her heart to bleed out into the ground.

But she couldn't do it. Val needed her. Keely and Alanna needed her. And, even if she had been alone in this, she had already decided that she would never give up.

She rubbed her forehead, trying to ease the throbbing headache behind her eyes, and forced herself to concentrate. "I'm guessing you've considered going out the windows?"

Alanna rolled her eyes so quickly that she would have missed it if she hadn't been looking directly at her. Ha. She liked the other woman more and more.

"There's no way out," the queen explained. "We're at least thirty feet above the ground, assuming you can get the bars off the window in the first place. The doors are just as difficult. There has to be someone outside prepared to open the bolts."

"So, all we need is for someone to open the door?"

"The guards never will. Not even if they thought we were on fire."

"We just have to sit here and wait for Grendel and Ballanor?" Nim asked, and then immediately regretted the question when Alanna's already pale face became even more blanched. Gods. How many hours had the woman spent doing exactly that?

"I, um… I don't know if it helps," Alanna suggested uncertainly, "but I have some opium sleeping powder…. Maybe once Grendel and Ballanor are here, we could convince them to take it somehow? It's bitter, but I don't think they'd taste it in a glass of wine."

Nim sat down heavily on the side of the bed, her arm hanging at an uncomfortable angle in the air where she was joined to Keely. She wished that the two men would come in and happily drink a glass of wine offered to them by their captives. But she knew that life didn't work like that.

And she could tell by Alanna's face that she knew it too.

"I also have embroidery scissors and a small piece of razor."

"How big?"

"Maybe as long as my nail?"

Nim shook her head. That wouldn't be any use against the swords and daggers carried by Ballanor and Grendel.

If Val or Tristan were there, they would use the chain between her and Keely as a weapon. But she and Keely didn't have the skill. Or the strength. They would only end up hurting themselves.

Her talents lay elsewhere. Her talents... herbs, medicines, chemicals....

"Wait, did you say it's a powder?"

"Yes. I have it in a packet."

Thank the gods, maybe they had a chance after all. "We could burn it. That would slow them down. But we'd have to be careful not to breathe it ourselves."

Alanna looked down at her, a thoughtful, considering look on her face. "We can burn it in my room. If we close the door and build up the smoke, while we cover our faces with scarves and hide in Ballanor's room, we'd be away from the worst of it."

"Wouldn't it be easier to burn it in Ballanor's room and hide in yours?" Keely asked and then grimaced and shook her head, answering her own question. "No, then we'll still be trapped in here."

"We need to somehow convince them to come into your room though," Nim replied. The whole plan was worryingly tenuous.

Alanna gave her a rueful smile. "If they see the door is unlocked they'll come in to check on me. Ballanor will never allow me the chance to open it."

Keely nodded slowly, and so did Nim. It wasn't much, but it was better than nothing.

Tentatively, as if afraid of being rejected, Alanna put out her hand. Nim didn't hesitate; she reached out and took it. They spent a moment, hands clasped, taking strength from each other.

They quickly ransacked Alanna's wardrobe for clothes—tunics, breeches, socks, and boots—and scarves to cover their faces. It was difficult to get dressed while shackled to Keely, and it didn't help that Alanna was taller and thinner than them both, but they did the best they could, tearing seams where they had to and using Alanna's small embroidery scissors to cut holes for Nim's wings.

Alanna knelt to shove a bundle of rags into the chimney and then set a massive fire while Nim and Keely finished dressing and then wrapped bits of fabric over their chain to stop it clanking. As soon as it was blazing, she stepped away, wiping her sooty hands on her dress.

Nim watched the queen work, her regard for Alanna going up yet another notch. Whoever thought she was arrogant and spoiled had obviously never met the woman.

The room was rapidly becoming sweltering, the air thick with trapped smoke, and as soon as they were done, they covered their faces, tipped the powder onto a decorative bronze plate that they'd ripped from the wall, and then shoved it onto the coals.

The three women hurried into the fresh air of the king's chamber, closing the door behind them, and looked around for somewhere, anywhere, to hide. There weren't a lot of options.

It was a magnificent suite of rooms, far grander than the queen's single bedroom. On one side was a large seating area of velvet sofas and leather armchairs. Beside that, a small nook with piles of books and a rolltop desk of polished mahogany. A screened-off dressing area flanked a massive wardrobe, and an archway led to an opulent marble washroom with a sunken bath.

But none of it offered anywhere for three grown women to hide. In the wardrobe, under the bed, the attached bathing room… all the kind of options that would appeal to a six-year-old.

Gods. This was never going to work.

She looked at their options again, mind spinning and coming up hopelessly blank.

"We need to make them go straight into my room, to the smoke," Alanna observed, her voice muffled by the fabric over her face.

Nim grunted, feeling a sharp pang as the sound reminded her of Tristan. "There's no way to do that. We just have to hide and hope they notice the door's unlocked and go to investigate."

Alanna frowned, her eyes bleak, as aware as Nim that there was nowhere for them all to hide. "I'm sick of hiding, sick of hoping."

Nim's chest burned at the sight of the grim desolation in the queen's gaze. "I understand, truly, but it will get better. As soon as we're out of here. I promise."

The queen dipped her chin. "And Val's out too."

"Of course; that's the whole point," she agreed softly.

"Yes, that's the whole point." The queen gave a small, decisive nod and rested a slim hand on Nim's arm. "Please promise me something."

"Of course."

"When you see Val, tell him I'm sorry. And tell him…." Alanna glanced at Keely, and the two women shared a look.

"Tell him thank you for the snowdrops, and I wish he'd been right about them."

Nim blinked. Presumably it would mean something to Val. "Firstly, there is nothing for you to be sorry about. Secondly, you can—"

Nim was cut off by the noise of boots in the corridor outside, and the rumble of male voices giving orders. They were out of time.

She flew into the wardrobe, the only vaguely viable option, dragging Keely with her by their chain. Her heart hammered and her breath labored against the scarf, as she pushed against the king's clothes with one hand, forcing enough room in the cramped wardrobe for Keely to go ahead.

The chain between her and Keely was stiff and awkward, but somehow, they managed. Once they were both in, she held the door open a couple of inches and frantically waved to Alanna, where she stood in the middle of the room watching them. They only had seconds left.

But the queen shook her head and took a step away.

No. That wouldn't work. Nim whispered a loud "No!" gesturing frantically for the queen to join them.

Alanna dropped the hand holding her scarf, bit her lip and gestured for them to close the door.

What the hell was Alanna doing? Nim met the other woman's wide green eyes and saw her mouth, "Tell him," before Alanna straightened her spine and turned. The queen swiftly opened her door, coughing desperately in the billowing smoke, and then disappeared back into her room, closing her door behind her with a rough click.

Gods. Beside her, she felt Keely tensing to fling open the wardrobe door, leap out, and grab her friend. But the lock was already turning in the outer door. They only had a second to pull the wardrobe closed before the king's door flew open, and they both froze, muscles trembling with the thwarted need to follow Alanna and the fear of discovery.

She turned her head to look at Keely in the dim space and saw desperate tears swimming in her eyes.

Nim's chest felt like a giant hand had closed over her ribs and squeezed. What had just happened?

"I thought I told you to put them in here." The king's voice, petulant and whining.

"Where are those fucking women? They were here." Grendel's oily reply sent an acidic burn of fear through her veins. Her own breathing was loud in the close darkness of the wardrobe.

"What happened to them?" The king's voice, slightly further away.

"They never came out, Your Majesty. I swear." The guard's voice was rough and adamant. Probably terrified.

"Don't just stand there. You—take the guards and sweep the corridors."

Boots stamped away.

A different door slammed, and Nim knew they were looking in the bathroom. Grendel growled from nearby, and her gut clenched painfully as sweat broke out down her back. She remembered the feel of him. Rough hands on her throat. Hot breath on her face.

She wanted to slide to the floor and curl into a ball, but she forced herself to stand still. She would face him on her feet.

Suddenly there was a muffled thump. Gods. Had Alanna done something in the other room to call their attention?

There was a moment of stunned silence before Ballanor spat out, "Why the fuck is that door unlocked?"

She heard the men stalking angrily toward the queen's room. The door crashing open. Loud coughing and wheezing.

Acrid smoke seeped through the cracks around the wardrobe door, scratching her throat, and she had to swallow repeatedly to stop herself from coughing.

"What the fuck?" the king rasped from the other room.

"Why is the queen…?" Grendel's cold tones broke into a spluttering fit of coughs.

Nim risked a peek out around the side of the door. Ballanor and Grendel had their backs to her and Keely, hallowed in wreaths of smoke, both choking on the pungent fumes. Ballanor went down onto one knee in the doorway as Grendel mumbled something vague and stumbled into Alanna's room.

It was their only chance.

They crept out of the wardrobe, quickly and silently.

Ballanor gave a rough, confused order, and the shock of hearing his voice so close spurred them into action. They flew across the room, dropping the scraps of fabric from their faces, and desperately praying that the disorienting smoke was masking their escape.

And then they were out, into the blissfully clear air of the corridor. The guards were gone, sweeping the corridors. But for how long?

Holding hands over their chains, they ran like deer in a hunt as Nim tugged Keely along, forcing her faster.

She could hear the other woman sniffing and knew that she was devastated to leave the queen. It was agonizingly awful to run away and leave Alanna behind, but she had no idea what else they could do.

They flew around a corner, and Keely pulled her through a servants' door onto narrow stairs, lit only with small pools of intermittent light from lamps in recessed sconces. They were both wheezing from the smoke and pounding terror.

Keely was weeping openly, angry tears, leaning against the wall as she shuddered. "Oh, Bard! Oh, how could we? We left her!"

Nim leaned against the wall next to her and felt her own throat clench tight with horror and shock. "We didn't have a choice."

"We did! We have to go back!"

Nim took a deep breath, and then another. "If we go back now, all they'll do is catch us and put us right back where we were. She did this to save us. Don't make a mockery of her bravery."

And then, in an ice-cold shock of realization, she finally understood the truth and slowly added, "Sometimes you have to walk away to survive. Not because you want to, but because there's no other choice. Because if you don't, then hope is utterly lost. Then everyone dies."

Gods. Tristan.

She was still going to kick his ass. He deserved it. But she knew, deep in her soul, that he would never have left her if there had been any other choice.

Tor had blindsided them both. Had he betrayed them? Tor had been disowned, rejected by his entire family when the Hawks were exiled. Would he sacrifice her to get them back? Were his family ties to the crown more important to him than she was? A woman he hardly knew. Maybe.

Tor had been furious with her, entirely convinced of her guilt. Maybe he'd gone along with their plans because it was the easiest way to get her back to the palace? Gods. The thought made her stomach roll. Could Tor, a man who had stepped in to save someone he didn't know in the market, hate her that much? Hate Val that much? Or perhaps see them as less important than his chance to return to his family?

The answer seemed obvious—he'd handed her over to Grendel and been reinstated after all.

But Tristan would come back. She knew he would. He had walked away to keep them both alive, and she had to do her part and believe in him while he was gone.

Keely drew herself up, white-faced with rage and helplessness. "Your brother would be ashamed of you!"

Nim flinched, feeling the barb strike right where it hurt. But she shook her aching head and took a step away, letting the chain between them pull tight. "No, he wouldn't. He would want two people to live rather than three to die. And he would want me to look after his lover. While we're alive, we have a chance. A chance to save Val. A chance to come back for Alanna. If we go back now, those chances will be gone."

Keely looked as if she were about to argue, but sudden voices from below startled them and they huddled together in silence as a group of serving women chatted and grumbled about the late hour on the level below them.

A door opened somewhere and, finally, the stairs cleared.

Nim stared at Keely, and Keely stared back. Neither of them said anything, but somehow, in the silence, they reached a tentative truce.

Keely took her hand, across the chain, and led her swiftly down the stairs to another small door.

They eased it open a crack and peered through it. The corridor was filled with milling soldiers. They pushed back into the stairwell and waited. Every second weighed heavily as it passed.

Cold sweat trickled down her back between her wings, terror sliding through her as she wondered if the soldiers would use the servants' stairs.

Then the leader gave a command and they were gone. Thank the gods.

Keely gestured to a door on the other side of the corridor, and they bolted across and into a long, high-ceilinged room filled with books. An elderly cleaning woman was clearing out the fireplace, but they simply ran past her, grateful when she kept her head down to her work, and made their way out a far door.

Down more narrow stairs to an official corridor, flying past the portrait covered walls.

Finally, through a heavy door inlaid with silver and into a small antechamber decorated in plush ruby-colored velvets. With deep carpets and polished tables, crystal glasses gleaming in the light of a multitude of lamps. A massive, throne-like chair sat beside a fire, and Nim knew immediately that this was one of the king's reception rooms.

A decorative sword was hanging over the mantelpiece, its gold and black pommel highlighting the two fierce boars locked in battle at its center. She reached up and took it, pulling Keely's arm up with the chain so that she could use both hands. It was too heavy for her. And iron, which she hated. But it was a sword.

Keely pulled her across to a dark oak door at the far end of the room and slowly worked the massive bolt open. She tipped her head to the door and whispered, "The great hall. I don't know what's happening in there. Could be cleaners. Could be soldiers."

They both stared at the door.

"We can't wait here," Nim said quietly.

"You think?" Keely replied acidly.

Apparently, their truce was still evolving. Nim sighed. "Let's get it over with."

The door opened behind a small screen, which allowed them to creep silently into the great hall and then huddle together as they took stock.

The hall was dark except for a set of bright lamps placed around the dais. Their golden light glittered along the two ornate thrones, throwing long shadows along the swaths of burgundy brocade behind them. How dark and claustrophobic would it be behind those heavy curtains? It must feel like being buried alive.

She bit her lip hard, distracting herself with the pain, and took a deep breath to ground herself once more. They were there to free him.

Two guards stood in front of the dais, keeping a watchful eye over the now empty great hall. Otherwise the room was empty.

She looked back and saw that Keely was watching her closely. Probably reading every ounce of horror and desperation she was feeling written on her face. The other woman's expression was brittle as she glanced away, toward Val, but a fraction less accusatory than it had been.

A horn blew a sharp call from somewhere in the palace, and they both shrank back against the screen. The guard was being called. They were being hunted in earnest.

Through the screen they heard the soldiers debating how to respond. Nim looked at Keely and raised an eyebrow. The other woman gave a tiny nod, and Nim firmed her grip on the sword.

One guard left to check for further orders, and they heard his boots stomping through the hall. As soon as the door was closed behind him, they started running. Keely in front, pulling at the chain, Nim struggling to hold the sword behind her in her free hand.

"Help! Help me!" Keely called as they flew toward the dais.

The soldier spun toward her voice, his hand on his sword, already drawing. It took a moment for him to recognize them. And in that moment, he dismissed them as threats and let his sword hand loosen. A calculating look crossed his face as he realized that he would be the one to capture them for the king.

And then they were on him. "Please, sir, you must help us!" Keely sobbed dramatically, reaching up to grab his arm and pull him toward her with her free hand.

It was all the opening that Nim needed. She used their momentum to help her swing the heavy sword around and smash it hard into the soldier's head.

Her one-handed grip was too weak to hold it firm, and the sword turned in the air, hitting him with the flat of the blade. It was a brutal blow, but not enough.

Keely leaped to the side, pulling them both clear as the soldier stumbled forward and sank to his knees. He was only down for a second before he was pulling himself back up with an angry growl.

"Help me!" Her whisper was harsh, but she knew Keely had understood when the other woman stepped closer and wrapped her hands over Nim's on the hilt of the sword.

Working together, they whirled it overhead and down as hard as they could, into the Blue's vulnerable neck, splitting his armor and wedging deep into his shoulder, almost decapitating him in a sudden rush of hot blood.

Gods. Nim retched and felt Keely shuddering beside her. But they couldn't stop. They stepped back, away from the dying man, and then rushed up the dais and onto the stage, frantically working together to wind the handle that would release the brocade.

And then it was open, Val blinking, dazzled by the sudden light. She threw herself forward, dragging Keely with her, desperate to hold him but unable to find anywhere that wasn't injured.

"Gods. Val. Gods."

"Nimmy?"

She wiped his forehead with her sleeve. "I'm here. I'm here. I'm so sorry. What have they done to you?"

He blinked slowly, confused. "Nimmy?" His rasping voice was almost too low to hear. "You shouldn't be here."

"I know." What else could she say?

Val's hands were wrapped in a long chain that was thrown over a high beam and attached to a hook, holding him dangling. Ordinarily she would just fly up and undo it, but how could she with Keely attached to her arm?

The other woman understood immediately. "If you can get us both up there, I'll unhook it."

Nim had no idea if she could even lift Keely, let alone fly her up to the beam, and she had a moment of terror. What if she failed?

She pushed the thought away. There was no time for doubt.

She wrapped her arms around Keely's waist. She had no other option but to pin Keely's chained arm behind her back, but they managed to leave her other arm free.

"On three. One, two—" They both leaped, and Nim flared out her wings, using the momentum of their jump, forcing her screaming muscles and battered wings to carry them both up and then, impossibly, to hold them as Keely fought with the chain.

It had started to rust. Keely tugged and pulled frantically, but it didn't budge.

And then it was too much, and they were falling.

Nim crashed into the ground, barely holding the other woman safe as her arms shuddered in exhaustion. She let go and stepped back to catch her breath.

She shook out her arms and then stepped forward to wrap them around Keely once more.

"Again."

This time Keely counted, and then they were flying again, up, up to the beam.

Nim's wings juddered, and she gritted her teeth over her hissing pants, clamping her arms around Keely, holding her, trying to focus on staying in the air for one more second. And one more.

And then, by some miracle, Keely worked the whole knot over the hook. The chain was off the beam, and they were dropping, out of control. Nim only just managed to keep a grip on Keely as they tumbled into a staggering, jarring crash landing.

Val fell to his knees with a low groan as the chain released, his arms stretched out along the cold ground in front of him, forehead on the floor. His wings hung limp and gray and tattered over his back.

Nim could only imagine the agony he was in after being held in that position for so long. The shackles on his ankles were attached to the wall by short chains that had pulled tight as he fell, and she knew the iron must be cutting his flesh brutally on top of everything else he'd endured.

And she was about to make it even worse.

She gestured to Keely, motioning to her to grab Val's arm on one side while she took a firm grip of the other, quickly telling her what she needed to do. Then, on another hurried count of three, they each pulled, dragging his arms back down beside his body.

Val's agonized whimper, as if he didn't have the strength to scream, almost broke her. But there was no time to stop and comfort him.

A glance at the iron manacles was enough to know that they would not come off easily, and every passing moment put them one step closer to being caught.

"The guard?" Keely flicked her head back to the dead soldier, and Nim caught her breath. It was worth a try. They ran together, dropping down next to him, uncaring of the blood all over the floor.

For a few seconds they battled each other, both trying to use arms that were still chained, but then Keely took hold of her hand and they started again, anxiously searching for a key with their free hands.

Nim's heart was in her mouth as she checked the dead man's belt, his coat pockets, even his trousers. Nothing.

She wanted to scream in frustration. How long did they have before the guards realized they weren't in any of the upstairs rooms? Or the Blue from the hall came back? Not long.

He had to have keys. Where else could they be? She pulled the bloody sword out of his body and shoved it awkwardly into her belt. "Help me roll him."

They worked together to push the heavy solder onto his side. There, under his lower back, was a set of iron keys.

Val was how they'd left him, still kneeling with his forehead on the ground. They ran back up the dais, clutching the keys. The key was cold and rough, the iron immediately sapping strength from her fingers, and her hand trembled. The key wouldn't fit the lock. She tried again, but still couldn't get it in. Oh, gods.

"Give it to me." Keely held out her hand, and Nim passed her the keys. The other woman took a deep breath and then inserted the key in one smooth motion. The grinding click as the manacle opened was the best sound she had ever heard.

It took a few seconds to get the other manacle off and then to work their way around to find the best position for lifting Val. Even with all the weight he'd lost, he was still a big, heavy man, and almost unconscious. They managed to get him strung between them, their chain tight around his back, beneath his wings, his arms over their shoulders, and to take a few stumbling steps.

They almost fell getting off the dais, then Keely slipped in the bloody footprints surrounding the dead Blue, only just managing to right herself in time.

Slowly they moved forward, one step after the other.

That was when they heard it. Booted feet tramping right outside. The palace guard was in the courtyard and would be on them in any second, their bloody footprints leaving no doubt as to where they'd gone.

They hauled Val urgently back the way they'd come, only just reaching the screen as the first soldiers burst through the door.

The cry went up immediately. The guard had seen the corpse, the gory trail. Orders were shouted as their broken trio reached the door to the king's study and fled through it, turning to drag the heavy bolt closed just as the first Blues reached them.

The room was meant to be a safe retreat for the king, and it was heavily protected with a multitude of bolts. Nim and Keely frantically slid them closed, flinching as soldiers began thumping into the door.

Something about the booming thuds seemed to reach

Val even in his almost catatonic state, and he stood stronger, taking more of his own weight, as they rushed him across the room toward the only other exit.

And stopped. The sounds of more boots thumped through the air. More men. The sound of rough orders being briskly delivered, too low to hear clearly.

It was the sound of the end.

Nim glanced at Keely and Val. Between them, they had one sword. All of them were beyond exhausted. Val could hardly stand.

Would it be better to give in, accept the inevitable, and do what they could to survive, even if just for a few more hours? Survive, however broken, and wait for Tristan to come?

She gritted her teeth. She wanted to survive, but not like that.

Somehow, in the long dark night under the pier, the woman who had sat at home waiting, even as she slowly lost hope, had gone. And in her place was a woman who had been forged in the fires of her own rafters. A woman who truly, finally, trusted in her own strength. Who came all this way to rescue her brother. A woman who fought for herself and what she wanted.

As if sensing her decision, Keely gave her a small, resigned smile of agreement. She lifted her arm, and together they swung their chain back over Val's head.

He swayed at the sudden loss of support and went down onto one knee, head bowed.

The two women stepped together, in front of Val, and gripped the sword together, lifting it high between them just as the door crashed open.

Chapter Twenty-One

EVERYTHING TOOK TOO FUCKING LONG.

The cavalry guards at Court Gate couldn't understand why a squad of Palace Blues was heading back into the palace they had just left and tried to send them back to the barracks. Tristan had been entirely comfortable with killing them all where they stood, but luckily for them, Mathos's parade ground bellowing had convinced them to stand back.

The cobbled bridge seemed to have stretched impossibly as they clattered their way to the gate.

The discussion as they left Jeremiel and Garet with the horses was interminable. The men would wait for ten minutes and then quietly lead the horses away to join up with Rafael and Reece. There was no way anyone was coming back out the front. Why did it take so bloody long to explain?

And then the guards on the inner gate gave them another round of skeptical looks as Tristan strode forward flanked by Mathos, Tor, and Jos.

He ignored them. They could see the fucking blue tunic. "Halt."

He narrowed his eyes and slowly turned to face the soldier. The same one that had had his eyeballs glued to Nim's chest. It would be a pleasure to end this asshole just for the way he'd looked at Nim.

"I knew I recognized you, you're the captain that got sent back down to the stables." He nudged his friend with his elbow and chortled.

Tristan took a step forward, and another, until he was looming over the guard. The soldier swallowed heavily as Tristan slowly raised his hand. His fingers were still tipped with brutal curved claws; he had no idea how to get rid of them. And, at that moment, he wanted nothing more than to slowly sink one into the guard's eye.

His thoughts must have shown on his face, because the man stepped back with a strangled sound, and then Mathos was there, hand back on Tristan's shoulder, eyes flicking up to the archers focused on them from the unfinished walls in a silent message.

"We came back," Tor answered for him as the soldier gulped and then wisely stepped aside.

And then they were moving again.

Before they could reach the great hall, the wooden doors swung open and a great rush of people came pouring out. From the snatches of conversation that he could overhear, it sounded as if the king had retired for the night and the guests now felt safe to make a run for it. The cleaners were already busy in the hall, and everyone there wanted to get far away as quickly as they could.

It was chaos as everyone pushed and shoved, trying to get back to their carriages in a great heaving mass. A few brave, or stupid, people whispered about Val and the queen, but they were quickly shushed by their panicked friends as they hurried away.

This was where their blue uniforms finally helped. A large, empty circle formed around them as everyone tried to avoid them, chatter dying away into brittle silence and anxious glances.

Tristan's fingers ached as his claws lengthened impossibly further and the dark pit inside him gaped wider. This was where he had to choose a direction—hall or chamber, Val or Nim.

The thought of leaving Val hanging in the hall burned like acid. But with the king already in his chambers, Nim had to be his priority. If he could ask him, Val would agree.

They peeled away from the crowds, down a covered walkway, past the pair of guards that stepped back with a suspicious look, and into the palace proper.

A wide marble foyer filled with art, gleaming in the soft lamplight, led up to a long corridor carpeted in plush blues, which Tristan knew led to official chambers, libraries, and studies.

Ahead there was a set of stairs, carpeted and flanked by lamps glowing in their sconces, leading up to the royal sleeping chambers.

An alert palace guard in an immaculate blue tunic stood at the bottom of the stairs, watching them suspiciously as they strode over to him.

Tristan recognized his face. A good-looking Tarasque, the sheen of copper-colored scales creeping around his jaw. He'd been climbing remarkably swiftly through the ranks, just promoted to work with the Lord High Chancellor a few months before the Hawks had been demoted to the cavalry. It must have been bloody lonely to be the only competent man surrounded by Ballanor's cronies and relations for so long.

Did the Blue have any respect left for his former captain? Would it be enough to get them through?

A quick look at the man's set jaw and narrowed eyes ended that hope.

Although, if he were being honest, Tristan was sick of this game that they were playing. It would be a relief to finally acknowledge exactly whose side he was on and act on it.

"Stand aside. We have palace business." Mathos's tone could have cut glass.

But the guard stood his ground. "None upstairs."

Mathos waved a hand toward Tristan. "Show some respect to your captain."

The guard widened his stance, his lip curling. "He's no captain of mine."

Tristan grunted. They had finally found a palace guard with backbone. Exactly at the worst time. "What's your name, son?"

"My name is irrelevant, and I'm not your son. My orders are that no one goes upstairs. Therefore, no one goes upstairs."

"When a superior officer asks your name, you fucking give it!" Mathos roared, a vein pulsing in his temple. Damn, when his second-in-command finally stopped joking, it was brutal.

The guard seemed to recognize the danger of antagonizing a squad of extremely angry, well-armed soldiers and decided to answer. "Lieutenant Dornar. But that doesn't change my orders. No one goes up. Especially not men that haven't been in the Blues for months. Go away, and next time come back with an order from the king."

Tristan pinched the bridge of his nose. By the obstinate look on his face, Dornar was never going to let them pass.

Tor stepped forward, his massive bulk looming threateningly over Dornar, and opened his mouth to argue. But before he could start, a harsh trumpeting blared from the floor above.

Dornar didn't flinch; he was too well trained. Instead he rested his hand on his sword and firmed his jaw. But he was clearly listening to the mayhem above them, his attention split for just a second as he waited for further orders from the rooms above.

Mathos gave Tor a nod, lifted his fingers to his lips, and let out a piercing blast of a whistle, the kind of noise you'd expect on the docks, not in an opulent palace. Dornar's eyes flickered his way. It was all they needed.

Tor reached out, took hold of the soldier with one big hand, and, before Dornar could do more than slide his sword from its scabbard, threw him roughly into the wall, knocking him half unconscious.

Tristan hit him on the head once more, just to be sure. Then they grabbed the limp body and dragged it down the corridor and shoved it into one of the nearby studies as all hell broke loose above them. Trumpets blared, boots thudded, orders were shouted.

Gods. Nim. Fuck. Something had happened.

The stairs were a blur as they sprinted up, two at a time, and around a corner into the king's wing to find Grendel and Ballanor in disarray as soldiers swarmed around them. Both men had wide, blown-out pupils, and there was a sickly-sweet, acrid smell in the smoky air.

"Find them!" Ballanor sputtered, coughing loudly as a

soldier rushed up with a glass of wine, while another opened a window to the crisp night air.

Between the chaos and the guards' frantic search, no one seemed to care about the strange arrival of the Hawks as they smoothly joined the other Blues in their hunt.

Palace guards flung open doors and tramped through rooms. They stripped beds, pulled luxurious gowns from wardrobes, threw dripping courtiers from their baths.

The king looked apoplectic with rage. And Nim was nowhere to be seen.

Tristan felt like laughing. And simultaneously howling in horror.

Nim had escaped. Of course she had. But now anyone could get their hands on her.

And when one of these men, fear and rage pumping through their systems, each one desperate to redeem themselves in the eyes of the king, got hold of her... what then?

He forced himself to slow down and consider what the options would have looked like to Nim. What would have been going through her mind as she looked down the long corridor filled with rooms and lots of little hiding places?

Would she have crept into one of those tempting dark spaces? No. She knew better than to cut herself off from an escape by hiding.

She would run.

A tendril of icy realization worked its way down his spine as he followed the thought. She would run. But she wouldn't run away from danger, not Nim. Gods. He knew exactly where she would run to. The worst fucking place in the palace. His beast snarled within him as his scales closed over his skin.

"You!" A red-faced guard, most likely one of those that

should have been guarding the door by the look of congealed horror on his face, pointed right at him. "Stop standing around and help! How far can two women go?"

Fuck, there were two of them. He remembered how Nim had moved her body protectively toward Keely. She would have taken the other woman with her. That made it exponentially harder to get her out. Get them out. Nim, Keely, and Val.

He kept his face blank and silently returned to his task as the Hawks ripped into the closest room and started pulling it apart. The destruction helped to soothe the crawling itch burning his skin from playing this game of charades when all he wanted to do was turn around and run after Nim.

But he couldn't. Not without everyone noticing.

He moved on to the next room, further away from the king, hardly caring what he was doing, what destruction he was wreaking. Knowing all the while that Nim wasn't there.

The weight of time pressed heavily. Each passing second meant that Nim was that much closer to being discovered. And not by him.

But each room took them a few precious paces further away from the king and Grendel.

A guard emerged from yet another destroyed room and shook his head. The king, flanked by Grendel, turned away to face the soldier, his back rigid with rage as he ranted and swore.

And Tristan knew that it was their best chance. While the king was distracted. Before someone got it together enough to start questioning why they were there. Tristan nodded to his men, and in seconds they had ducked around the corner and started to run.

They sped down the stairs, passing troops and staff as the search spread out, and back through the marble foyer.

Around them men were shouting. A horn blew loudly, and orders were called. By the sound, a fresh team was just entering the great hall.

And then he heard the sound he had been dreading. A roar went up in the distant courtyard.

They'd found her.

Too far away. Too late. There was no way through the troops. Their only hope was to turn back and take the king's personal entrance into the hall. And pray that they got there before the rest of the guards.

He spun around and sprinted down the empty corridors where the court met and the stewards, chaplains, and marshals could be found during the day.

He pushed himself harder, flinging orders to the Hawks as they skidded to a stop just outside the door to the king's private study. There was no time for finesse, he simply drew his sword with one hand while reaching out to throw the door open with the other.

The sword in his hand saved him.

The sword and reflexes born of thousands of hours of training and battlefield experience, combined with that deep, primal awareness.

He flung his arm up and deflected the crushing downward strike whistling toward his head, swinging both swords in a locked arc down and away.

As he swung, he stepped forward, meeting the attack, combining the momentum of the descending swords with a sharp flick that sent the enemy sword spinning away.

The whole thing happened in slow motion. The swinging swords. His horror as he realized that it was Nim and Keely behind the attack. The jarring shudder as the swords met in the air. The wrench that traveled through the two swords as someone, Nim, tried to pull back, to check the blow. The crash as the women's sword smashed into a table. The tinkling crackle of broken glass falling to the stone floor.

And then silence.

Nim stood frozen, a chain stretching between her and Keely. Both women were bone pale, their eyes wide with shock and prolonged terror. Val was behind them, on his knees, swaying, seconds away from complete collapse.

It all happened in slow motion, and then stopped. And he froze too. Fully battle scaled, sword still tightly gripped in his hand, he froze. For the first time in his life, he had absolutely no idea what to do.

Then Mathos was there, pushing past him. "Thank the gods! Nim, we've been looking for you!"

She turned to his friend, still silent. Stunned.

Mathos threw his arms around her, and Tristan saw her soften against him, just a fraction.

He wanted to rip Mathos's head off his shoulders. Wanted to snap his neck and fling his body into the Abyss. But Mathos was comforting Nim, and gods knew, he'd lost that right when he took the blue tunic and walked away from her while she called his name.

He looked away, focusing on Jos as he followed them into the study. He jerked his chin. "Get Val. Everyone else, move out."

Mathos wrapped a firm arm around Nim. "Come on, darlin', time to go."

Nim took a hesitant step forward, bringing Keely with her on their chain. Fuck. They'd been chained. His inner beast howled in fury.

But then Nim stopped dead, her breath going shallow

and uneven as she stared in dismay at the doorway. Tristan spun round, lifting his sword once more, ready to rain down hell on whoever had threatened her. And then hesitated. It was Tor she was staring at.

Tor's face was like granite, his massive shoulders rigid with tension.

"No. No, it's not like that," Mathos was murmuring to Nim, trying to drag her forward as she locked her knees. Keely took a shuddering step back, tangling them all further.

If Tristan had to see that look of distress on Nim's face for one more second, he was going to lose his mind. But he couldn't punish Tor either. And they had to get the fuck out of there.

He reached down and grabbed the fallen sword, recognizing it as King Geraint's as he lifted it. Once, that might have bothered him, but none of that mattered to him anymore.

He spun it swiftly and pressed the grip into Nim's small hand, gently closing her fingers until he felt them tighten.

She was still standing circled by Mathos's arm, but he leaned as close as he dared and looked her in the eye. "He's not here to hurt you. No one will hurt you. I promise."

Nim never stopped looking at him. And for a moment, it felt as if they would stay, staring at each other like that, forever. And then she gave a tiny nod and took a small step forward.

Her trust nearly broke him.

Tristan spun around before he could do something fucking stupid, like rip her out of Mathos's arms and kiss her, standing right there in the king's study. He got himself under control and grunted the order to move out.

Tor moved first and then quickly gestured through the

door that everyone should follow. Tristan joined him, sword drawn, Mathos and the women behind him, and then Jos, supporting Val.

Tristan turned them away from the clattering chaos of the distant courtyard and led their battered little group at a run down a richly carpeted hallway, past a series of shadowed reception rooms, and into the bleak stone and gloom of the servants' wing.

As soon as they were all moving, Tristan fell back, letting the others pass him until he could bring up the rear, trying to keep their bedraggled group together while propelling them forward as fast as possible, all while keeping a lookout for anyone coming up behind them.

They pushed their way into the shadowy kitchen, sweltering despite the banked fires and eerily quiet with most of the staff already asleep or having wisely made themselves scarce when the first horn blew.

Those few night servants still working rapidly averted their eyes and ducked their heads at the sight of four Blues and three prisoners.

Tor swung open the back door, and the brisk night air flooded in, fresh with the smell of herbs from the kitchen gardens, clearing the air and making the fires spark. Shadows rippled along the walls as they hurried forward.

"Hey! You can't go through there!" an indignant matronly voice demanded behind them.

Tristan spun, already forming a vaguely polite response, but his movement cleared the way for the woman to see behind him. Her eyes widened at the sight of Val being half carried through the door by Jos, and without taking a breath, she started to scream.

Her panicky shrieks triggered something in her staff, who immediately joined in a loud howl of outrage and fear, and a small boy ran for the kitchen door screaming for the guards.

"Move!" Tristan threw himself through the door, pushing the others in front of him, and whirled to slam it shut behind them.

Fuck, all the bolts were on the inside.

He was torn. Should he stay and try to hold the door closed or run with the others? It would be a matter of only minutes before the screeching in the kitchen brought the guards.

He hesitated for only a moment. There was no way he could hold the door alone. But he could carry someone.

It took mere seconds to catch up to Jos and Val. They were moving so slowly that it looked like they were stuck in treacle.

Without stopping to explain, he grabbed hold of Val and swung him up into a rough carry hold over his shoulders. He grunted under the weight, struggling to find a good grip on Val's skin as his friend's tortured wings flopped brokenly toward the ground.

They had wrestled hundreds of times as boys. Thousands, maybe. Picked each other up. Stumbled around carrying one another. Dumped each other in the icy water of the nearby river.

But never had he imagined carrying Val's broken body as his friend shuddered and groaned in agony.

Or, in his worst nightmares, considered that he might one day so misjudge his friend. That his own lack of faith would leave Val alone, abandoned to the cruelty of two sadistic torturers.

He had brought Nim to the palace to prove to her that she was wrong about her brother. That people lied and betrayed. And instead, he had to face the truth—*he* had betrayed Val when he had walked away.

A deadening bitterness that settled over his heart as he recognized that there was no way that he could ever atone for what he'd done.

Nim and Val would never—should never—forgive him. But he could still get them free. And he could spend the rest of his life keeping them safe.

He half ran, half staggered down the graveled paths as Jos rushed forward and threw an arm around Keely, dragging her faster, while Mathos helped Nim. The women struggled to run, restricted by the clanking chain strung between them.

A massive wall loomed above them in the darkness and Tristan knew they were nearing the Old Tower, the ancient castle keep that the rest of the palace had grown up around.

Almost there.

Horns and whistles blared frantically in the distance behind them, mingling with the crunch of gravel under their boots and their grunting pants as they flew between low beds of vegetables and herbs toward the Old Tower and the ramparts it guarded.

And, more importantly, their only way out of the palace.

Somewhere above them along the stone walkway, a voice called out. Then more. Beacons flared along the walls, and the garden was thrown into stark, flickering light and deep shadows.

A horn blasted from the wall, joining the cacophony in the palace behind them, and suddenly the air was alive with the crunching thuds of arrows hitting the gravel paths.

A woman gave a low scream of pain, and he nearly went to his knees as Val jerked violently on his shoulders and then slumped, completely unconscious. He righted himself with a grunt, got a better grip on Val, and continued their mad flight.

And then they were there, huddled up against the inner wall. Arrows clattered harmlessly a foot away as the archers on the wall failed to compensate for the fortifications that were designed to withstand invaders from outside, never considering a threat from inside the garden.

Water sloshed in the small alcove beside them, and Tristan knew from his time as a palace guard that a set of worn stone steps led down to a tunnel protected by an iron portcullis.

The last time he'd seen it, the gate had opened into a lamp-lit tunnel under the ramparts of the Old Tower, through a second portcullis, and into the grassy field that flanked the Tamasa, where the court used to picnic and practice their archery and falconry on the banks of the wide green-brown river.

Now that was all underwater, the field dug away to allow in the muddy river waters that filled the new moat.

They would have to make it through both gates and across the moat with Val unconscious and the women chained.

Beside him, Tor was already cranking the windlass, the portcullis grinding on its gears as it rose. Thank the gods that the fortified gates, like the walls, assumed attackers on the outside, not the inside.

He ordered them forward, and everyone scrambled down the narrow steps. He staggered behind them, sweat running down his neck as he balanced Val on his shoulders while trying to navigate the slippery wet stone stairs.

His foot caught a slick growth of moss and he slid helplessly, only just caught by Tor's iron grip as they continued down into a shallow pool.

Cold black water lapped against their legs, and thick mud sucked at their boots as they rushed into the dripping darkness of the tunnel.

No lights shone in the freezing stone passageway, and the dark was deep and ominous, the icy water rising with each step that they took until it was swirling chest-deep.

Mathos went ahead, and Tristan could hear him cursing as he fought to crank the second windlass that would raise the outer portcullis. Everything was under frigid black water, and he could hear soft female whimpers that cut into his heart with every beat.

"Nim?" His voice was a rough whisper that echoed through the darkness of the tunnel. Gods, please let her be okay.

"Not me," she whispered, understanding his concern. "Keely was hit by an arrow."

Fuck. He knew he shouldn't be so relieved that a woman was hurt. But he didn't think he could handle hearing Nim whimpering.

He grunted, not knowing what to say.

"It's rusted." Mathos's voice cut through the dark.

There was a swishing noise as water lapped. "Do it together." Tor's rough voice.

"One. Two—" The final count was lost in a harsh male curse and loud screeching squeal as the crank finally moved and the portcullis scraped its way slowly upward.

And then stopped.

"Fuck. Fuck." Tristan had heard Mathos's voice range from snide jokes through to battleground weary, but he had never heard that degree of horrified dismay.

"Report."

"It's stuck."

"How high?"

"Two feet. Maybe a little more."

"We can swim." Nim's disembodied voice.

He didn't waste any time wishing it was different. "Do it. Tor first. Jos, take Nim and Keely. Mathos, help me."

He could hear Tor muttering under his breath. Water lapped and echoed. The sounds of soldiers shouting in the garden drifted through the tunnel.

Then Tor was through, calling quietly. He heard someone take a deep breath. Another swirling pull of icy water. The seconds dragged by.

And then he heard a shuddering gasp on the other side. Jos whistling the signal. The women were through.

Mathos followed next.

Val was shivering where Tristan still held him on his shoulders. But he couldn't hold him out of the cold water any longer. They were out of time.

He swung his friend down and into the moat, feeling like a brute as Val gasped in shock. "Wake up!"

"Tris?" Val's rough voice was confused.

"We have to swim. I'm going to pass you to Mathos, but you must keep your mouth closed. Do you hear me?"

Nothing.

"Do you understand?"

He felt a small nod. It had to be enough.

Tristan took hold of Val's shoulders and pushed him down, following him into the icy, muddy, silted bottom of the tunnel. The water was so cold that not even his scales could protect him, and it would be infinitely worse for Val. It was pitch-black. There was no way to know where they were or which way to go, other than to recall where they'd been.

He could feel the shudders wracking through Val's body as he gripped him and hauled him forward through the water. Agony ripped into him as the spikes of the portcullis tore into his shoulder, but he was grateful for the focus the pain gave him. It helped him know exactly where not to put Val.

And then another pair of hands nudged his, and he let go. Felt as Mathos pulled Val out of his arms, the rest of the way through the portcullis and away.

He forced himself through, then up to the surface, only allowing himself a second of relief when he heard Val spluttering and coughing.

They had escaped the palace.

But they still had the moat ahead of them and the archers looking down from the ramparts.

Chapter Twenty-Two

Nᴵᴹ's sᴋɪɴ burned with the cold as the water lapped around her neck. She and Keely clung to the broken stones along the outside edge of the rampart, trying to keep their heads out of the water, the heavy sword abandoned somewhere in the garden behind them.

In reality, she was doing most of the clinging. She had one arm around Keely, helping to prop her up; the other hand gripped the rough stone.

The ground had dropped away sharply after the tunnel, and there was no way they could stand, or even swim, with the chain dragging them down. And Keely couldn't use her free arm with the arrow lodged in it. It was all they could do to clutch onto the tiny jagged bits of stone and keep their heads up.

At the tunnel entrance, she could just make out Mathos taking a deep breath and diving back down to the portcullis to help Tristan with Val.

She held her breath, scanning the silty black water again and again.

And then they were up. Mathos dragging Val out of the water and thumping him hard on his back as her brother spluttered weakly.

A few seconds later, Tristan followed, and she was finally able to let out a shuddery breath of relief.

Archers and soldiers called orders on the ramparts above them, a whispered discussion carried over the water as the guards debated whether it would be better to kill the escapees outright. No one wanted to take responsibility for making the wrong decision.

And then she heard a sound that she honestly hadn't ever expected to hear again. The high-pitched hunting whistle of a hawk.

Beside her, she heard a low rumble from Jos that could almost be a chuckle. And then something even better. Oars, dipping and sliding almost silently through the water nearby.

Jos gestured her forward, silently urging her off the ramparts.

Gods. "I can't." She mouthed silently.

Jos gestured more urgently.

"I c-can't let go," she whispered as quietly as she could, shuddering with cold. "Keely's hurt. And the ch-chain…."

Jos turned in the darkness to murmur, "Captain…."

Before Tristan could reply, a dark shape swam in close beside them.

"Give Keely to me." It was Tor.

Nim shivered helplessly. Her body was exhausted, and she knew she was in shock. Too much had happened. Too much fear, too much grief.

And now Tor was there, and she didn't know how she felt. Frightened of him? Or was she frightened because he reminded her of Grendel? She still felt sick when she thought of him standing beside Tristan in the great hall, pointing her out to Grendel. But had he genuinely betrayed them? He was helping, wasn't he? She didn't know.

Her whole body shuddered as she clung helplessly to the rock wall, one arm hooked around Keely's waist, the other woman slumped against the slimy, wet battlement beside her.

"Nim," Tor's voice was gentle, "can you pass her to me?"

She closed her eyes and tried to think. This was a man who had sacrificed himself for an unknown woman in the marketplace. Everything else, she didn't understand.

Tristan said that Tor wouldn't hurt them. And she trusted Tristan.

"C-can y-you help me?" she whispered through her frozen lips. "I'm trying, but I c-can't let go."

Big hands reached out through the water, and Tor took hold of Keely, holding her cradled against his chest in the water. Jos put his arm around Nim and supported her, just enough, that she was able to force her fingers slowly open.

He was warm and strong and keeping her safe. But he still wasn't right. Wasn't who she wanted. "T-tris?"

"He's helping Val. Come now." Jos's warm body buoyed hers as the two men helped her and Keely cross the short stretch of water, the chain tight between them, to a large rowboat. The men boosted them up together to fall noisily into a shivering puddle at the bottom, beneath the heavy tarpaulin being held up by Reece while Jeremiel and Garet manned the oars.

A loud cry went up on the battlements, and there was a flurry of activity. Was the king there? Or had they seen the boat?

More bodies fell into the boat in a heap of limbs and armor; someone groaned in agony.

Was it Val? She couldn't move under the pile of people. And she couldn't see him in the dark chaos.

And then they were moving, bodies sorting themselves into a rough order. Oars dipping and pulling. Whispered commands.

The tarpaulin was pushed away, and she knew they must have made it to open water, out of reach of the archers.

Jos pulled her and Keely to sit at the bottom of the boat, Val unconscious beside them. She lifted his head into her lap and leaned back against the wooden hull, staying out of the way as they flew down the dark river.

Everything became a blur. Time passed, but she didn't know how much. Her shivering was out of control, and her lips felt completely numb. Val had stopped shivering, and somewhere in the recess of her brain, she knew that that was worse. She lay down over his body, trying desperately to keep him warm.

Eventually they stopped at a small jetty, and she and Keely were lifted out, shaking with cold, by Jos and Tor, and carried up a small beach to a treelined path. Everything around them was soft in purple and gray as the sun slowly rose, lightening the darkness.

They made their way, side by side, to a low shed where Jos and Tor placed them gently on the ground. Nim felt her legs wobble with exhaustion, and she allowed herself to fold slowly, going onto her knees.

"Wait here a moment," Jos said quietly before moving into the shed.

She leaned her head against the wall behind her and

waited, her chained arm held up beside her to where Tor stood, cradling Keely.

Within a few minutes, Jos was back with a large ax. He directed her to run their chain over a nearby rock and to cover her eyes as he swung. There was a loud clang, and then another, and suddenly the tension released as the chain snapped. She fell back, sitting in a heap, and then simply stayed where she was. She was vaguely aware of Keely groaning and Tor lifting her to carry her inside, but she didn't have the energy to follow. Days of exhaustion and terror had suddenly become too much.

She shivered slowly and let her cheek rest on her bent knees, the remaining few links of the chain dragging down from the manacle still around her wrist.

"Can you walk?" Jos asked gently.

She shrugged.

His face crinkled with worry. "Shall I carry you?"

No. She could manage. She pushed herself up, leaning heavily on Jos when he put his arm around her, and tried to keep control of her trembling limbs.

They made their way slowly into a large farmhouse and down to the kitchen, where he nudged her to sit on a long wooden bench.

It was achingly similar to her own lost home, with its wide hearth and scarred kitchen table. Dried herbs hung from the rafters and filled the room with the soft scents of lavender and thyme.

It hurt something inside her to know that the place that she'd grown up, the homestead that her parents had built and nurtured, was gone. Sitting in the warmth of someone else's kitchen reminded her of just how much she'd lost.

Jos interrupted her melancholy thoughts by asking her to hold her arm over the table as he pulled out a slim blade and slipped it into the lock on her manacle. His eyes narrowed as he probed and wiggled the long blade. Nothing happened.

She rested her free arm out across the table and then laid her head down on it, watching Jos frown as he twisted the blade inside the manacle, muttering about breaking the tip.

"Is this why we had all the drama with the ax? In case it doesn't open?" she asked quietly.

"Nah, I'll get it, but it's much easier to do in the light. And we wanted Keely to go straight up and see Rafe while Tor opened her manacle, the ax was the quickest way to get you apart."

His eyebrows scrunched together. "Just about—" There was a loud grating click and the lock opened, "—there."

Jos gently pulled the manacle away, and finally, she was free.

Having the iron away from her body was like stepping out of the rain. The sudden relief almost made her cry. She blinked heavily, working to keep it together.

Jos seemed to sense her struggle and her need for space. He turned to take the manacle away, fiddling with the kitchen dresser as Nim took a set of slow breaths.

"I need to see V-Val." Her lips felt numb with cold.

"Sure. But get changed first. You can't stay in those soaked clothes."

He led her up a flight of wooden stairs down a short corridor and into a cozy room with a small fire lit in the hearth and a soft-looking bed covered in yellow blankets.

"Can you get your clothes off?"

Honestly. No. Not with her numb fingers. She shook her head.

Jos sighed. "Captain's going to kill me. Turn around."

She turned, faced the wall, and lifted her wings out the way as she tried to ignore Jos's friendly grumbling as he tugged at the wet and tightly knotted laces of Alanna's jerkin.

She heard a snick of a knife and then the sudden relief of air filling her lungs as the wet leather fell forward and she caught it against her chest.

"Can you do the rest?"

She nodded, not looking at him.

"Look in the wardrobe, there might be something. I'll be back to check on you."

Two minutes later, wearing a long shirt that she had found in the decidedly male wardrobe, she was standing next to the fire and slowly trying to take stock. She still felt completely dazed and weirdly dissociated. She needed to get to Val. But she also needed her fingers to thaw enough that she could pull on some trousers. Then they needed to somehow get back to Alanna.

And mostly, above all of that, she wanted Tristan.

There was a quiet knock at the door, and Jos was back. She should have felt embarrassed, but she was too far past exhaustion to think of it.

"Can you help me put on some trousers so I can go to Val?"

"No."

"No?" She blinked in confusion. Jos didn't seem like the kind of person to refuse to help.

"I'm absolutely not helping you get dressed, or undressed, any more than I already have. Gods, imagine the captain walked in while I was putting you into trousers."

His look of genuine horror made her huff out an almost giggle.

"Val is sleeping," Jos continued, "and I have strict orders that you need to rest."

"I have to see him." Nim grabbed one of the blankets off the bed and wrapped it around her shoulders, letting it fall to her knees as Jos let out another beleaguered sigh. But he didn't argue, simply took her elbow and walked with her to a nearby room and tapped gently on the door. "Rafe?"

"Come in," a low voice answered on the other side of the door.

The room was bright with lamps and heavy with the pungent steam of something herbal boiling over the fire. Mathos was there, and Tristan, both men working quickly under Rafe's direction.

At a glance, Nim could see that Val had been cleaned, his wounds already wrapped in soft bandages and a smooth sheet draped over his body up to his waist. But gods, he was so thin, his face gaunt beneath the dark beard. And there were so many bandages.

He let out a choking groan of agony as his body shuddered, and Nim pushed past all the men to grab his hand, kissing him gently on his heated forehead as she murmured, "You're safe, Val, you're here. I'm here."

His eyes opened, glassy and dazed. "Nimmy?"

"I'm here."

"Where…?"

"We're in a safe house."

"No." His frown deepened, the muscles in his neck standing out in long cords as he strained to sit.

"Shh, shh." She stroked his hair from his forehead, helpless, trying to push him back to the bed without hurting him.

His voice was so thin and rasping that she almost didn't hear him. "We left her."

Oh gods, he didn't know. "Keely's here with us; she's okay."

He didn't seem to understand, instead he became even more frantic, and he started pushing weakly once more. Then Rafe was there with a mug, directing Mathos to hold Val up as he tipped it against her brother's mouth. Val swallowed reflexively, and again. And then, as if slipping into a dream, his muscles slowly softened and he lay back, eyes flickering closed on a long, broken sigh.

It was as if his collapse had given her permission, because, finally, the tears came. So many tears. She lay her head down on Val's limp arm and sobbed.

Male voices whispered behind her. But none of them were Val. Or Tristan. So she didn't really care.

She still didn't care when Jos wrapped an arm behind her and another under her legs and lifted her like a baby.

But when she saw that he was carrying her back to her room, she started to wiggle to be let down. "I have to stay with Val."

"No." Jos's voice softened. "He's safe here, and Rafael is with him."

"He needs me."

"Rafe is doing everything that Val needs."

"But I—"

"No. You're dead on your feet. You're no use to him like this. Sleep for a few hours."

"What if—"

"I'll get you. I promise."

Nim let her head hang. She wasn't going to win this. And truthfully, she knew he was right.

"Fine. Just for an hour."

She climbed into the softness of the small bed, almost whimpering with relief.

"Do you need anything?" Jos asked quietly from the doorway, the perfect big brother stand-in.

"Just… I…."

He took a step back into the room.

"Never mind."

"Ask me."

"Is Tristan…?" She didn't know what exactly her question was. She only knew that she needed him. And he wasn't there. He'd saved her. Come back for her, as she'd known he would. He had been in Val's room. Hadn't he? But now he was gone. And she was all alone.

The look on Jos's face was unreadable. Or maybe she was too tired to understand. "The captain is checking the perimeter and then he's coming back to check on Val."

That was different. Tristan would know that Val was her priority. "Okay."

"Go to sleep now." Jos was definitely using his big brother voice. Val spoke to her in precisely the same way. The thought made her want to smile and cry at the same time.

She exhaled slowly and lay back, closing her stinging eyes, huddling in the covers as Jos left the room and closed the door behind him with a quiet click. It was less than a minute before she was fast asleep.

She woke up with early morning sunlight streaming around the edges of not-quite-closed drapes. The fire had burned down to embers, but the room still felt pleasantly warm. She lay for a moment, getting her bearings and remembering everything that had happened.

Somehow, she had imagined that Tristan would be there when she woke up, but she was alone.

Her tired body felt weak and shaky as she opened her eyes and forced them to stay open. She needed to see Val.

And they needed to plan. She counted to ten and then made herself roll over and climb slowly out the bed.

Someone had left a cup of water and a bread roll on the bedside table, and she took rough bites as she rifled through the room's wardrobe once more. Her search revealed some men's cotton trousers, which she pulled on over the shirt she'd already taken, followed by a short woolen cloak and a pair of thick socks. The leather boots she'd borrowed from Alanna were still soaking wet, so she left them off.

She let herself out of the room and padded quickly down the wooden floorboards to Val's room.

The door opened with a slow squeak, and she paused at the entrance while her eyes adjusted to the warm darkness of the room. The air was thick with fragrant steam, and she could easily identify musk mallow and sage, and something mustier, hemlock perhaps. In capable hands, a small dose could help with pain relief, if the need was great. Her heart mourned the enormity of what had been done to Val—that he could be in so much pain.

She stepped into the room to see Val, huddled over on his side in the wide bed, wings twitching behind him as he moaned almost silently.

Rafe sat beside him, watching her calmly.

She stepped as quietly as she could up to the bed and laid a soft hand over Val's forehead. It was slightly cooler than the night before, but still too warm.

Val shuddered but otherwise didn't respond, seeming locked in his fitful sleep, and she looked up to Rafe questioningly.

"Valerian," he said softly, as if that explained everything. And it did, to a degree.

"You're keeping him asleep?"

"He needs rest. I've cleaned and treated his wounds, and

I don't want him pulling at the dressings. We've warmed him from the chill he had in the water, and I've also been treating him more directly myself. Right now, our biggest concern is his fever."

Rafe was right, and she appreciated the professional respect shown by discussing his treatment plan with her. And the gift of his Nephilim healing. But it was still hard, so very hard, to see her brother lying unconscious and in pain. "How can I help?"

"He doesn't need anything right now. In fact, you should be sleeping too."

"I slept already. I want to help Val."

"Get your energy back; he'll need you strong when he wakes up."

Nim sank onto the bed next to Val and picked up his big hand between hers, wishing he was awake, even while she knew he was better off asleep.

"Where's Keely?" she asked softly so that she didn't disturb Val. Why wasn't she taking care of her lover? Were they even lovers? Or had that been part of the lie to Ballanor too?

"Keely had her wound cleaned and bandaged and then took the last bedroom. I saw her briefly last night, but since she was stable, I left Tor to check on her."

Nim looked around the room, taking in the fresh bandages hanging ready near the fire, the jars of poultices and ointments that had been made during the night. All the work that had been done while she was resting. Guilt prickled—she shouldn't have left him.

"Do you want to take a break? I can sit with him."

"I just had a break. Mathos sat with Val while I slept. I've only been back long enough to check on his dressings and settle in. And whatever you're thinking, you're wrong.

You were of no use to anyone last night. It was wise to recognize the strengths of others and to trust us with your brother."

Nim nodded slowly. She didn't know about any kind of wisdom, but she did recognize that the Hawks were full of strength. And she knew she could trust them with Val's life.

But why Mathos? Why not Tristan? She thought he'd been with Val. Honestly, the only reason she'd been able to go to sleep was because she thought he'd been looking after her brother for her.

She wanted to ask, but hesitated. Why had he still not come to find her? Where was he?

"Where are we?" she asked instead.

"Reece has a friend…."

She rolled her eyes. Of course he did.

Rafe snorted softly and continued, "…who has a brother in need of some quick cash, happy to loan us his farmhouse and take his family out of the city for a few days."

Thinking about Reece and his friends reminded her of the carriage drive to the palace. It was the last time she'd really spoken to Tristan. So much had happened since then. And now he was avoiding her.

She tried to shake it off, the stab of hurt. She should be worrying about Val, Alanna too, not Tristan. Shouldn't she?

Rafe watched her steadily, not speaking. As if he knew exactly what she was thinking. Gods, he probably did.

She lifted Val's hand and gave it a small kiss before settling it back on the covers and then gently sweeping his hair out of his face.

"He's doing as well as we could hope," Rafe murmured gently.

"Yes," she agreed and then added softly, "I can't ever thank you enough."

Rafe shook his head. "We should never have left him."

Nim smiled sadly—everyone had made mistakes. The Hawks had never had any kind of real choice, if they had stayed when Val was arrested, they would simply have been imprisoned with her brother. Val should have trusted them, trusted her, with the truth of what was happening at the palace, long before it got to that point.

She had already forgiven them all, now they needed to forgive themselves.

She leaned over and gave him a quick hug. "Thanks, Rafe, for everything you've done."

He nodded against her hair. Understanding. Then leaned back and gripped her shoulders to look at her intently. "You'll need to fight for him." Rafe's voice was low, but his expression was serious.

"Of course—"

"Not Val. Tristan."

"I, uh…," she stuttered and then closed her eyes and let her head fall forward as understanding slowly crept in. He was so convinced he was unworthy. So certain that the people who should have loved him would leave. He had thought Val's regard for him low enough that he could betray him. Maybe he had never allowed himself to trust that when she said that he was hers, she'd meant forever. And he would be punishing himself viciously for what had happened.

"Where is he?"

"He spent the night securing the farmhouse, setting up watches and working on escape plans. In between, he helped with Val. He checked on you several times."

"He didn't sleep?"

"No, and he won't let anyone treat his wound. Did you know that he got caught on the spikes at the bottom of the portcullis?" Rafe rooted through his pocket and then held his hand out toward her, passing her Val's ring. "He asked me to give you this."

Gods. It was worse than she thought.

"What about his nails?"

Rafe chuckled, his teeth showing white in the gloom. "You noticed."

She didn't bother to respond. And Rafe didn't seem to expect her to. Instead, he gave her a gentle nudge with his shoulder. "Val's sleeping and won't move for some hours. I'll watch him."

"You'll call me if anything changes?"

He dipped his chin. "You know I will."

Chapter Twenty-Three

STANDING on top of the ramshackle old mill gave Tristan a good view of the farmhouse buildings, with their picturesque red bricks, thatched roofs, and low eaves.

Looking further, he scanned the copse of woods leading to the small dirt road, the nearby wheat fields lying bare since the autumn harvest, the tinkling stream running beside the path that led to the jetty, and the wide, muddy Tamasa river.

The pale morning sky, streaked with clouds, contrasted against the dark reds and golds of the ancient oaks and beech trees surrounding the homestead, while a woodpecker drummed a rolling tattoo somewhere in the distance.

He supposed it could have been beautiful, probably was beautiful, if it didn't all seem so unreal. Like a scene in a play or a book.

A moment of stillness, outside reality.

The reality that he had lost Nim. That Val was broken. And somewhere not that far away, outside this strange bubble, there was an army bearing down on them all.

He swept his eyes slowly over the woods and river, checking for threats. He would not fail them again.

It was the only thing keeping him going after two nights without sleep and enough fear, loss, and anguish to bring him to his knees.

He had put everyone else onto a roster, sleeping in shifts and working in teams. The two Mabin had taken the boat downriver and flown back while the others cared for the horses, took turns as sentries, and worked in the damp darkness of the tumbledown mill house. Thank the gods that the owners had let it go to ruin.

He had worked alongside them. Taken lead on every task. But skipped the sleep. There was no way he could rest until they were finished. Until he knew that she would be safe.

Now, they were finally ready. Mathos and Jeremiel had laid the last stone and slipped quietly into the house to rest. Leaving him alone. Watching.

Rafe had been clear that moving Val would set him back days, if not kill him. His fever was raging, and he needed to sleep. He needed to stay cool and dry and still; they could not risk him on the river. Otherwise Tristan would have had them moving already.

Instead, he made plans. Kept watch. And worried.

He scanned the forest once more. With a bit of luck, they would have a few days before the king could find this isolated homestead. And he'd already told Rafe that they would be moving out in the morning—Val had to be ready.

The back of his shoulder throbbed relentlessly. He knew he'd have to get it seen to soon if he didn't want it to fester. But he'd needed the pain to help him stay awake and focused during the long hours before dawn.

The front door of the farmhouse opened, and he

watched for Rafe or Tor; both would be joining him soon. Jos was supposed to be finding food for everyone, and the others were either watching the perimeter or sleeping, their bedrolls spread out over the floor of the large formal parlor at the front of the house.

But it wasn't any of his men that walked through the door.

Her dark chocolate braid fell over her shoulder, wings held softly at her back, her chin tilted as she looked around, getting her bearings. Nim.

It shouldn't have hurt to see her standing in the weak sunlight, but it did.

She took in the farmhouse, the surrounding farmland and woods, and then swept her gaze along the small tributary that fed into the wide Tamasa. She paused at the old mill, taking in its mossy stone walls and abandoned machinery, and then, inevitably, looked up.

Her face set, and she took a step toward him.

He knew that he could climb down and walk away before she reached him, but he couldn't bring himself to do that to her.

Or he could do what he really wanted, which was fall to his knees at her feet and beg her to forgive him for abandoning Val. For abandoning her. But he didn't deserve her forgiveness. He didn't deserve her at all.

He had gone to check on her in the night, long enough to see that she was completely passed out each time, sleeping the deep sleep of shock and physical exhaustion. And then he had turned away, filling the long hours with everything he could think of to keep her safe. To keep Val safe. And to avoid them both.

Now he stayed where he was, waiting for her judgment.

She walked slowly away from the house, toward the mill,

head down. He wished he could see her face, have some idea of what she was thinking. But he couldn't. He could only watch from above, chest aching.

She paused at the bottom of the mill, assessing. And then surprised him by unfurling her wings and launching straight up into the air.

Gods, she was so beautiful, strong and powerful as she sailed smoothly through the air. Yet still so delicate and vulnerable, almost lost inside too-big men's clothes, no boots, dark rings circling her eyes.

He reached out a hand to catch her as she landed on the ancient thatch and left it circling her waist for just a moment too long before letting it fall slowly away.

Being next to her was torture. The overwhelming conflict between wanting to wrap himself around her and wanting to get far away from her before she could say the words that finished whatever they'd had between them was killing him.

He was desperate to step back and give himself some space, but he didn't want to leave her standing on the roof without support. She was tired, and the roof was old and slippery.

"I have wings," she said softly.

He raised an eyebrow. He had no idea what she was talking about.

"If I fall, I'll just fly down."

He grunted, not knowing how to reply. She was right. She could fly. And he should step back. And he would. Very soon.

"Show me your hands," she demanded in her low, slightly husky voice.

This conversation was not going as he'd expected, in any way. But he couldn't say no to her. He lifted his hands slowly, fingers pointing up, palms toward her, surrendering.

She stretched out and gently laced her slim fingers between his, her hands warm and soft against his, locking him in place in front of her. Trapping him. Now he couldn't step back, despite needing to even more desperately.

He closed his eyes so he didn't have to look at her. That serious look on her face. So sad and tired. And so determined.

And then opened them again immediately when he felt a soft warmth against his fingertips. She had leaned forward to kiss them.

He shuddered helplessly, falling into the blissful absence of pain. The dull throbbing in his hands that he had simply ignored for so many hours was gone.

He twisted his hands gently, still intertwined with hers, and saw that the brutal claws had finally retracted. Leaving bruises and dried blood, but, thank the gods, his own normal hands.

She leaned her smooth forehead against their clasped hands. "I came to say I'm sorry."

"What?" Fuck. He felt like a caveman. He literally had a one-word vocabulary. And he hadn't meant to grumble at her. But nothing was making any sense.

"I'm sorry for how I reacted when I saw Tor."

How was this something they were even talking about? "You had every right—"

"No." Her smooth cheek rubbed against his fingers as she shook her head. "I didn't. I knew you would come back for me, and when you did… well, I reacted badly, and I'm sorry."

He couldn't get his head around what she was saying.

"You knew I'd come back?" Was it even possible after how she'd looked at him? Called for him?

"Of course."

"You didn't think I betrayed you?"

"Well. Maybe for a moment." She gave him a rueful look, eyes soft and shining. "It was very hard to see you standing there, just letting them…." She must have felt how all his muscles clenched, because she paused and gave herself a shake before continuing. "But then I saw your nails."

"My nails?"

"Your claws. Didn't you notice?"

"Only later. But I don't—"

"If you had known what was coming, you would never have reacted like that. And I realized that sometimes you have to leave a person so that you can live to go back. You have to trust in their strength until you return. And that's what you did."

She leaned forward and kissed his fingertips again. "I knew you would come back. I just didn't know whether Tor was trying to help or…." Her voice shook, and it broke his resolve. He tugged her closer, against his chest, and rested his cheek against her soft hair.

Her body nestled against his, warm and soft. Completely unguarded.

Everything he wanted. And couldn't have.

He pressed a tender kiss on the top of her head, soaking her in before he forced himself to say the words. "Nim, I did betray you."

Her head shook under his chin. "I know you didn't."

"Not then, no. But the truth is…." He pushed her back just far enough that he could, finally, look her in the eye. Those beautiful, silver-flecked midnight blue eyes. "The truth is that you would never have been there in the first place if it weren't for me. And neither would Val."

He kissed her forehead and then pushed her slowly back. "I don't deserve your forgiveness."

She was silent for a long time, her eyes searching his while his heart thudded hard against his ribs and he waited for her to recognize the truth and step away.

Eventually she sighed softly and leaned her forehead against his chest, their hands still clasped together between them. "I was very angry with you."

He couldn't find it in him to even grunt a response.

"But then I remembered Val, that last time he came home. So different. So angry and sad. He refused to tell me what was happening, and I still don't properly understand… but what I do know is that he refused to talk to you too. You were lied to by your king, Tris, without the benefit of whatever it was that Val already knew."

She raised an elegant shoulder in a small shrug of helplessness before continuing, "The last thing Val told me before he left was that if I ever needed help, I should go to you. It wasn't you that burned down my house or chained up my brother or wanted to… to…."

Suddenly he couldn't stand the space he had created between them. Without thinking, he let go of her hands and wrapped his arms around her, pulling her tightly against him. Not so firmly that she couldn't step back, but tight enough that he could feel her, know she was safe.

"All you've done is try to help," she said quietly against his chest. "You came all the way here to get Val, and you've exiled yourself and your entire squad to get us out."

"No. Nim, I came with you to show you… fuck, I don't want to say it."

"You were going to prove that Val was guilty. I know. I

always knew. But it was enough that you believed in *me*, you wanted to help *me*. When you saw what was happening, you saved us both. We're only alive because of you."

He wanted to accept her words. To think that there was any way that she didn't hate him. But he couldn't see how that would be possible.

"Has it occurred to you that if you stayed with Val after Ravenstone, they would have imprisoned you too? And then who would have come to save us?" she asked gently.

He stilled. Maybe, just maybe, there was a chance.

She looked up at him, still so serious. "I forgive you for the mistakes you made, Tristan."

He looked back down at her, almost daring to hope. This was Nim, and she never lied.

And then she turned her face and kissed him right over his thudding heart. And then again, on his sternum, as if following his frantic pulse, and then, rising to her toes, on his neck and up to his jaw.

It was too much. He wrapped his hand around her braid and tugged until she lifted her face and he could seal his lips over hers. She opened immediately, pouring herself, her light, into him, and all he could do was hold on, revel in having her against him.

He lost himself in the feel of her, the warm, clean scent of her skin. The rush of overwhelming joy that she was, inexplicably, unbelievably, somehow still his.

He tugged at the small ribbon on her braid until it opened and her hair fell loose down her back in a shining wave of silk that he buried his hands into, angling her head so that he could take her mouth more thoroughly as she moaned, that same low, husky sound that drove him insane.

Her wings came up and around them, creating a cocoon

of privacy as he ravished her, standing in front of all the world up there on the roof.

Fuck. The thought had him pulling away, breathing hard. "Not here. It's not safe."

Her swollen lips quirked up at the side, her eyes twinkling, and he took that as agreement.

He climbed down the side of the mill, jumping over piles of old stone left from some long-forgotten project as she flew down far more elegantly. Then he took her small hand in his and pulled her at a half-run back to the house.

Mathos and Jos were standing together in the hallway, and Tristan had a sudden strong urge to shove Nim behind him where they couldn't see her. Couldn't see her mussed hair and flushed cheeks.

She was *his*.

His men knew better than to push him when he was so close to the edge. Neither one of them so much as glanced at her.

Mathos cleared his throat. "Captain, we've assigned a roster of watches. You're off duty."

He gave a rough grunt, grateful and hoping they knew it, and then pulled Nim up the stairs.

"Val is still asleep. I'll call you if anything changes," Jos called from behind them.

He didn't know if the reassurance was for him or Nim, but he appreciated it. Especially when he saw Nim's shoulders soften ever so slightly.

And then they were in her room.

He pushed the door shut and locked it before turning slowly. She was standing next to the bed, waiting for him, and he stalked slowly toward her. The beast inside him dropping its relentless vigilance for the first time since their carriage had reached the palace gates.

He no longer had the rush of danger flooding his veins. Instead he had a roaring hunger. And only one person in the world could sate it.

She must have seen it in his face, because she laughed and then took off running around the bed.

His response was entirely instinct. He flung himself at her, catching her as she reached the corner. He pulled her against his body and then threw her onto the mattress as she giggled breathlessly.

He crawled over her, his beast pushing hard against his skin, as she squirmed beneath him, caged between his arms. He lowered his head to suck hotly at her neck. Mark her as his.

Her giggles faded into panting breaths as he moved lower, running his open mouth down her throat, over her pulse, tasting her skin.

He lifted a hand and stared hard at his fingers, willing claws, and the beast responded. He gave a satisfied grunt and then ran the blade-sharp points ever so slowly up the middle of her shirt, tearing off the buttons one at a time until it fell open, revealing the soft creaminess of her breasts, the dark rose of her puckered nipples.

He drew one perfect nipple into his mouth and worried it with his teeth, sucking and laving against it until he released it to stand hard and wet. He turned to her other breast as she arched and whimpered beneath him.

A slow flush spread over her chest as she groaned, and a deep, possessive rumble vibrated through him. Fuck, she was beautiful.

He retracted his claws and ran his sensitized fingertips over the soft curves of her waist and into the band of her trousers, reveling in everything about her. Her smooth skin, her hungry moans.

She lifted her hips, and he drew the too-loose trousers down, taking her socks with them, off her body in one movement before returning to lay succulent kisses over her belly, flicking his tongue through her belly button and along the ridges of her lower ribs before meandering slowly down again.

He slid down and pushed her thighs open, and she let her legs fall apart, her blue eyes half-closed with lust. His cock ached as he nuzzled against the sublime skin of her inner thigh and bit gently on the apex of her leg, then nosed, slowly, through her tight curls, luxuriating in her scent, her intoxicating flesh, before running his tongue, hot and slow, through her folds.

Her hips jerked, and he wrapped his arms around her thighs, holding her open as he tasted her again and again, relishing her soft whimpers, the way her hips shuddered and pushed up against his mouth.

Releasing one thigh, he used his free hand to hold her open as he swirled his tongue around her clit, twisting and torturing as she panted, and then, achingly slowly, sank a finger deep into her.

Her hips pushed restlessly against him as he drew his finger back out and then added a second and smoothly thrust again, searching for just the right.... Her eyes closed, fists clenching in the bedding beneath her as she arched her back and moaned helplessly. That was it.

He thrust again, pumping slowly as he flicked his tongue against her clit, the sweet musky taste of her arousal flooding his senses as he took her right to the edge, and then before she could go over, he pulled back. He had to be inside her when she came.

She whimpered in protest and he ran his tongue up her quivering belly, through the channel between her breasts, soothing her with hungry kisses and the vibrating rumble of his beast, before returning to her mouth to ravish her with open, panting kisses. Kisses that tasted of Nim and hunger as she kissed him back, her tongue sliding against his in an all-consuming sensuous dance.

He pulled himself completely over her, and then balanced on one arm to guide her legs onto his shoulders, first one side, then the other, until he was holding himself over her. Nim completely open beneath him, his aching cock nudging at the wet heat of her entrance. This was what he needed, to feel her under him, held within his arms, connected to him in every way.

"Open your eyes, Nim." His voice was half beast. "Look at me."

Her eyes fluttered open, pupils wide with lust, her lips swollen and cheeks flushed, dark hair spread all around her. He had never imagined anything so breathtaking. It was the first time he had ever said the words to another person, but he couldn't hold them back. "I love you."

She smiled, the slow, glorious smile that he had never thought to see again, and whispered, "I love you too."

Her hands ran slowly up his arms to grip his shoulders, as he sank, devastatingly slowly, into the clenching heat of her body. Never once losing that scorching eye contact.

It was exquisite. Overwhelming. Ecstatic. And he lost any kind of control as he impaled her, twisting his hips and ravishing her in a relentless sensual rhythm of two bodies meeting each other in every possible way. Desperate for each other.

Sweat broke out on his back as he pumped into her, her breathless moans becoming sharp little cries and grunts that penetrated all the way down to the beast in his soul.

He shifted back to grasp her legs, pulling her closer

while he thrust, his eyes still locked on hers, until she shuddered, crying out his name, and then clenched around him, convulsing.

He rode it as long as he could. Surrounded by her. Almost entirely lost in her. The base of his spine tingled, and he started to pull away, but she tightened her grip, holding him close. "Stay." Her voice rasped breathlessly as she held him deep inside her body.

Gods. She was everything. This moment was everything. He lost his rhythm, his body shuddering as he flew right over the edge with her, climaxing together in a wave of helpless ecstasy.

He eased back, letting her legs drop, and then rolled them to the side to wrap his arms around her, holding her tight against him.

Their breaths slowed, muscles relaxing, her heated body entwined with his. He had never lost control like that before. Hadn't imagined it would be possible.

He lowered himself down her body, reveling in the delicate smoothness of her skin, until he could lie between her legs and spread soft, adoring kisses over her belly. Gods. She had given him everything.

She propped her head on a pillow to watch him before letting her hands sink into his hair, running through the too-long strands, scratching delicately at his scalp.

Never in his life had he experienced such a powerful rush of feeling.

Both overwhelming protectiveness—the need to keep her safe drove every decision he would ever make—and also the knowledge that she forgave him, accepted him. Wanted him. Stayed with him.

Tristan lifted his head so that he could watch her face as he said it again. "I love you. Don't ever forget." The warmth of her smile was everything he could ever have dreamed of hoping for.

He nuzzled her belly again and then rested his cheek against her softness. "I didn't take any precautions."

"I know." He could hear the pleasure in her voice.

"If there is a child, you know that every single one of the Hawks would treat him like their own family."

"Or her." She chuckled, and he felt the vibrations through her body like the physical manifestation of joy.

He grunted. Or her. Gods. A little girl with dark hair and blue eyes. He wrapped his arms around Nim's thighs and held her tighter.

Nim curled her slim fingers around his chin and turned him to face her. "And the best daddy in the world."

He couldn't reply. And he didn't want her to see the hot moisture in his eyes. Instead, he crawled back up her body and kissed her again.

Chapter Twenty-Four

NIM TOOK another bite of the sandwich Jos had brought and nudged Tristan with her knee. She had cleaned and bandaged his shoulder before they got dressed, and now they were sitting together beside Val's bed, Tristan's long legs stretched out next to hers as they ate.

Her brother twitched restlessly, sometimes speaking in garbled, panicked tones, and she wished there were something, anything, that she could do. But even though her heart hurt for him, she still felt better than she had for weeks. Tristan loved her, and she had Val back.

The only shadow still hanging over them was having had to leave the queen behind, but Tristan had agreed that they would sit down with the squad that evening and decide what to do.

A sharp series of whistles cut through the air, and she felt Tristan go instantly from peaceful and relaxed to ominously stiff, his scales rippling up his arms in a dark wave.

She tried to keep the worry out her voice as her heart rate picked up. "What's happening?"

He turned to look at her, his face a mask of shocked torment. "They found us."

"Already?" How was that even possible?

Tristan stood. "I thought we had longer. Hoped for enough time…." He glanced down at the bed, and she knew what he didn't want to say. They would have moved already if Val had been in any fit state to travel.

Nim climbed to her feet, joining Tristan as footsteps thumped up the stairs and Mathos crashed into the room.

"You have to move." Tristan's second-in-command wore a harsh expression that ramped up Nim's fear more than anything else. She had never seen him look so serious.

"Thirty seconds." Tristan's voice was rough and low, and he didn't take his eyes off hers.

Mathos was not impressed. "There's no time!"

"Thirty. Seconds."

"Fuck. Fine. I'll get the stretcher." Mathos stalked out the door, calling orders.

Tristan tilted her chin up with his thumb and then leaned down to brush his lips over hers. "I love you."

She gripped his arms, feeling the muscles clench under her hands, and wished she could fly them all away somehow. Wished, desperately, for more time. "I love you too."

"Do you remember your promise? That you would do what I say if there's danger?"

She dipped her head slowly, heart thudding even more heavily. She remembered. Even if she was certain she was going to regret it.

"I need you to honor that promise now."

She looked into the dark green of his eyes, the jagged

scar on his left cheek an angry reminder of the brutal life he'd lived. He was formidable. And so easy to hurt.

Her voice was subdued. "I don't want to."

"You must do this. For me. For Val."

She took a breath and released it slowly. She wanted to fight, but she was untrained and would only distract him, and she knew he was right: Val needed her. "What do you want us to do?"

The relief on his face squeezed her heart more painfully than Grendel's chains ever had.

The door swung open, Mathos was back with Garet, carrying a rough stretcher between them, Rafe following closely behind. In seconds they had Val lifted and were carrying him out the door as Rafe threw all the jars of ointments, bandages, even a blanket into a large leather satchel.

Tristan guided her after the stretcher as Rafe did a last sweep of the room. It was as if they had never been there.

They ran down the stairs as doors slammed behind them. After each slam, a loud voice called, "Clear!" and Nim knew the whole house would be pristine within minutes.

They reached the front door just as Tor dragged a pale Keely through it, and they followed at a jog. Everything happened so fast. The squad coordinating with each other effortlessly, as if they'd evacuated a hundred times before. Nim followed, slipping into a strange sense of calm as they flew across the courtyard and into the old mill house.

It was damp and gloomy inside. A single lamp stood on an old barrel, its dim light throwing flickering shadows along the rusted cogs and gears of the abandoned mill.

Ahead of her, she saw Tor guide Keely to a small

opening in the back wall. The other woman ducked and crawled forward.

Tristan dropped a fleeting kiss on the top of her head and then nudged her to follow.

Nim could feel her hands shaking as she dropped to her knees and pushed her way into the shallow opening. It was a small hollow between the two stone walls—the existing outer wall and a new false wall inside the shadowy mill—creating a safe hiding place.

But it was not big enough for everyone. Gods. The thought rose, and then had to be set aside as the stretcher carrying Val was passed in. The men grunted and cursed as they struggled with the narrow opening, and Nim tried to guide it into the constricted space. The stretcher caught on a stone, jostling heavily, and Val gave a long, pained groan.

Nim ran her fingers down his face soothingly, whispering that he would be okay, and he settled back into a fitful sleep.

Finally, the three of them were in. Rafe appeared, kneeling at the entrance, and passed her the bag of bandages and ointments. He disappeared for a moment, then returned to pass her an unlit candle, another blanket, several flasks of water. And then he was gone.

Tristan's face appeared, scales gleaming on his clenched jaw in the dim light, deep forest green flecked with pewter. She wanted to touch him, but she couldn't reach him over Val's stretcher in the tight space.

"I'm sorry." His voice was grim. "You can't risk a light."

"Okay." She tried to keep the waver out of her voice.

"Take this." He passed her a thin blade. It had a curled pewter hilt set with a trio of rubies, and she knew it had been his grandfather's. He'd played with it as a boy, so many years before.

She gripped it tightly. "Thank you."

"When it's time, you can kick away the stones we're going to lay—there's no lime between them, and we've put in a support beam so that the rest of the wall will hold. I'm putting some old wheat sacks in front of the new stones to hide them. You'll need to move them."

His scales were over his face, and his claws were back. Gods.

She wanted to cry and beg and demand that they all hide. Or that they might run, now, together. But she knew that Val couldn't be moved, and that this was Tristan's last resort plan. If he thought this was their best option, then it was. She did her best to keep her voice from shaking as she replied, "I understand."

"Remember what I said. I love you. And I want you to know that I will never walk away from you, Nim—but I will fight for you."

Nim nodded, not trusting herself to reply.

He closed his eyes for a moment, throat working as if he was going to say more. But he didn't.

And then he was gone.

There was a rough scraping noise as stones were quickly added to the wall, the gap narrowing and then disappearing with a final thud. She had expected total darkness, but the old stone wall had small chinks and cracks that let in dusty shards of dim gray light.

The low voices of the Hawks murmured in muffled conversation, at first in the mill, and then outside the farmhouse as they finished their speedy preparations.

It had been less than ten minutes since the first sentry's whistle.

She looked over at Keely. Her ashen face was smeared

with dirt where she had wiped it after their crawl, and she was holding her bandaged arm protectively.

Val whimpered, and the horrifying thought occurred to her that someone might hear him. She passed a blanket to Keely, who wrapped it around her shoulders, and then they spread the other one out over Val. Next, she rifled through the bag Rafe had given her and found the sleeping draught. She lifted Val's head and poured a little into his mouth, waited for him to swallow, and then gave him more.

She was giving him the last mouthful when Keely went rigid next to her. A few seconds later, she heard it herself. Hoofbeats.

She leaned back against the cold stone and waited, wishing she could see what was happening, or do something to help. But she knew that being found with the Hawks would only guarantee their deaths.

Outside, everything was still for one last moment.

Then there was a thundering of hooves and horn calls. Shouted commands, jangling of bits, and then the thuds of men dismounting in the dusty courtyard.

"I thought I'd find you here." She shivered at the sound of that hated voice. Grendel.

Keely's small hand nudged her arm, and she took it thankfully, and they clung to each other in the darkness.

"Where else would I be?" Tristan's voice sounded cool and arrogant.

"I told you to go to the barracks."

"We tried it. Liked it better here."

"And where is here exactly?" Grendel asked.

"The home of a friend of my father's. He loaned it to us while we found our place back among the Blues."

"Is that so?" Nim could just imagine Grendel's oily sneer as he raised his voice and commanded, "Search the house!"

Boots thudded, doors slammed, something smashed. None of the Hawks responded.

And then a new voice. "It's clear."

"What?" Grendel demanded, voice dripping with annoyed disbelief.

"There's nothing."

"Try the outbuildings."

More boots stomped past, men shouted. The door to the millhouse slammed open. Something thudded, perhaps a barrel being tipped. Chains clanked, and the rotting floorboards shook under the onslaught of stamping boots. Dust filtered down through the tiny shards of light.

Beside her, Val twitched restlessly, and Nim pressed her free hand firmly over his mouth, bending to kiss his forehead silently, trying to reassure him and keep him still.

Long moments passed as she desperately willed him to stay quiet.

And then the noises faded, footsteps receded.

"Clear."

"Clear."

"Nothing here, m'lord, sir."

Nim felt her aching shoulders drop ever so slightly.

"They must be here!" Grendel's voice snarled as he ordered, "Archers, cover them."

The Hawks, wisely, remained silent.

"You were seen last night," Grendel announced.

"I was in the palace last night." Tristan's voice gave away nothing. "It's entirely to be expected that I'd be seen."

"You were seen in the kitchen with the prisoners… helping them to escape."

"The Hawks were helping upstairs, nowhere near the kitchen. Plenty of people saw us there."

"The cook identified you. She saw a Tarasque captain

escaping with the prisoners." Nim could imagine the smug look on Grendel's sneering face.

"She could have seen anyone. Surely there is more than one Tarasque officer in the palace guard? How would she have even known a captain in the dark? Or particularly identified me?" Tristan still sounded calm and logical. "Why don't you tell us how they escaped, and maybe we can help you?"

The silence stretched for so long that Nim wondered if Grendel might be convinced. But then he laughed, an oily, patronizing sound.

"Ah, Tristan, I do like watching a man squirm. But it doesn't matter now. We know it was you. A young noblewoman and her brother had an audience first thing this morning with the king. You might remember Helaine?"

Nim raised an eyebrow to Keely, who gave a single shake of her head.

Grendel continued, "Apparently she had a most fascinating visit from young Corporal Reece. He was looking for somewhere safe for his squad to stay. Somewhere on the river, not too far from the palace, easy to reach by boat... all very urgent and secret. I believe they were able to help."

Gods. That was how they found them so quickly. Poor Reece was going to be devastated.

"You know, Corporal Reece," Grendel mocked, "you really shouldn't break a woman's heart and then expect her to help you. Women are very... fragile.

"And now, well... you know what the penalty is for conspiracy. Guards, take Corporal Reece into custody."

"No." Tristan's voice rang out clearly, and Nim knew. Knew exactly what he was about to do. What he had always meant to do.

Remember everything I said... You promised... The Hawks will treat him like their own family... I love you.

She wanted to hold her hands over her ears so that she didn't have to hear what he would say next. She wanted to scream and drown out his words. But she didn't. She held her courage together by a thread and listened as he spoke.

"This has nothing to do with anyone else. Corporal Reece had no idea what the house was for; he was simply following orders. Your prisoners are not here. I sent them away. *I* freed them, and *I* put them on a boat to escape. And I did it by myself."

A rough grumble followed his words, but Tristan grunted, loudly, and the noise died away, leaving only the snuffling of the horses.

"Follow the river. Find the boat," Grendel ordered, and several horses thundered away.

"You don't want to arrest the whole squad. It will look bad for the king. People will think he has no loyalty among his men," Tristan reasoned, voice gruff and low.

There was a moment of loaded silence.

Finally, Grendel spoke. "That's true. Consider your men dishonorably discharged. As for you, Tristan, you can join the queen in the cells. It turns out that Alanna set a fire in her rooms with the intention of drugging and murdering her husband. She's already been found guilty of attempted regicide and sentenced to death. Isn't that nice? Now you can hang together."

Nim felt herself go cold with devastation and remorse, as Keely began to shudder beside her. They were going to kill Alanna after all. Alanna who they'd left behind, thinking that they had time. Thinking she was safe from Ballanor and Grendel's machinations. Gods.

Alanna was not safe, not at all, and now she was going

to be executed. And Tristan too. Her fists clenched painfully as she fought her need to get to Tristan. Get to him and save him.

A chain clanked, and something thudded. Tristan groaned, a harsh grating noise, and she closed her eyes helplessly. They were hurting him.

A scuffle broke out, and she wished desperately that she could see what was happening. But then Tristan spoke again. "Stand down. All of you."

"No, I don't trust you to stay out of this. Go into the house," Grendel ordered.

There was another scuffle. Swords being drawn.

"Archers, shoot anyone that isn't in the house in the next ten seconds."

"Do it," Tristan ordered. "Move!"

There was the sound of boots marching over the sand. A door slammed. Keely shivered relentlessly beside her. And Val twitched restlessly in his sleep.

"Bar the house."

She could hear scraping and banging as the doors were barred, windows shuttered. Then hammering as if they were being nailed closed.

Nim stroked Val's cheek and counted seconds. Surely by now Grendel knew that no one could follow. He would leave at any moment. Surely.

The banging stopped and she let out a shaky breath. And then gasped at Grendel's horrifying next order. "Archers. Fire the roof. Aim through the upstairs windows."

"No!" Tristan's hoarse cry was anguished. "You have what you want!"

"Give me Lanval and the girl, and I'll let them out."

Nim felt her breathing go shallow and panicked, her

palms slick with fear. How could Tristan possibly make this choice?

"I can't!" He sounded broken.

Gods. She couldn't do it. Couldn't leave him out there alone. She climbed over Val and started to kick at the fresh stones of the false wall, praying that no one would hear her in the chaos outside. Praying that Keely and Val would remain undiscovered when she was gone.

The men in the house were shouting, beating at the door.

And then she heard a soft, infinitely terrifying crackling. The thatch had caught.

She kicked harder. One stone fell free. A few smaller stones tumbled down, but the rest held.

She paused for a few seconds, waiting to see if anyone had heard her, but the men's bellows and the hissing, snapping flames drowned out the noise.

Someone was shouting orders, but she couldn't hear what was said over the sound of her own heart beating and the thump of her feet against the stones. Two more hard kicks, and the next big stone fell forward.

It was small, but it was a hole.

She looked over her shoulder to see that Keely had moved into her place, holding Val's hand. "Stay here," she whispered, and Keely nodded, ghostlike in the dim light.

She furled her wings as tightly as she could and then slithered desperately over the rough stones. The skin on her hands tore on the ragged edges, and her wings caught and scraped, but she didn't stop.

She had to get out. Get to Grendel. Hand herself in. Save Tristan.

Her heart thudded in her ears as she pulled herself the

last few inches and tipped forward into a mildewed pile of old sacks. And then she was up and running.

Daylight blasted her eyes as she scrambled out of the mill and into the dusty courtyard.

It was empty.

Gods. She was too late.

No. Not too late. The house was blazing, flames leaping from the roof in a hellish play of heat and smoke. But it wasn't down yet.

The door and windows were barred with heavy slabs of oak roughly hammered into the frames. As she watched, the door bulged as if hit by a ram, but the bars held.

She couldn't get in that way.

She ran around to a side window. The shutters were nailed closed, but it been done too quickly, most of the effort going into the sealing the door. She ripped at the wood with her hands, cursing at the splinters tearing through her already broken skin.

It didn't open.

She called out to the men but couldn't hear anything over the vicious crackle of the flames.

Then she remembered. She ran to the side of the house and found the ax, right next to the stone, left there the night before. She hefted it in a frenzy, sprinted back to the window and brought it down in a wide swing, smashing it against the shutters. The wood flew apart in a storm of splinters, and she swung again, crashing the ax into the thick leaded glass and shattering it into a thousand shining pieces.

Smoke billowed from the opening, but she didn't hesitate. She climbed over the broken shards into the house, screaming for the Hawks. The first face she saw was Tor's. Thank the gods. He turned, still holding the end of the table they were using as a battering ram on the front door, and noticed her.

He shouted something that she couldn't hear, and then they were all moving, a flood of Hawks. The men she was coming to see as brothers. Tor passed her and dived through the small opening, and she leaned over, resting her hands on her knees as she coughed in the smoke and heat, thankful he was out.

She waved Mathos forward, but he simply picked her up and threw her out the window to be caught safely by the huge Apollyon and gently placed on her feet as the others poured out around her.

Without thinking, she reached up, wound her arms around Tor, and hugged him. He was safe. They were all safe. She felt his arms circle her tentatively and then, slowly, hold her tighter.

They stood like that for a moment, lightheaded with relief and still coughing from the smoke, and then stumbled into the courtyard with the rest of the men.

They watched, transfixed, as the roof beams collapsed and the whole house shuddered before slowly falling in on itself.

"Well. Fuck," said a familiar voice at her ear. She turned to see Mathos give her a wink. "Thanks, darlin'."

She started to laugh, a hysterical half sob that turned into a choking wheeze until Rafe threw Mathos a dirty look and rubbed her back gently as he pulled her toward the mill stream.

Keely emerged just as they got there, and the two women folded each other in a brief hug, grateful to be alive.

Garet and Jeremiel followed, carrying Val on his stretcher, and Nim kissed her brother gently on the forehead before collapsing to her knees next to the stream, joining the men in taking great gulping sips of the cold, clear water.

All except Reece, who was standing a few paces away. Blue scales covered his folded arms, up his neck and on to his cheeks—and his face was grim and bleak. Her heart ached for him, but there was no time to go to him. Tristan was her priority.

She lifted a last handful of water to her face and tried to wash away some of the soot and grime, wincing at the sting in her shredded palms, then hauled herself up to standing. She had to get to Tristan before Grendel got him back to the palace.

Before she could take a step, Mathos was there, blocking her way. "No. Whatever crazy plan you're hatching, the answer is no."

She laid a hand on his arm, grimacing as her torn flesh protested. "I'm not leaving him."

"He wouldn't want you to go back there. You stay here with Keely and Val, and we'll get him."

Nim took a breath and did her best to stay calm. "Absolutely not. I'm not staying here to be coddled while Tristan needs me."

Mathos folded his arms, scales rippling up the defined muscles. "Tristan would want me to keep you safe."

Nim lifted her hand to cup Mathos's rough cheek, feeling the rigid tension in his jaw. "That's true, but it doesn't mean he'd be right. Tristan has spent his whole life constantly expecting to be abandoned—I'm going to show him that I will always come back to him. This is something I need to do. For him, and for me."

The Hawks frowned down at her, listening intently.

She turned slowly, making eye contact with all of them. "As far as Grendel's concerned, the Hawks just died in a fire.

This is your chance, your only chance, to get out of this. If you go back and are seen, they'll be coming after you for the rest of your lives. And anyway, someone needs to stay here to take care of Val. And Keely."

"We can't let—"

Nim raised a dirty eyebrow—no one "let" her do things, not anymore.

"Fuck. You really are just like each other," Mathos grumbled.

"I'm better on my own anyway," Nim added. "They'll see a squadron a mile off. But the last thing they'll expect is me on my own."

"No, I still can't accept this." Jos had his wings folded back rigidly; his teeth gritted, the consummate big brother. "Tristan would never forgive us. Honestly, I wouldn't forgive myself. And if you do rescue the captain, well, then we'll all be hunted along with him anyway."

Damn. He had a point. If she got Tristan free, soldiers would come back. They'd see that there were no bodies in the ruined farmhouse, and then they would all be hunted anyway. And the king would never stop looking for Val, whatever happened. She had wanted to keep them safe, but they would be better off working together.

She looked around the squad. "What if I go ahead with Garet and Jos? We'll make good time in the air. The rest of you can help Keely and Val and then follow."

Jeremiel nodded. "It makes sense. Grendel only brought Apollyon and Tarasque soldiers. If anything goes wrong, they can't follow you into the trees."

The men were silent as they all turned to look at Mathos.

Mathos nodded slowly. "Okay. You go ahead, and we'll follow."

She gave him a two-fingered salute that was only very slightly sarcastic.

"But you better fucking stay alive or the captain will kill all of us himself."

Nim dipped her chin. He didn't need to worry. She had every intention of staying alive and bringing Tristan back safely.

"Keely, pass me that bag."

Keely handed over the bulging satchel that Rafe had packed, and she rifled through it to find the small pot she knew was somewhere at the bottom. Then she pulled out Tristan's slim dagger and started to prepare.

She knew exactly what she had to do.

Chapter Twenty-Five

TRISTAN STUMBLED AGAIN. The last kick had caught him right on the knee, and he was struggling to bend it. It didn't help that he almost certainly had at least one broken rib. His shoulder throbbed where the previous night's gashes had reopened, while the long chain wrapped around his wrists and tied to the horse in front of him had rubbed his skin raw within the first few minutes of this hellish forced march.

But the pain in his body was nothing compared to the agony of seeing those flames licking the thatch on the farmhouse roof.

Grendel hadn't waited to see the end, and Tristan couldn't decide which was worse. To stand helplessly watching while his friends died—knowing that he had sent them to their death—or to be dragged away, leaving them to their fate.

At least Nim was free. And Val. Keely too. Although how long that would last was impossible to guess. An apothecary, an injured personal maid, and a half-dead

former soldier with nowhere to go, and the might of the
kingdom arrayed against them.

The broken boat they'd abandoned in the rapids during
the night, crashed into a rock and smeared with blood,
might fool the soldiers into thinking they were drowned. But
more likely not. At best it bought them a few hours.

He tried to remind himself that Nim was strong and
intelligent, and she was absolutely devoted to Val. She
would always prioritize him. If nothing else, her need to
save her brother would drive her.

It gave him a slim hope.

That, and the fact that Grendel had no idea how to lead
an army.

Take something as simple as leaving the burning
farmhouse. If he had ever sunk so low as to set fire to
unarmed men, Tristan would have stayed and made damn
sure that they were dead.

Not Grendel; no, he wanted to get back to his palace
comforts. He had been so quick to leave that he hadn't even
sent anyone to look for the horses, barely hidden in the
small woods behind the farmhouse.

Never mind that he and Ballanor had filled the palace
guard with so many of their cronies that they'd completely
forgotten about looking at anyone's actual abilities or skills.

Tristan had been able to send his Mabin flyers down the
Tamasa, but Grendel didn't have any. He'd had to split his
force and send riders to try and follow the river as it became
narrower and faster, increasingly difficult and dangerous to
ride alongside. They might take hours.

And it also meant that of the ten men that had arrived
at the farmhouse, only Grendel and five others remained.
And of them, only one seemed to be at all disciplined and
well trained. Pity it had to be the grim-faced Tarasque from

the bottom of the palace stairs, Dornar, who did not look at all pleased about their previous meeting.

Grendel wasn't just a sadistic tyrant, he was a fucking poor leader, incapable of putting together a decent squadron even for his own protection.

It was profoundly disturbing. This was the man that, with Ballanor, was taking the country to war.

A war that should have already been over. Was already over. Treaty signed. Marriage vows spoken.

Except that Ballanor had obviously never had any intention of keeping to the treaty. The whole thing had been a lie while he waited for the perfect moment to rid himself of King Geraint and take power for himself.

What a fuckup.

Tristan stumbled again and silently cursed bloody Val's hard head. If his friend had just confided in him, shared whatever it was that he had known, maybe they would have had some idea of what was coming. Been able to prepare for the lies that Ballanor and Grendel told.

He wished he'd known. Wished that he could go back in time to that terrible night and wait long enough to speak to Val, force him to tell him the truth about what the hell was going on.

Not that it changed anything. He still should have trusted his friend. At least he'd made it right before the end.

And Nim had forgiven him. Nim had loved him.

The chains around his wrist tugged hard, breaking into his thoughts as he almost fell. He only just managed to stumble into a lopsided jog, fast enough to almost reach the horse in front of him and gain some slack.

He tried to angle himself closer to Grendel. If there was a chance, anything at all, to take the bastard down, he would do it. He had nothing left to lose.

But Grendel side-stepped his horse and nodded to a nearby soldier, someone Tristan didn't recognize, who rode up beside him and whipped him hard across the shoulders with his riding crop while Grendel chuckled.

Fuck, he hated these men.

He looked at the smirking Apollyon soldier brandishing the crop and considered using his chain, wrapping it around the man's leg and pulling. It would break the soldier's leg at the very least. His beast rumbled in approval.

It was damn tempting. But it wouldn't be Grendel's leg. He'd rather wait. He looked away and tried to distract himself.

He didn't have long left, and he wanted to spend it remembering exactly what Nim's skin tasted like. What she smelled like. Her face as he sank into her. Those soft little husky whimpers.

The crop lashed him again, but he hardly felt it. He was imagining the feeling of her hair in his fingers. The warmth of her soft body pressed against his. The way she looked at him when she told him that she loved him.

Nothing else mattered.

They had almost reached the main road when Tristan began to feel an ominous prickle in his gut. His scales had covered him at the first sign of Grendel and his men, but now his new claws lengthened and the fine hairs on the back of his neck lifted.

He ran his gaze carefully up and down the dirt road but saw nothing.

Birds still sang. The wind rustled through the autumn leaves. But some deep part of himself knew that something was coming.

He let his eyes wander, slowly, over the surrounding woods, all while jogging relentlessly forward. Then immediately dropped his gaze and focused on his feet, anxiously hoping that no one was looking at him.

He lifted his eyes long enough to cast a quick look around the soldiers. Dornar watched him intently, eyes appraising.

Tristan blanked his face and looked toward the horse in front of him.

Don't look up. Don't look up. He repeated the litany in his head as if he could somehow force the soldier to keep his eyes away from the trees. Away from shivering branches of the massive beech tree near the road.

The perfect spot for a Mabin hunter. Surrounded by the last red-gold leaves of autumn. Difficult to see into from the ground unless you knew what you were looking for. And, for the hunter, no telltale noise of horses on the road, no suspect shadow to give them away.

Was it possible that Garet or Jos had made it out of the flames? Was there any chance that his friends could be alive?

It was almost too much, the bright torture of hope. He felt his breath catching on his broken ribs and tried to prepare himself. Whatever came next, he had to be ready.

But he was not ready. Not in any way.

When he saw Nim fling herself from the tree, wings arrowed as if she was a Hawk herself, or perhaps an avenging angel, he thought his heart would stop.

She fell fearlessly from above, smashed into a shocked Grendel with brutal force, and ripped him right out of his saddle, their momentum taking them both crashing to the stony ground.

Hard behind her came Jos and Garet, wings beating in huge sweeps as they hurled themselves at the soldiers that surrounded him.

A wild roar erupted, and Tristan vaguely realized that it was his own fierce howl of outraged fury as he threw himself into battle.

His chains were wrapped around the leg of the soldier next to him, and the man's shin shattered before he knew what he was doing. He hauled the soldier down from his horse and threw him bodily toward the melee as he screamed.

Stallions reared and neighed loudly as men bellowed, suddenly unseated. Somehow, in the chaos, his chain came free of the saddle horn it had been tied to and he was free to move.

He swung it in a wide loop, building up power as a massive Apollyon soldier stepped up in front of him. The guard's red and black tattoos rippled as he drew his sword, and his black eyes gleamed with satisfaction at Tristan's bloodied face and battered body.

But he didn't know that Tristan had trained with Tor nearly every day for years. Or that he stood between Tristan and his woman.

It was brutal and bloodthirsty, but the Apollyon didn't stand a chance. Tristan used his chain to whip and crush, dancing away from sword and fists, ignoring the grunting, clashing battle around him.

The guard swung hard, and Tristan jumped back as the sword whistled past him. Then, taking advantage of his attacker's moment of imbalance, he flung the heavy chain at the man's unprotected face, hearing the crunch of facial bones, the soldier's scream of agony as he collapsed. Good.

He spun back to see Jos deliver a brutal strike, almost decapitating the guard he'd been battling.

Garet's opponent turned and ran, throwing himself into

the saddle of the nearest warhorse and fleeing in a cloud of dust and flying hooves.

Garet took one step toward the fleeing man and then stopped, the color draining from his face.

Tristan gripped his chain and whirled to see what Garet was looking at just in time to see Dornar violently shoving Nim to the ground with a wicked blade pressed against her throat, forcing her to kneel in the dust. Beside them, Grendel heaved himself back to standing, face mottled puce with rage.

There was no way Tristan could attack either of them without risking Nim. One glance at Jos and Garet's horrified faces showed they knew it too.

Dornar narrowed his eyes, gripping his sword in one hand, the dagger against Nim's throat in the other. "Don't move or she dies."

They all froze. So close that Tristan could almost touch her. But still too far away.

Dorner gestured with his head. "Drop your swords, then get on your knees next to her. Hands behind your heads."

They dropped their weapons and slowly lowered themselves to the ground just a few feet from Nim. Tristan's chain dragged brutally as he linked his bleeding hands behind his head.

Dornar circled Nim, his dagger teasing a line around her slim throat as he pointed his sword at Tristan. Then, with one smooth step, he shifted his weight behind the men, pulling his dagger blade from Nim to Tristan's jugular, his sword still held high.

Grendel stepped up in front of them. He was covered in the dust of the road, his clothes ripped, a dark graze marring his temple where he'd fallen, insane with rage.

Grendel nodded to Dornar. "Keep them still."

Tristan's scales flickered in a roiling wave, and his hands throbbed where his claws had unsheathed, but Dornar had his blade pressed tight against his jugular, his sword arm extended toward Jos and Garet.

Grendel stepped in front of Nim and gripped her face, his fingers pressing brutally into her pale skin as he tipped her head back. "I should have killed you when I had the chance."

Tristan could see a tear rolling slowly down Nim's face as Grendel reached down with his free hand and started to loosen his belt.

Gods. There was no way he could watch this. He would rather die.

He slowly unlaced his fingers, tensing, as the beast inside him howled and Dornar pressed his dagger harder against his throat.

"Tris," Nim whispered, her eyes fixed on Grendel as he pulled his belt free. "Now!"

Tristan didn't think to question. He simply launched himself up and back, cracking his head back into Dornar's face as brutally hard as he could.

Dornar grunted in agony, rearing back enough to allow Tristan to duck and spin under his arm. He used his momentum to rip Dornar's knife hand around behind his back and force it up high between his shoulder blades.

Dornar dropped to one knee in Tristan's relentless grip as Jos and Garet rocketed to their feet, launching themselves toward Grendel.

But they were too late. Nim had hurled herself forward the moment the words left her lips, swept her arm up in a vicious undercut, and plunged a gleaming dagger, his grandfather's dagger, deep into Grendel's chest.

The king's favorite stood, shocked, hand still reaching

for his sword. He hadn't seen Nim as a threat—and he'd paid for it with a blade between his ribs.

But only a small blade. And Grendel was still standing.

Dornar thrashed wildly at Tristan's feet, trying and failing, to escape the brutal shoulder lock.

Jos and Garet lifted their weapons and circled Grendel, their faces drawn in savage bloodlust.

They would never allow Grendel to threaten Nim, nor any other woman, ever again. And nor would he.

The beast inside him crowed at the coming death of the monster that had terrorized his woman. But he didn't want her to watch. "Nim. Step back."

She did as he asked and stepped back as Grendel reached up and slowly drew the small dagger out by its hilt and dropped it in the dirt.

"Nim. Run."

His voice was dry and cracked, but he knew she had heard him. Yet she made absolutely no move backward. Fucking stubborn. They were going to discuss that. As soon as she was safe.

And then he saw Grendel falter. An unhealthy sheen broke out over his sneering face, and he began to tremble violently. Grendel swallowed loudly and then clutched his chest, his breath wheezing as he staggered to the side and then sat heavily, looking stunned, as Jos and Garet watched him warily.

Tristan wrapped the chain around his hand and used it to crack his prisoner hard on the back of the head. Dornar fell facedown into the dirt, unconscious.

He glanced at Nim where she stood, pale and trembling, and then back at Grendel as the Lord High Chancellor collapsed onto his side in the middle of the narrow road.

Nim wiped her mouth with the back of her hand as if

ridding herself of something rotten, but she never lost her focus on Grendel.

In seconds, Jos and Garet were beside Dornar where he lay unconscious, and he could go to her. In two big strides he reached her, pulled her hard into his arms, and wrapped himself around her. Gods.

Each sawing breath dragged over his broken ribs like fire, but he had never felt anything more wonderful in his life than Nim, safe, pressed against him.

She looked up at him, her voice low as she explained, "Hemlock. On the blade."

But he was still remembering the horror of seeing her dive out of the tree. "Surely Jos or Garet—"

She cut him off. "I wanted to do it. I had to know that you were safe, but I also needed to make sure that he… was gone." She looked up at him with wide blue eyes. "He took something from me, that day in my house. And then he took you… I needed to know that I could take it back. And I needed you to know that I would come for you."

Gods. She was the strongest woman he'd ever met.

Grendel's lips were blue in his ash-gray face, but Tristan heard him clearly as he glared at Nim and whispered, "This isn't over. Ballanor will find you—he won't rest until he does."

Grendel panted, staring at Nim, struggling for air as he forced out the last words. "He will execute you all. Starting with Lanval. And their deaths will be on your head."

Nim's face lost the last remains of any color, but she didn't falter. She stepped out of his arms and reached down to pick up his grandfather's dagger. "Fuck you, asshole. It's your death that's on my head, not theirs, and I'm perfectly happy that I'm the one who purged you from this world."

She *was* an avenging angel.

And she was his.

Tristan saw her take in a shaky breath as she wiped the blade clean. She had killed a man. For herself, and the harm Grendel had caused her. But also for him.

His beast rumbled possessively, wanting to be near her, to hold her against him and never let go. But they had to get away before Dornar woke up or the coward that had run away came back with reinforcements.

He felt a flicker of sympathy for Dornar. The lieutenant had been following orders, just as Tristan had done for so many years, and he would certainly be punished for this debacle. But there was nothing they could do about that. Dornar would have to be grateful that they'd let him live.

Nim was shivering more forcefully as they hurried down the dusty road and around a corner. He wasn't sure how far she could walk after everything she'd been through. And he was even less sure that he could carry her. But his beast would not tolerate her leaning on Jos or Garet.

"The Hawks?" he asked slowly as they stumbled away.

The dark terror that only Jos and Garet had managed to fly from the burning house, that the others were lost, tore at him. He had to know.

Nim smiled apologetically. "Sorry, I should have said something, they're on their way—"

He cut her off with a rough grunt, needing to be clear. "They're alive?"

"Yes, everyone is fine, they'll be here soon."

The relief flooding through him was almost overwhelming. Thank the gods. His men—his brothers— were safe.

But there was another important point that she had missed entirely. He led her off the road and spun her to face him. "Let me understand. My squad is alive, and yet they let you go after Grendel with only two men for backup? They had one job—keep you safe."

Her eyes narrowed. "I can keep myself safe."

He glared back.

"They wanted me to stay back with Val," she added softly, "but I refused. Once they had Keely and Val ready to travel, they were going to follow. This was a good plan, Tristan. The right plan."

He wrapped his arm around her, too glad she was alive to argue. Too glad that the Hawks were alive. She was safe, she had come after him, and now they had a chance at a future.

No, he wasn't going to argue with her.

But that didn't mean he would accept insubordination from the Hawks. They had been given clear instructions to protect Nim. He understood she had needed to be the one to kill Grendel, but the squad needed to be damn clear that in future, their priority was keeping her safe.

They were only walking for a few minutes before hooves thudded through the woods nearby and the rest of the squad arrived, their horses kicking up dust as they pulled up beside them. They'd unearthed a rough farm cart to carry Val, and Keely sat beside him holding his hand as he groaned, only half conscious.

Tristan's heart lifted in his chest. Just seeing the Hawks again, after being so terrified that they had all been lost, nearly overwhelmed him. But it didn't mean they would avoid the blistering they were about to get. "What the fuck were you thinking!" His roar echoed off the trees. "Mathos, report!"

"See, Nim, I told you he wouldn't be happy." Mathos sounded almost cheerful.

Tristan kissed Nim gently on the forehead and then

stalked up to his second-in-command, staggering slightly as his weight landed on his throbbing knee, caught between wanting to grab his friend to check that he was well, and wanting to wrap his hands around his neck and throttle him.

Before he could do either, Nim was there between them. She pressed her cool hands into his cheeks and forced him to look at her. "It's not Mathos's fault. I already told you that they didn't want me going after you. I made them."

He looked her up and down, the top of her head just touching the bottom of his chin, her body still trembling in shock, inside the too big clothes. "You *made* them. You're not even wearing any boots!"

She gave him a small smile as the men around them chuckled.

The beast inside him was not appeased. "Mathos needs to realize—"

"Tristan, I love you." Nim's smiled widened. That beautiful, glowing, smile. "Now shut up."

And then she stood on her toes and kissed him, right there in the middle of the road, in front of all his men. And, gods help him, he couldn't be bothered to shout at them anymore.

He threaded his fingers through her hair and kissed her back.

Epilogue

V<small>AL</small> <small>GROANED</small> and tried to open his eyes. Someone had their hand on his chest, and he could feel waves of warmth unfurling through his body. A twisted knot of pain somewhere deep inside him pulled tight and then unraveled, and he sighed in relief as another gnawing ache ebbed.

Slim fingers smoothed his brow, and a gentle voice shushed him.

"Nimmy?"

It didn't make sense. She was at home. He'd kept her out of it. Hadn't he? Was he dreaming?

Everything was blurred and distorted. Strange shapes loomed over him.

"I'm here." That was definitely her voice. Gods, no. Please. He thought he remembered seeing her in the palace. Like a nightmare come to life. But if it was real, then… what the fuck had happened?

He'd fallen. Had someone carried him? He remembered the ice-cold water. The shock. Trying not to breathe. And then, nothing. Was he still in the palace? "Where…?"

"We're in a safe house." Nim's voice, trying to be reassuring.

No! He couldn't be. They couldn't. What had they done? "No!" He couldn't make his voice any louder. They had to listen.

"Shh, shh." She stroked his hair.

Couldn't she see that it was urgent? He had to get up. He tried to get his cramping muscles to move. Tried to make them understand. "We left her."

Nim tried to soothe him. "Keely's here; she's okay."

Her words made him even more frantic. He had to get up. Had to convince them. No one understood. Gods. What had he done?

Then Rafe was there with a mug, something to drink. Yes. Then his voice would work. Then he would explain.

But instead he felt his ability to fight drain away. His eyes were so very heavy. He tried to push himself back up, but his muscles were too weak. His eyes closed, and he slipped into darkness.

Strange dreams came and went. He opened his eyes and saw Nim kissing Tris.

That couldn't be right. He closed them again.

Something jostled him, and his wounds burned. His body was on fire. He groaned and shifted his legs. Why was it so dark? And cold. He shivered restlessly, waves of heat and cold shuddering through him. Nim poured something cool into his mouth. And he was gone again.

He came back to consciousness slowly, aware of the sounds of muffled activity. Camp sounds. A woman's voice said something, and deep voices chuckled.

He forced his eyes open and looked around. He was in a tent, the kind they'd used on campaign, wrapped in a bedroll.

He stretched his legs and arms gently, gingerly circled his shoulders and shuffled his wings against the blanket. Everything worked. The hot, shivery fever seemed to have faded. He had to get up. Find out where he was. Get back to the palace. Fuck. How long had he been out?

He pushed the blanket back and sat up. Too quickly. The sides of his vision went black as the world spun, and he had to drop his head and breathe deeply to avoid passing out.

The tent flap lifted, a firm male hand landed on his shoulder, and a soothing freshness flowed over him, like a soft breeze on a summer's day. "Take a minute."

He turned his head to see Rafe beside him. Supporting him. He'd been alone for so long that he didn't know what to say. A strange feeling of grief flowed over him, and he shook his head, at a loss.

Rafe seemed to understand. He dipped his chin briefly and then stood and stuck his head through the tent flap. "Nim! He's awake."

"My sister's here?" His voice hardly worked anymore.

"What do you remember?"

Before he could reply, Nim was there. She looked tired, thinner than he remembered, with dark rings under her eyes.

She threw herself into his arms, and he only just managed to catch her. His heart broke as he felt her sob, her small body quivering against his chest as if she was a young girl again. His baby sister, and he'd put her in so much danger.

Then the tent flap lifted again, and Tristan was there, gently prying Nim away, his voice a low rumble. "Here, sweetheart. Give him some space."

He expected her to say something tart to Tris. Slap him maybe.

But instead she curled her body into Tristan's lap as he wrapped his arms around her and kissed the top of her head.

And was that a hickey on her neck?

What the actual fuck?

Nim lifted her tear-streaked face and glared. Not at Tristan, no, at him. Had he said it aloud? Maybe.

He had no idea what the fuck was happening. But he damn sure didn't like the way that Tristan was rubbing Nim's back. Possessively. No. Worse than that. Familiarly. As if he had done it before. A lot.

He pushed himself up, ready to demand an explanation, when he realized that he was completely naked. He hesitated, trying to decide whether it was worth punching Tristan with his dick hanging out. Yes. He took a step forward, it would definitely be worth it.

"You'll open your wounds." Rafe's voice was firm. It made him pause. But not for long.

He opened his mouth to reply, but Tristan beat him to it. "I love her. I'm not giving her up. Not even for you."

Nim lost her death glare and rested her cheek against Tristan's chest and, just loud enough to be heard, she murmured, "I love you too."

He took a moment to look at her. Really look at her. She did look tired and too thin. But she also looked happy. He had seen, for all those years, how she followed Tristan around. While his friend had seemed completely oblivious.

He didn't know how he felt. It was too much to deal with, and he didn't have the time. He'd think about it later. After.

He pinched the top of his nose and shook his head as the roll of dread crashed over him. "I need my clothes."

Rafe shook his head. "You're still healing. I've done what I can, but you're not ready to get up."

"No choice. I have to go."

"Go where?" Nim asked, anxiety threading through her voice.

He stood, wrapping the blanket around his waist. Someone would have clothes. "Back to the palace."

"Fuck, no." Tristan's voice was a rough growl. "We only just got the two of you out of there."

Nim leaned out of Tristan's hold and laid a reassuring hand on his arm. "Keely's here. I'll get her."

He shook his head and then wished he hadn't when the world started to spin.

He had tried so hard to keep them out of it all. To keep them safe. To keep his promises. And look how well that had turned out.

His shoulders sagged. "I need to get back to Alanna."

"Alanna?" Nim's voice was confused, but he saw the moment that she understood.

He waited for the questions. The judgment. The outrage. But it didn't come.

"Okay." She gave a brisk nod as she got to her feet. "We were going to start planning later tonight anyway, but let's get the squad. We have to do it now."

She was out of the tent before he could stop her, shouting orders like a drill sergeant.

Val shook his head, trying to get his head around the idea of his baby sister bossing the Hawks around.

Tristan chuckled at the look on his face, but then he grew serious. "There's something I have to tell you."

The conflicted look on Tristan's face sent a spike of

horror through Val's veins like a shot of black ice. Whatever it was, it was bad.

But he hadn't begun to imagine just how bad.

Tristan sighed and put his hand on his shoulder. He might have thought it was to support him if he didn't know better.

"They're going to hang your princess."

Thank you

Thank you for reading *Tristan*, I hope you enjoyed it! I loved writing it, and I'm so excited to share it with you. I'm also completely in love with Tristan, and if I could have one wish, it would be to have wings like Nim's.

Would you like to know when the next book is available? Or maybe just feel like chatting about romance books of all kinds? You can sign up to my e-mail list at:

www.jennielynnroberts.com

like my Facebook page

https://www.facebook.com/Jennie.Lynn.Roberts. Romance

or follow me on Instagram

https://www. instagram.com/jennielynnroberts_author/

Everyone who **signs up to my newsletter** will receive a password that takes you to a hidden page on my website where you'll find **a *bonus epilogue*** for Tristan and Nim:

Tristan buried his childhood pain under thick scars and the determination never to think of what he'd lost again—until new fears bring back the old demons.

He promised Nim he'd never run again, but can he keep that pledge? Especially when she insists the demons might be real?

This short story takes place in parallel with the early part of book 2, but there are no plot spoilers, I promise.

Please Review this book! Reviews help authors more than you might think and they also help readers to find books they would like. If you enjoyed ***Tristan***, please consider leaving a review—I would be very grateful.

Val (The Hawks - book 2)

He'll do anything to save her. And then he'll say goodbye...

Being framed for murder, captured, and tortured for weeks didn't break Val. But seeing Alanna every day, knowing she didn't love him as he loved her, surely would. So, he'll do whatever is necessary to stop the king from executing her...then he'll walk away. Forever.

Queen Alanna gave up everything—including her soul mate— to secure the treaty that would end the war. Now, her husband wants her dead and any chance she had for true happiness with Val is ruined.

The king's new guards are arrayed against them, the threat of war looms large, and their enemy has the upper hand. When all is said and done, will Alanna choose to sacrifice her own happiness to save her kingdom? Or will she risk it all for a second chance at happily ever after with Val?

Mathos (The Hawks - book 3)

All he has to do is find the princess, help her claim the throne, and not fall in love with her. Easy…right?

Mathos's task was straightforward. Find Lucilla—while evading the Lord High Chancellor's military, of course—and deliver her safely to the Hawks. He was ready for anything…except how she made him feel. Now, the stubborn beauty with the courageous spirit has awakened a hunger in him, and it's driving him *and* his beast wild.

Lucilla is *done* with her gilded cage. She's ready to truly live and experience everything she's been denied. She's determined to have her independence, not blindly follow the grumpy former palace guard who looks at her like he wants to eat her for dinner. Even if she's starting to think she might like to take a bite out of him, too.

Mathos, however, isn't the only one who wants Lucilla. The most dangerous man in the kingdom will stop at nothing to have her. And if Mathos and Lucilla don't learn to trust each other and work together soon, they'll be in danger of losing a lot more than their shot at happily ever after.

Tor (The Hawks - book 4) - coming soon

**What is it about her that makes him lose his mind?
Every. Damn. Time.**

Tor's world is falling apart. The king he'd sworn to guard? Dead.
The family he worked so hard for? They certainly wasted no time
disowning him. All he has left is the Hawks… and an intense
desire to win Keely's heart. It won't be easy—especially not after
the mistake he made when they were last together. But he has to
try, because the alternative, living without her, is unthinkable.

Losing someone you love leads to nothing but pain. Keely learned
that the hard way. But there was something about Tor that made
her wonder if loving him was worth the risk… until he opened his
mouth and ruined everything. Now her best option is to create a
new future on her own—no matter how much she might wish her
relationship with Tor could be different.

But all is not well in Brythoria. The treaty still isn't ratified, and
the mountain border is filled with enemies poised to destroy them.
Can Tor and Keely find their way back to each other? Or will
their second chance at happily ever after burn in the fires of
impending war?

About the Author

Jennie Lynn Roberts believes that every strong, kickass heroine should have control of her own story, a swoony hero to support her at every turn, and a guaranteed happily ever after. Because that doesn't always happen in real life, she began creating her own worlds that work just the way they should. And she hasn't looked back since.

Jennie would rather be writing than doing anything else— except for spending time with her gorgeous family, of course. But when she isn't building vibrant new worlds to get lost in, she can be found nattering with friends, baking up a storm, or strolling in the woods around her home in England.

If you want to talk books, romance, movies, reluctant heroes, or just about anything else with Jennie, feel free to contact her on Facebook or Instagram.

Printed in Great Britain
by Amazon

65511517R00196